BAIT AND SWITCH

THE ADVENTURES OF ELSABETH SOESTEN

NO GOOD DEED...

BAIT AND SWITCH

FORTHCOMING

PRIZE PLAY

THE GONNES OF NAVARRE

THE CONFESSION AT GODRA

THE ADVENTURES OF ELSABETH SOESTEN

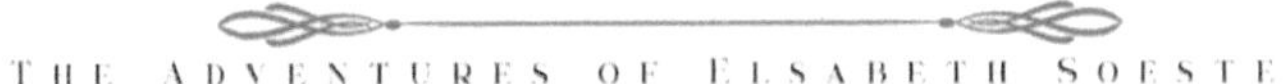

BAIT AND SWITCH

D. E. WYATT

Wyrmfyr Press
St. Louis, Missouri
2022

This is a work of fiction. Some characters, settings, and events
have been inspired by historical record, but any direct depiction
of historical events and individuals both living and dead is
unintentional.

The Adventures of Elsabeth Soesten: Bait And Switch

Copyediting by Debbie Manber Kupfer
Cover Art by Rebecca Frank, Bewitching Book Covers, LLC
(bewitchingbookcovers.com)
Heraldry image resources sourced from HeraldicArt.org

Second Edition

ISBN-13: 979-8-9853905-0-6

To Mom, Laura, and Jenna, whom I swear I didn't put up
to it.

A NOTE FROM THE AUTHOR

A number of terms contained within this work may be unfamiliar to you, the reader. As such, I have provided a glossary at the end of the book for your convenience, along with a quick guide on how to read the blazons for the coats of arms described herein.

THE ADVENTURES OF ELSABETH SOESTEN

BAIT AND SWITCH

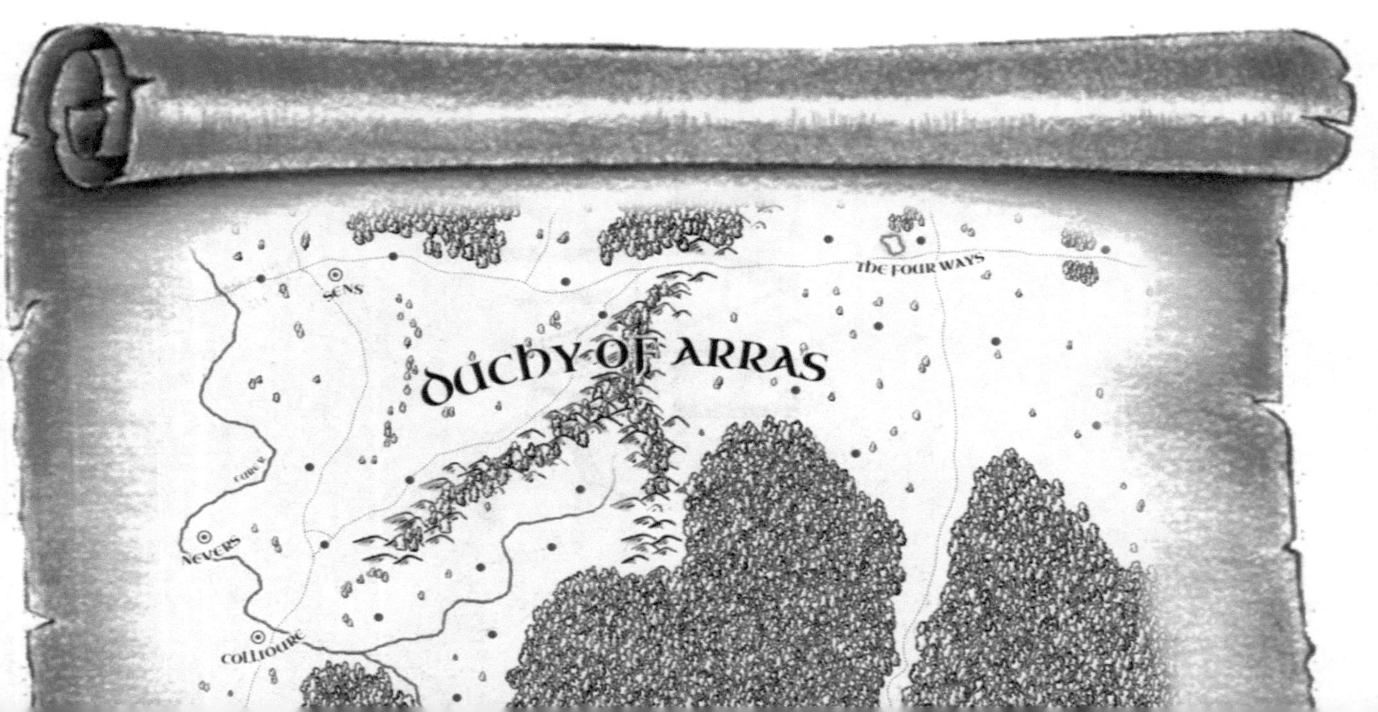

DUCHY OF ARRAS
THE FOUR WAYS
SENS
NEVERS
COLLIOURE

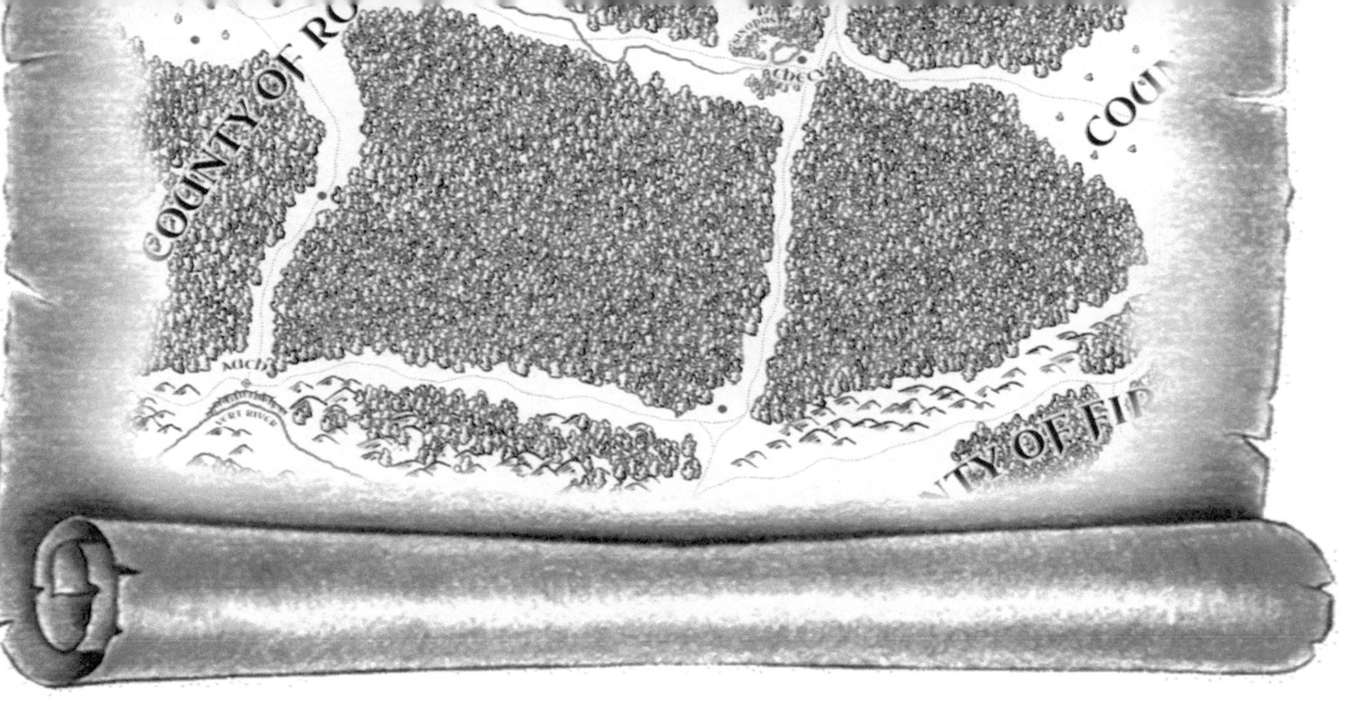

COUNTY OF RO
COUN
COUNTY OF FIP
MICH
RT RIVER

1

HE BLUR OF SOMETHING RATHER LARGE and heavy flying towards her caught her eye, and in one fluid movement Elsabeth spun away from her horse, her sword flashed from its scabbard, and she cut the melon aimed at her head neatly in two. The halves spun harmlessly past her in a shower of juice and pulp that splattered a broad streak across her heart-shaped face.

She was not exactly certain from which direction the missile had come but, judging from the chorus of curses raining down on her from the approaching villagers, she needed no specifics. If her deft defense against the unexpected attack startled any of the crowd, they did not show it. If anything, the failed assault only enraged them further. This was especially evident when a hasty shower of stones followed the melon and sent her scrambling to the far side of her old Lizarran jennet, Felis, who danced nervously and snorted at the commotion.

Hieronymus, his portly round face framed by an unruly mane of graying hair and beard, clutched his carved wooden staff and stepped between Elsabeth and the crowd, pleading for their attention. "Peace, sons and daughters, peace!" he said in his passable Navarrese, touched with a heavy Boehman accent. "Don't give in to wrath. Remember what the Son of the Lord would say of forgiveness!"

Neither the travel-and-ale-stained black woolen habit of his order, nor the arming sword and buckler hung at his hip, made an impression on the crowd. A hail of insults answered him, most directed at her to judge by the count of "whores" and "harlots" screamed by the women of the village. The men mostly kept to the rear and well out of the way, more than a few with looks of utter embarrassment on their faces. The village priest, a handsome man somewhat younger than her twenty-three summers and dressed in a brown woolen habit, stepped forward to join the friar's efforts to mediate the situation.

"I beg of you, my children," the priest said, "let justice prevail, not anger. If this woman has wronged you, then let the Lord of All cast his judgment and she will be punished accordingly."

He turned to Elsabeth. "My child, will you come forward?" he continued, and Hieronymus looked askance at her as well, as if waiting for her response. She gave the slightest nod towards his horse, and Hieronymus slowly inched his way over to Josephus. The old Hackney took the excitement in stride, and browsed on the grasses on the village outskirts where they stabled. "There need not be any violence if you will consent to answer to their charges."

Elsabeth wiped the melon pulp from her face with one elbow and swept the tail of her brown leather coat back behind her hip to clear her scabbard. She rammed her sword home and flashed the priest a mischievous smirk.

"Oh, there is no need for that," she said. Her own Navarrese was mostly clean with little in the way of an accent. She swept her black felt hat from her head and held it over her heart. "Bless me father, for I have indeed sinned, and lain with several men of the village. And if the women here are as skilled in their beds as they are at flinging stones, then 'tis small wonder I found them so willing to join me."

Hieronymus rolled his eyes as a fresh volley of stones, curses, insults, and oaths filled the village.

"Well, that will certainly smooth things over," he said in Boehman, as he hurried to ready Josephus for flight.

"We already got paid for the job," she replied in kind in a low voice, "so there is no need to come back again, anyway. Let us just go before they light the torches."

The priest managed to contain the crowd again with great effort and turned back to her. "I beg of you, my child," he pleaded. "For the good of your soul you must make amends to those whom you have wronged!"

Elsabeth tsked at him and set her hat back atop her head at a rakish angle. The broad brim, pinned up at one side, shaded her eyes from the sun. "Oh Father, and I thought my soul was already in such good hands when I was on my knees before you last night. I would think all of Navarre heard your prayers with the way you were carrying on."

The priest's face turned a brilliant shade of crimson, and for a moment he sputtered and could not find the words for a rebuke. "Succubus!" he finally spat, and jabbed an accusing finger in her direction. "There for certain stands a servant of the Dark One himself! See how her tongue weaves salacious lies?"

"Well, now you did it, Tetty," Hieronymus muttered.

"Yes," she said, "I may have pushed this one a tad too far."

"In the name of the Lord, seize the witch so she might be hanged, and her corruption lifted from our village!" the priest screamed.

"Time to go?" Hieronymus said.

Elsabeth vaulted into the saddle. "Time to go!"

As the townsfolk surged forward, Elsabeth gave a cry and jammed her heels into Felis' flanks. Felis snorted, reared, and took off like a shot away from the village. Elsabeth's copper hair streamed behind her like a gleaming banner, with only a glance over her shoulder to be sure Hieronymus was with her and to check for signs of pursuit. However, the villagers had no riding horses to speak of, and thus little hope of catching them.

They rode hard for several miles. Only when the village lay well behind them, hidden by a turn of the road as it passed through a small wooded area, did she pull up Felis and check her pace. Hieronymus rode up beside her and shook his head.

"Well, that was another fine mess you got us into," he grumbled.

"Me?" she protested. "This whole adventure was another one of your schemes. I only tagged along to keep you out of trouble."

"Yes, you. God in heaven, girl! What has gotten into you lately? I have seen you leave a trail of broken hearts — and I suspect very angry wives — from one end of Boehm to the other, but this has been excessive even for you. Did you lay with every man there, or just the ones whose wives were throwing stones?"

"It was actually only two of them. Well, and the priest, but he was a strange one, and insisted only that I—"

He cut her off abruptly. "Enough, girl, enough! That is all I really can bear to hear."

She rolled her eyes. "You did bring it up."

"Only because you nearly got yourself hanged for it! And likely me with you. Now something has been bothering you ever since we crossed into Navarre. I am your priest, such as it is, am I not?"

Elsabeth eyed him incredulously. "Are you saying you want me to give confession now?"

"Who said anything about confession? I am merely offering you the comfort of my ear. And I rather hope you take advantage of it before the next village you scandalize sees fit to lock up our only means of escape before coming to hang you."

She sighed again. "If you must know, though 'tis rather none of your business, it has been nigh on six weeks since I have had satisfaction by means other than my own hands, and I am trying very hard not to think of Cuncz and his magic wand. I am likely to get more enjoyment from bumping along in the bloody saddle. And now here I am telling you about it on top of it all."

"I happen to think 'tis a message. For too long you have willingly opened your body to any man with a pulse. The Lord of All does not wish to see you flitting from bed to bed like a common bawd, 'tis unbecoming."

Elsabeth glared at him. "And what about you? I am sure He thinks highly of the sort of 'indulgence' you offer the laywomen."

Hieronymus harrumphed and looked towards the sky. "Lord, grant me patience with your wayward daughter! I offer her advice and she responds by questioning my piety!"

"Your piety deserves questioning, and you well know it. Nor did I ask your advice. The sort of bed I make to lie in is none of your concern, so if you don't like it, you can go and bugger yourself."

At that they rode in silence for some time. After a mile or so they passed through the wooded area and broke out into open fields stretching out for some distance in all directions. No sign of pursuit followed them, and they passed no one else on the road, though at times they saw laborers at work in the fields. The road itself ran westwards across Navarre. It was a rutted and hard-packed dirt track crossed at times by little streams gurgling in stony beds spanned by fords or bridges of crumbling and weathered stone. Here and there they saw the remains of old paving stones peeking through the dirt and turf like old, bleached bones, a rare sign of the great Imperium Valentium that once stretched out of the Free City-States to the south, to cover much of Navarre and Coventry further to the northwest.

It was already midday by the time they set out from the village, and it promised to be well after twilight before they reached their destination, which Elsabeth noted Hieronymus had not been forthcoming about. Finally, she could take no more of riding with only the singing of birds and the steady clatter of their horses' hooves to break the silence.

"Where are you taking us, anyway?" she asked.

"Somewhere to get a drink," Hieronymus replied, "and maybe a bit of work to keep you occupied and out of trouble, though you seem to have a knack for drawing it wherever you go."

She rolled her eyes. "Any time you go looking for a drink and a bit of work, I always end up having to get you out of trouble. Like that time you tried to hustle those gents in Aue and ended up hung by your ankles from the village church."

"That was not my fault! They were easy marks, and I would have had them if you would have just done as I asked."

"My sleeping habits are suddenly much less objectionable once you think you can use them to your advantage. Now, what are you planning this time?"

"My plan was to head for a place a bit up the road the priest back there—" he jerked his thumb over his shoulder and motioned vaguely back towards the village "— mentioned before you were nearly hanged. He called it the Inn of the Four Ways."

Elsabeth let out a groan of exasperation. "Oh good God, not another inn. Why is it always a bloody inn?"

"Do you know of anywhere better to look for someone needing a sword arm or two? The Four Ways is right at a major crossroads so anyone on the road will be passing through. I am sure there will be no lack of merchants and travelers looking for protection."

"And 'tis also a good place for you to lose all our money on drink and dice. How long did it take before you had been through your share of the reward from Cuncz?"

Hieronymus glared at her. "As I recall you enjoyed your fair share of the libations along the road, Tetty."

"Tch. What makes you think I paid for them from my own purse?"

"I wonder. Every innkeeper between here and Leyen I am sure has been singing your praises after we passed through. Not to mention your name, among other things, has been on the lips of every bard and minstrel as well. Now, will you just trust me? I know what I am doing."

She sighed and shook her head. "It terrifies me every time you say that."

The rest of their ride was uneventful. Midday passed into afternoon, and soon the sun was sinking into the west, setting the sky alight with brilliant golds and reds as the pale blue ceiling overhead slowly deepened into indigo. The silver-white points of stars ignited in the gathering dark as the golden lights of their destination loomed up ahead of them.

The Inn of the Four Ways was a substantial structure nestled in the northwest corner of the meeting of the two roads whence it took its name. The greater of the two ran north and south across Navarre, and was worn and deeply rutted by the passage of merchant wagons. The road Elsabeth and Hieronymus followed westward from Boehm was less well-traveled these days, though once had been a major passage for goods moving overland. In summer months the hard dirt surfaces were a sea of choking dust, making the Four Ways a welcome respite for travelers.

The Inn was virtually a town in and of itself, enclosed within a wooden gated palisade atop a low grassy rise overlooking the road, backed by a small, wooded area with a clear bright pond beside it. A broad path branched off the westward road to run up to the main gate to the south. It bisected the grounds behind the wall before it exited another gate on the north side to rejoin the main highway. Brightly painted half-timbered homes and shops lined both sides of this path, creating a maze of crowded alleys with merchant stalls and several open squares dominated by the Inn itself at its heart.

The Inn straddled the path, with a long, two-leveled wing with peaked roofs and many windows on each side, connected by a central section, through which the road passed by means of an archway. Beneath the main wing were stalls for the sheltering of horses, and a doorway in each of its four corners led inside.

Elsabeth left Hieronymus to arrange the stabling of their horses and made for one of the doors.

She entered through the southeast doorway and found herself on a well-lit landing at the foot of a steep stairway. Golden light filled the room above, and there was music and the fragrance of cooking food along with the sour odor of beer in the air. Elsabeth started up the stairs and soon emerged in the inn's common room, a wide chamber that filled the entirety of the main wing above the stables below. Glass windows looked north and south out onto the road, and thick timber columns supported the ceiling above. A door on either end led to the east and west wings.

Trestle tables ringed an open space in the middle of the common room floor, where men and women danced to a jaunty tune played by musicians on pipes, drums, and lutes, while serving girls glided between tables and spun out of the reach of grasping hands. Elsabeth flashed one of the pipers a smile when he looked her way, then swept her eyes across the common room. She spied an empty table in the southwest corner, near another stairwell much like the one through which she had entered. She sighed and made her way across the room, keeping to the wall and out of the way as she slipped past tables full of drinkers. Some were stained and worn from the road. Others were locals visiting the Inn to share news of the day and join in the revelry of the evening.

She reached the table, dropped heavily onto the bench with her back to the wall, and propped her sword against the table. Before long, a serving girl appeared bearing a platter of the evening's meal and a tankard of ale for her, which she set down with an uncertain eye on the sword leaning against the table. Elsabeth handed her a silver *pfennig*.

"I have a companion joining me shortly," she said. "Be a dear and have a plate and tankard brought for him as well. If 'tis not here before he is, I'll be dealing with his grumbling all evening."

The serving girl inclined her head slightly and hurried off to the kitchens. Hieronymus arrived presently. He leaned his staff against the table and dropped heavily onto the bench beside her. He frowned at the platter in front of her.

"Well, that is courteous of you; leaving me to contend with the horses and boarding while you sit down to eat."

"Oh, don't start with me. The girl will be back in a moment, though God knows you could stand a fast. So, are we just sitting around and hoping for someone to turn up?"

"More or less."

Elsabeth sighed and rolled her eyes. "Wonderful. We could just spend the night at ease and move on somewhere work was publicly posted. Instead, we hang around just hoping for something to turn up on its own. Brilliant plan."

"Show some faith, my girl, and do keep your sword in view."

"Fine. But I wager our meal and board for the night that nothing turns up."

Hieronymus smirked over the rim of his tankard. "Wager accepted."

“I HATE YOU,” SHE MUTTERED INTO HER tankard.

“I would think you should have more faith in me by now,” Hieronymus said.

Elsabeth rolled her eyes. Two figures had emerged from the nearest stairwell: a boy of perhaps fifteen, and an older man with a pronounced limp somewhere between her and Hieronymus in age. The elder man caught sight of her sword and started towards them with his companion trailing nervously behind him. “I just better not find out you had this whole thing arranged from the start and took advantage of me for a free meal.”

“I am deeply wounded you would even suggest such deception on my part, Tetty. Why I swear this is merely the Lord of All providing for us.”

“Right...”

Elsabeth trailed into silence as the newcomers approached. The elder was rather tall and powerfully built, with unkempt black hair flecked with silver, a rough beard to match, and a perpetual scowl. He shifted his weight off his bad leg. His companion was not much taller than Hieronymus, but thin and wiry, with a fair face and a mop of golden-brown hair. Both wore rough woolen trousers and doublets in faded colors, and short cloaks to their knees. A battered old sword a little shorter than hers hung at the hip of the elder man on a belt of cracked and aged leather. The boy appeared unarmed, though his cloak could conceal a knife at his back.

"Good evening, my sons!" Hieronymus said merrily. "The Lord's blessings be upon you both. Please, by all means sit and share our table." The friar gestured to the bench opposite them with both hands. "All travelers are friends upon the road."

"Thank you, Father," the boy said, and dropped onto the bench across from Hieronymus. His companion eyed Elsabeth for a long moment before he, too, seated himself across from her, with his bad leg extended out from the table. His eyes fixed upon her chest in a predatory manner. Elsabeth shifted uncomfortably under his gaze, and her hand edged closer to her sword.

"'Tis my first time away from home," the boy continued after a few moments of awkward silence passed. A pleased expression crossed his youthful features, and Elsabeth could not help but smile at his pride in the statement. The serving girl returned almost as soon as they were seated with platters of bread and meat for the newcomers, a tankard of ale for the elder man, and small beer for the youth.

The elder took a long, slow drink from his ale. "How well do you know this area?" he said casually. His voice was as rough as his countenance.

"We are both strangers here, I am afraid," Hieronymus said.

"Out of Boehm by your talk, I would guess."

Hieronymus nodded cautiously. "Yes, indeed."

"A long way from your province then, eh, Brother?"

"My Order calls upon us to wander and spread the word of the Lord. And so I wander."

"I see," the man said. He turned his eyes back on Elsabeth. "And you are a long way from your convent."

Hieronymus guffawed into his tankard, and Elsabeth glared at him. "If my companion ever spent time in a convent 'tis because she snuck in, likely to avoid being hanged for any number of offenses I can imagine."

He gave her a toothy smile. "A nunnery, then?"

"That is more believable." She gave Hieronymus a quick kick in the shin. "Ow! 'Twas uncalled for, Tetty."

"Oh, enough. You can play innocent another time," she said, then looked back at the others. "Is there something you were looking for?"

The elder man flashed her a greasy smile and did not bother to hide the look of appraisal he gave her. "I think I found it, love," he said.

"In that case you can keep looking. If 'tis a bawd you want, try out back."

"Please," the boy said. "My name is Maerten, and this is my guardian, Husson. I am looking to hire someone to help safeguard us on the road."

"And where are you headed, my son?" Hieronymus asked.

"There is a village a few days' travel south of this Inn. I have heard there is a man there who may be able to answer some questions for me. All I ask is your help reaching it safely, and perhaps on the journey back again. We can pay."

"How much?" Elsabeth asked.

"I have a modest savings," he said. "'Tis not much, but I can offer you five *sous*."

She frowned and folded her arms across her chest. "Just who exactly is this fellow you are looking for?"

Maerten leaned in and lowered his voice conspiratorially. "They say he is a wizard."

Elsabeth's brows rose incredulously. "A wizard."

The boy nodded, his eyes wide with excitement. "Can you believe it? An actual wizard! They say he has lived for hundreds of years, and can even see the future."

She glanced in disbelief at Hieronymus, whose own expression was unreadable. Maerten seemed not to notice her skepticism. "Just who are 'they?'" she asked.

Maerten shrugged. "People who spoke of him while passing through my village. They tell stories of him performing miracles and bringing good fortune to those who seek him."

Elsabeth shook her head. "'Tis more than likely just that: tales and stories. If there were truly a man claiming to be a wizard about, the local bishop would almost certainly see to it he could not make such a claim for long."

The boy gave her a wounded look. "I know they spoke the truth; I just need to find him."

Hieronymus put a hand on her arm before she could speak again. "Why do you seek this man out? What answers can he give that the Lord of All cannot provide?"

Maerten glanced at Husson, who merely shrugged, and continued watching Elsabeth over the rim of his tankard. The boy hesitated, before continuing in a low voice. "I wish to know where I come from," he said. "I never knew my parents. Husson has cared for me since I was a babe, but he could tell me only that he found me abandoned."

Maerten reached beneath his doublet, withdrew a golden disk hung from a silver chain, and held it out to her. Elsabeth took it and studied it closely. Markings like some form of writing ran the circumference of one face, which also bore an elaborately engraved design made up of beasts intertwined in a knotwork pattern filling the center. On its reverse was another design that looked heraldic in nature, but the device was one she did not recognize: a flowering tree with rampant lions on either side.

"This is all that I have," he continued once Elsabeth returned the amulet. He tucked it out of sight beneath his doublet once more. "Husson said 'twas round my neck when he found me, but he could not recognize the markings. I had hoped the wizard could tell me its meaning, and perhaps tell me who I really am."

Elsabeth rolled her eyes. "Now this is a story I know I have heard somewhere before..."

"Tetty! Be polite!" Hieronymus said sharply. "There are many unfortunates adrift in this world with no place to claim as their own."

She merely grunted and shook her head.

"Well, my son," Hieronymus continued, "I would first take great care to whom you show that bauble. There are more than a few ruffians upon the road who shan't think twice about cutting off your head to get hold of that little bit of treasure."

"That is why we seek protection," Maerten said. "Husson is a greatly skilled fighter, yet he is but one man."

Elsabeth appraised Husson for a moment. "Russdorffer?"

Husson's lip curled in disgust. "Ludovico da Lucca."

She smirked into her cup. "Both only suited for entertaining simpletons at a village fair. A clown with a willow branch would be of more use if it came to a real fight, though the fool would not nearly be so amusing to watch as someone who practices da Lucca's hapless flailing."

He glared at her contemptuously. "And you, I would guess, follow some student of that uncouth, inelegant, and crude braggart, Soest."

Elsabeth took a sip of her ale. "I learned from the Master himself, who taught me how to fight, not dance about like some screwed and tottering strumpet."

Husson leaned over the table and glared. "We can step outside if you need a lesson."

Maerten looked between the two with his features twisted into an expression of alarm and confusion. "I don't understand..."

Hieronymus took a swig of his ale. "Swordsmen, my son, tend to be a rather touchy lot on the subject of their masters. Though I, myself, am above such conceit, for which I have the wisdom of the great Leonardus to thank. Don't worry overly much; they are merely measuring one another's blades."

Elsabeth chuckled into her tankard. "Mine is bigger."

"Yes, but I don't think 'tis a time to demonstrate how well you handle it," the friar said. "But in answer to your offer, my son…"

Elsabeth set her tankard down and laid her hand on Hieronymus's shoulder before he could finish. She took a firm grip on the fabric of his habit. "Before we accept, I would rather like a word alone with my companion before he makes a rash decision."

She stood and practically dragged Hieronymus from his seat, and along one wall out of earshot of the table.

"Are you daft, girl?" he growled in protest, shaking her grip off, and uselessly straightening his rumpled habit.

"Are you?" she asked. "Do you realize how ridiculous this story of theirs sounds?"

"Of course I do, Tetty. I am not a child. But the last bit of work we had has not exactly been much to live on." He thumped one thick finger against her sternum. "And the less time you spend around inns the better 'twill be for both of us."

Elsabeth gawked. "Me? Who got us thrown out of that run-down shack near Albi?"

Hieronymus folded his arms across his chest and glowered at her indignantly. "That was hardly my fault. I did not start that disagreement with the girl's father."

She rolled her eyes. "Oh no, of course not. You certainly did not get drunk and blather on about your 'ministrations' in the barn to anyone who would listen. But this whole matter sounds completely mad. Oh, 'tis a fine fancy to tell over a round of ale, but I can't believe you are actually considering going along with this."

"Curiosity, my dear. Even you must be intrigued by even the rumor of a real wizard."

Elsabeth made a face. "I am sure the Master of your order would be quite pleased should he hear of this. Unless you were planning on a burning once you have discussed his craft over a few pints."

Hieronymus merely grunted. "I think the Master would rather like to compare notes with the man on the subject himself."

She sighed and pinched the bridge of her nose. "I just know I'll end up regretting this."

The friar chuckled, threaded an arm around her waist, and led her back to the table. "Come now, Tetty, do try and show a little optimism. At the very least, think of this poor lost boy who knows not whence he came."

"And here comes the regret. I reserve the right to hassle you when this goes bad."

Hieronymus tsked. "My dear, when do my plans ever go bad?"

"Usually right after you say that."

They returned to the table and sat again. Maerten watched them expectantly, while Husson busied himself with his ale.

"Well," Hieronymus said. "My companion and I have discussed it, and we accept your offer."

"Wonderful!" Maerten said, smiling broadly. "We should leave immediately!"

Elsabeth could not help but chuckle at the display of enthusiasm. "Easy, love. 'Tis better to start well rested, and the hour is growing late. Besides, I am sure your wizard will still be there whether we set out tonight or wait 'til morning. How are you fixed for supplies?"

"Well, there are our horses, and we have a few days' worth of food left. And Husson is a masterful huntsman!"

"Oh, I am sure he is. And where exactly is this village?"

Maerten hesitated a moment. "To the south, as I have said. I imagine along the road."

Elsabeth sighed and rolled her eyes. "You did get its name, I hope?"

The boy gave her an indignant look. "Of course I did. It was..." he trailed off, and his features twisted in concentration. "Oh, what did they call it?" He glanced at Husson.

"Checy," the elder said into his tankard.

Maerten clapped his hands gleefully. "Ah! Of course, yes, that was it. 'Twas Checy."

Elsabeth turned to Hieronymus. "Do you think you can handle getting directions while I see to our provisions? Someone must know it a bit better than to just say 'Go south.'"

Hieronymus scowled at her. "And why would you think I would have any better luck of it than you?"

"Because joining this little adventure was your idea, and the last time I trusted you to restock our supplies I found you face down and unconscious with a barrel of ale at your side."

He harrumphed indignantly. "Don't go filling the lad's head with falsehoods, Tetty!" He glanced to Maerten and rolled his eyes with feigned innocence, and the boy stifled a laugh. "And to imagine I put up with her lying tongue every day."

"Oh, go play the saint another time. 'Tis time to work, now," she said. "Just see to it. And take that one with you." She waved at Husson with her tankard.

Maerten frowned. "Is there a problem?" he asked, looking between her and his guardian with some concern.

"Only that I rather don't like the way he has spent this whole conversation trying to sneak a peek down my doublet."

Husson flashed a leering grin. "I expect you will be letting me have a closer look before the trip is over, love."

"Your charms are a better fit for your horse, though I imagine even she is prone to bolting when you come for a ride. And whatever your horse's reaction, you should be warned I kick and I bite when approached by an undesired rider."

"Good, I enjoy breaking a mount with a bit of spirit."

Hieronymus groaned and rolled his eyes. "If you will excuse me, I think I'll go and see to those directions now, if only so I need not sit here and listen to any more of your courting. Come, my son," he added with a pointed look a Husson, "I think it best you come along as she says, as I would rather like to avoid being the one saddled by the annoyance of arranging for your burial."

"Do try and stay out of trouble," she said. Husson grumbled as the friar all but dragged him away from his half-finished dinner and ale. "'Twould be nice to leave a town for once without being chased by a horde of angry fathers and husbands."

"As opposed to a pack of screaming wives?"

"Oh, just get going."

Hieronymus rolled his eyes once more and departed in Husson's company, leaving her alone with Maerten. She watched the youth over the rim of her tankard. Her lip curled in amusement while he finished eating in silence, and watched the swirl of activity around him with an equal mix of unease and fascination.

"Should we not see to our supplies?" he asked as he finished his supper.

"Oh, I suppose," she said, and when one of the serving girls passed Elsabeth waved her over. "We shall be departing in the morning. Please send word to the master of the house we wish to arrange purchase of two weeks' provisions for four." She fished in her pouch for another *pfennig.*

The girl pocketed the coin, bowed her head, and hurried off to see to the request.

Elsabeth quirked a grin at him over the lip of her cup. "There we are."

Maerten gawked at her. "That is all there is to it?"

"When you spend time on the road, love, you learn a few things on how to make the journey a bit less of a bother."

"But what was all that about with your companion...?"

She chuckled into her tankard. "Oh, he knows the tricks better than I do. But Hieronymus also could not pass up a barrel of ale if it was being offered by the Dark One Himself, so I prefer to take charge of such arrangements to be sure that our provisions consist of more than just a cask from the basement of whatever inn at which we happen to be staying."

"Then what do we do now?"

Elsabeth finished the last of her ale. "Now we wait for Hieronymus to get himself into some sort of trouble, which we will spend the rest of the evening getting him out of again."

Maerten frowned. "You truly expect there to be trouble?"

"Love, one thing you will learn about me is that I am always in trouble."

IERONYMUS STEPPED OUT INTO THE NIGHT and breathed in the air of the stables beneath the Inn's central wing. He promptly wrinkled his nose in disgust at the stench of manure and too many horses crowded together in one enclosed place, and muttered a particularly unholy oath about the absurdity of the arrangement of such accommodations. It was not helped as his malodorous companion followed him from the Inn. Whatever priorities Husson held, hygiene was not chief among them.

"Come, my son," he said, as he gripped his staff, arranged the hang of his sword and buckler at his hip, and started forward into the crowd. "Let us see what our fellow travelers have to say about the village you seek."

"What about the boy?" Husson grumbled in response as he hobbled along behind him, with a look over his shoulder at the Inn towering above them.

"Have no fear for your ward's safety. Elsabeth can handle herself well enough. I must confess she is perhaps one of the finest sword-arms I have had the privilege to see.

And mind that I was tutored by the great Leonardus himself! Furthermore, her tongue is almost as good at getting her out of trouble as it is at getting her into it in the first place."

Husson grunted and flashed a toothy smile. "I imagine she must handle other things rather skillfully as well."

"That, I regret, I cannot answer from my own experience, not that I have not expressed my interest. But I have seen many a heart break when she has left a town behind. And seen many a sigh of relief from the local wives. If you wish for my advice, however, I would suggest you put any thoughts of conquest from your mind. My dear Tetty is actually quite particular as to her tastes, as seemingly indiscriminate as they may be."

The evening was rather young, and so the streets around the Inn were still crowded by travelers, the merchants who plied to them, and the unscrupulous sorts who preyed upon both. Hieronymus casually forced a path through them all with his staff, and kept a hand near to his purse on his way through the throng of traffic. A few of those he passed stopped him for a blessing or other kind word before hustling off on their own business, but most either ignored him or attempted to peddle some useless odd or end.

At times he paused and inquired among the travelers and residents as to the way to Checy. Most had not even heard of it, and those who had could say little beyond that it lay some days south of the Four Ways, and that road was seldom traveled since the wars with the Coventrish left much of southern Navarre greatly depopulated. Husson kept close by him as they pushed through the crowd, admirably keeping with his pace though he favored one leg. His glower and unkempt countenance lent him a wild and dangerous air that scattered much of the pedestrian traffic around them as they slipped among the hustle of the peddlers, performers, and pickpockets.

"So, tell me, my son," Hieronymus ventured upon approaching an open square nearest the northern gates, "how did you come to take guardianship of your young ward?"

"Is that any concern of yours?" Husson growled with impatience.

"Well, as we shall be traveling together for some time yet, I find it desirable to know something of my companions. I certainly wish to express my admiration for you taking the poor unfortunate under your care, and to bless you for this wondrous act of charity on your part!"

Husson grunted. "'Twas hardly charity, leastways not mine."

"Oh?"

"I was riding in the company of a woman I knew, when she heard the babe crying off the road. She sent me in to look, and I found him lying hidden in the weeds. There looked to be some manner of recent struggle about. I was content to move on, but she insisted on claiming him as her own."

"I see. Your wife?"

He grunted again, a sound somewhere between amusement and derision. "There was nothing respectable about her, nor us. She passed within two years and left me stuck with the whelp."

Hieronymus stopped as the crowd closed in to form a solid wall of bodies ahead of him, and momentarily blocked the way. "And yet, you kept him."

Husson shrugged. "He proved himself useful once he was old enough, especially as I no longer had the woman to keep my home. He works hard when you keep at him, and he earns his keep."

Hieronymus tired of waiting for the crowd in front of him to open enough for him to pass, and instead started along the edge. "Then he is more servant than ward to you."

"The boy has a roof over his head and food in his belly," Husson said in a rather defensive tone. "Not that 'tis any of your concern, Brother."

"It certainly is the Lord's," Hieronymus said, "so I think I am not entirely out of line saying that makes it mine, as well. I do wonder that you have not long ago sold that little trinket of his, or that you even entertain him on this quest."

"Because I am no thief, Brother, which if I know men of your ilk is more than I can say of you. I have been cheated by more than a few of you wandering clerics and your worthless indulgences."

Hieronymus glared indignantly at the man. "And I say such peddlers are no true servants of the Lord, and thank you not to slander me, unless you wish to argue the point."

"I thought such arguments were beneath men such as yourself?"

"My cheek can only be turned so far," Hieronymus said. "At some point it must stop lest my neck break."

Hieronymus found a place where the crowd ahead of them began to thin and led with his staff as he waded into it. Wary of the bodies pressing in around him, he took his purse from his belt and stuffed it down the front of his habit. Husson regarded him with a raised eyebrow.

"Faith in one's fellow man does not mean taking unnecessary risks, my son," he said. "Sometimes 'tis best to remove temptation rather than put it to the test."

After a bit of nudging and cajoling, he reached the opposite side of the crowd and found himself in an open square surrounded by market stalls and lit by lamps. The cause of the mob here was quickly apparent: a troupe of entertainers had chosen this square to set up for those lingering in the streets in the early hours of the night. Jugglers, dancers, and street musicians pandered to the traffic patronizing the market stalls encircling the square, and provided a distraction for the pickpockets sent round the unwary onlookers to relieve them of whatever coin they did not see fit to offer as remuneration for the performers.

"Ah, here we are," Hieronymus said, and forced a path into the audience.

"What do you mean?" Husson asked.

"If you seek information about the road ahead, who better to ask than those who live their lives upon it?"

"I thought the Church took a dim view of vagrants such as these."

"A man of God should not sit locked away with his eyes covered and ears plugged, and one cannot truly minister to souls in need without knowing what it is that they contend with in their daily lives. The Lord intends his world to be experienced." He smiled appreciatively at one of the musicians, a lovely, dark-haired, and olive-complexioned young woman, perhaps a few summers Elsabeth's junior. She sat at ease beneath a bright red canopy, her delicate fingers dancing lightly along the strings of a lute, filling the night air with sweet music. "And many times, the experience must be savored."

He and Husson stood by and watched her performance transfix the gathering audience, most of them men. The Lord of All had seen fit to grace this particular creature with an abundance of charm that was just constrained by the scandalous plunge of her cotehardie's neckline, a strategic choice to draw the attention of onlookers towards her cleavage and away from their purses. It was a task greatly aided by the pendant of colored glass nestled in a quite suggestive manner in between. Sure enough, from the corner of his eye Hieronymus spied a young cutpurse at work at the back of the crowd, taking advantage of her ample distractions. He quietly tapped Husson with his staff and pointed the fellow out, and his companion moved his purse to a much more secure place at his belt.

They waited for her song — a bouncy and quick rustic melody — to end, after which the crowd around them erupted into applause and tossed their coin into an upturned hat lying beside her. She smiled and bowed her head to them (granting a generous peek down her dress to buy her partner a few more moments with their purses) and, with her show at an end, the crowd began to disperse. Only Hieronymus and Husson continued to loiter while she laid aside her lute and gathered up her coin.

"A marvelous performance, my child," he said, his voice filled with all the solemn gravity he reserved for the occasions he chose to exercise the tenants of his office. "Why surely the Lord of All himself has blessed your gentle fingers!"

The woman looked up at him and smiled broadly. "Thank you for your kind words, Brother." she said, her Navarrese colored by an accent out of the Free City-States. "I am pleased you enjoyed my performance."

"Quite! And do my ears detect the melodious strains of Lucca in your speech?"

Her cheeks colored slightly, and she inclined her head. "Your ears are not only kind, but keen as well."

Hieronymus chuckled. "They have had much practice, though I fear many years have passed since I last visited that fair city in my many travels. I particularly miss the view of the blue waters from the markets along the seaside."

Her features brightened noticeably. "My father maintained a studio near the markets. I used to walk them to watch the ships when I was a child!"

Hieronymus smiled and leaned in with interest. "Your father was an artist, then? I fear I never had the opportunity to watch them at work, but you, I imagine, must have provided a wealth of inspiration for many a young master seeking to capture the perfection of Luccan womanhood."

Her cheeks turned bright crimson, and she ducked her head shyly. "You flatter me greatly," she said. "Yes, my father was indeed one of the masters of whom you speak, though he took a dim view to the thought of me posing. Alas I am here because it was the only way I might escape confinement to the home and be free to find a meaningful life of my own."

"A sad tale, but truly a blessing to the people of this fine Inn. Would you not agree?" he asked, with a look to Husson.

"Quite a blessing indeed," his companion said with a greasy smile. The woman, no doubt accustomed to such blatant lechery, took Husson's leer in stride.

"Have your travels taken you far?" Hieronymus asked.

She gave him a proud smile. "They have indeed, across the whole of Boehm and Navarre, and even into Coventry."

"Tell me, then, if you have heard of a village south of here named Checy? For we shall be departing on the morrow, and I regret our knowledge of the land is lacking."

The woman regarded him slyly. "And why would a servant of the Wheel have business in such an out of the way place?" she asked. "Is there something you seek there?"

"For myself, no, but my companion does have business which takes him there, and I shall be accompanying him along the road."

"Well, you shall want to continue south from the Inn. About ten days by foot along that road there is a fork heading west, and it leads right to Checy, only a few miles off the main road."

"I thank you, my child," Hieronymus said, and turned to Husson. "Be kind and pay the dear for her trouble, will you?"

Husson scowled at him. "Me?"

"Well, we are securing directions for your lad, are we not? Your generosity to this lovely creature would undoubtedly reflect well upon you in the eyes of the Lord of All." He fixed him with a look of well-practiced righteous command, which carried with it all the weight of his clerical authority. His companion glared at him in protest, but thumbed into his purse for a coin and casually flipped it at the woman with only a low grumble of argument. Hieronymus nodded curtly and released Husson from his gaze. "Very good. Now then, my child, I shall leave you to your evening. Thank you very much again for your time."

Hieronymus hitched up his staff and was about to start back from the square when the woman brought him up short. "Your pardon, Brother, but if I could beg your indulgence for a moment," she said.

He turned back and leaned on his staff. "What is it, my child?" he asked, in his most patient and ceremonial tone.

The woman clasped her hands in front of her, inclined her head, and looked up at him slightly from beneath her brows. "The company I travel with has been on the road for some time, and I fear I have not had the opportunity to give confession of late. Might I trouble your ear for a brief while?"

Hieronymus raised an eyebrow. "Indeed?" he asked with interest. "And what prompts such urgency?"

She favored him with a coy smile. "I fear I have sinned rather frequently on the road, and 'twould come as great relief to unburden myself."

He glanced sidelong at Husson, who watched the exchange impatiently, and still glowering over having his arm twisted into paying the woman for information she was not truly due remuneration for. Hieronymus smiled back at her. "I have some time to spare before I am due to return to our lodgings for the night." He looked at Husson again. "Be a good lad and wait for me, I shan't be long!"

And without awaiting Husson's acknowledgement, Hieronymus took the woman by the hand and allowed her to lead him to one of the enclosed pavilions set up along the edge of the market square. As she led him inside, he decided Elsabeth deserved his forgiveness for sending him out that night.

IERONYMUS AND HUSSON RETURNED JUST as the master of the Four Ways confirmed arrangement of their provisions for the journey to Checy. They then retired to their rooms for the evening.

They awoke early the next morning, and after breakfast gathered in the stables to ready their horses for departure. Husson's and Maerten's Hackneys were lively and of good disposition, though Josephus took little liking to both animals, and snorted and nipped if they strayed too near. He tolerated Maerten and allowed him to approach and offer him a welcoming scratch behind the ear, but met Husson with a sharp snap of his teeth, and an aggressive snaking of his head. Husson, for his part, wisely steered clear.

Felis took the strangers in stride.

The extra provisions were spread out amongst the four animals and, with everything stowed and ready, they set out with Hieronymus and Husson in the lead, quarrelling with one another as to their pace.

By horse, they would cover the ten-day walk to Checy in half the time. After some miles of running through farmland and open fields worked by peasant farmers, the road passed into empty grassland, and they soon left signs of human habitation behind them. In the distance, Elsabeth could just make out the darker shadow of woodlands ahead.

She spent much of the time riding alongside Maerten to make sure the boy kept up with their pace. He showed little sign of being troubled by the ride, however, and mostly they spent the hours in quiet conversation. Maerten chattered merrily about the doings of his home village, and Elsabeth could not help but smile in amusement at his wonder at leaving it behind, as if the journey to Checy were taking him to the far side of the world. He blushed at reminiscences of the miller's daughter and laughed uproariously over some mischief of the local youths.

There were no real stops along the road, and this far east little remained of the major settlements south of the Four Ways other than burned-out scars of the long conflict between Navarre and Coventry. A few scattered hamlets dotted the fields sprawling along either side of the road, but none were large enough to host a proper inn, or even welcome travelers into a private residence, so they were obliged to make camp for themselves.

The first day out passed quietly, and they made their camp in a sheltered place just off the road, where it turned aside to skirt a large, weathered gray bit of rock thrust upward from the depths of the earth. Stars winked to life as the sun descended in the west and the sky darkened, and the rolling grasses rippled like seafoam in the late-summer evening.

Elsabeth and Hieronymus laid out their bedrolls and tended to their horses. She frowned over her shoulder when she watched Husson put Maerten to work taking care of both their horses, while he sat on a log growling instructions between pulls from a flask. She finished her work with a gentle pat to the side of Felis' neck, and made her way over.

He grinned toothily as she approached. "Hello, love, come to your senses yet?"

"There is work yet to be done round the camp, 'love,'" she said, and with an irritable scowl kicked the log out from under him. Husson cursed when he slipped off. He landed in the detritus littering the ground, and the contents of his flask sloshed out to soak his lap. "So be a dear and get off your ass and lend us a hand."

"Stupid bitch!" he snarled. "This is good wine you spilled!"

"So sorry. Now, get up! We need a fire, and there ought to be plenty of firewood about, so even you might find an armful."

He glared up at her. "'Tis what the boy is for."

"You have two hands and two feet of your own, so put them to use. So long as we travel together you do your share."

Husson glowered up at her and she glared back. He backed down first, but muttered under his breath as he tucked his flask away inside his doublet, regained his feet, and limped off away from camp to gather wood for a fire. Elsabeth watched him go for a moment before she turned her attention to helping Maerten.

"What was that about?" he asked upon her approach. Elsabeth lent a hand in brushing Husson's horse. The horse nickered and bumped her welcomingly with its muzzle, clearly unaccustomed to such gentle treatment.

"Never you mind, love," she said as she worked a burr out of his coat.

Maerten frowned at her. "If there is something the matter with Husson, I would have you tell me."

Elsabeth glanced sidelong at him, and from the look in his eye knew the boy would not let the matter go easily. She sighed. "There is no time for tyrants in your camp when on the road. Everyone must do their fair share."

"At home it has always been up to me to do the work."

"Well, you are not at home now, are you? You have a poor example to learn by in that man."

He frowned. "Husson will not like to hear you say such a thing."

Elsabeth dismissed his veiled warning with a roll of her eyes and gave the horse a scratch behind the ears. "Husson's approval is hardly my concern."

"It should be," Maerten said. The tone of his voice drew Elsabeth's eyes back to him. "He has a frightful temper, and a long memory."

She scowled at that. "I appreciate the concern, love, but I have handled far worse. Now go on and set out your bedroll, I'll finish with the horses."

Maerten hesitated a moment, then nodded, leaving her to work. At times she directed a concerned look towards his back, but if Maerten caught her glances he did not show it.

The rest of the night passed uneventfully. Husson returned without a word to her or Maerten. He did his share of setting up the rest of their camp without further argument, and after dinner they slept fitfully under the stars. They started early again the next morning, and the day proceeded much as the one before it. However, the temperature soon dropped and thick gray clouds closed in rapidly from the west. By midafternoon a gentle drizzle began to fall.

Later in the day the drizzle slackened a bit, and for a few hours stopped entirely. However, as the sun sank into the west, the clouds turned black and threatening. At times lightning lit them from within, and distant thunder rolled across the plains around them. They stopped early that night to set their camp and shelter it as best they could against the rain. This time, Husson lent his aid without her encouragement, though Elsabeth felt the resentment in his eyes whenever he looked at her.

The rain started in earnest after nightfall. It fell in drenching sheets that their tarpaulins could not completely keep out, and made keeping a fire lit impossible. They passed an uncomfortable night huddled together in what little shelter they had, much of which Elsabeth spent fending off Husson's groping hands.

Things looked little better the following morning. By the time they awoke the canvas of their tarpaulins were thoroughly soaked through, and of no further use keeping out the rains. The horses plodded along miserably, and at times they were forced to dismount and lead them through a sucking morass of mud that nearly came over their pattens. If there was any mercy that morning, it was that the road soon delved into dense woodland, and the storm's biting winds were largely broken up by the trees on either side of the road, providing them at least a small respite from the weather. Nonetheless a cold breakfast of dried meat and hard bread after a cold wet night did little for their dispositions.

They rode some hours in low spirits. Even Husson's and Hieronymus's quarreling over the road quieted as they bobbed along with their heads bowed beneath their hoods. Maerten huddled quietly in his cloak in the saddle ahead of her, while she brought up the rear. Her longcoat helped keep most of the rain out, but her hat did little good for her head with the wind in her face, and she vainly mopped the water from her eyes. At times thunder rolled in the dense ceiling of gray overhead, but there was little other sound than the rain pattering on the foliage overhead.

Elsabeth gently nudged Felis forward until she was riding alongside Maerten. He clutched the front of his hood with one hand, his lip trembled, and he shrunk as deeply into his sodden cloak as he could.

"How are you fairing?" she asked.

Maerten glanced sidelong at her from beneath his hood. His expression was perfectly miserable, and he blinked rainwater from his eyes. "Minstrels' tales tend not to say much about the weather, do they?"

She chuckled and shook her head. "No, they don't."

"When I set out, I did not even consider that it might rain like this while on the road. I have seen storms before, and though the roof at home leaked a bit it at least rained less on the inside than out."

"Oh, this is nothing. I once spent a week trapped in a convent on an eyot outside Culsam, when a sudden storm swept up and washed out the bridges across the river."

"What were you doing in a convent?"

Elsabeth smirked at the memory. "Avoiding a rather angry fellow who lost track of the jewelry he had relieved his mistress of and had hidden down his pants, when next he was convinced to take them off."

Maerten's cheeks colored noticeably. "And the sisters did not object?"

"Considering a good many of the sisters were placed there by their fathers because of inconvenient dalliances of their own, I actually received a rather warm welcome."

Maerten blinked. "Minstrels' tales tend not to say much about that, either."

Her smirk widened into a full smile of amusement at his naïve discomfiture. "Well, then you are just not listening to the right minstrels.

"You see, love, the dirty little secret of the world is that people are always people. Just take our good, lecherous Brother," she said and motioned vaguely to where the fat friar was bobbing along on Josephus, who plodded with his head bowed against the weather, and the burden of carrying not only more than its accustomed weight in provisions, but Hieronymus's bulk as well. "He can take all the vows he likes, and you can hang a holy symbol round his neck, but he is still a man. A fact which he attempts to remind me of rather too frequently for my liking."

Maerten chuckled. "If I may ask, how did you even come to travel with him?"

"I rescued him, and I have been living with the regret of it ever since," she said with a laugh, content to leave it at that. The look in the boy's eye, however, quickly convinced her he expected a bit more of a tale.

Elsabeth sighed. "All right. About four years ago I was passing through a little town called Deba and came upon a mob gathered at one end. As I drew nearer, I learned a wandering Olivian brother had been taking indulgences in the town and, well, let us just say he certainly 'indulged' himself with the local magistrate's wife and daughter. At the same time, it would seem."

Maerten's eyes widened, and his cheeks burned even brighter.

"The magistrate was, for reasons I am sure you understand, quite intent on separating the brother's head from his shoulders," she continued. "Well, one licentious and imprudent friar against an entire town seemed hardly sporting, so I decided I ought to help the poor fellow out."

"So what did you do?"

"I arranged a little act of God to put the brother back in the good graces of the townsfolk."

"And how did you manage that?" Maerten asked several moments later when she did not elaborate further. He watched her expectantly, and Elsabeth felt distinctly uncomfortable as she tried to decide exactly how to respond.

"She stripped down naked and ran into the middle of the crowd, babbling like a thing possessed," Hieronymus called back over his shoulder before she could say anything more. Husson looked back at her with a greasy smile.

Elsabeth felt her own face heat this time. "Thank you, love, but I was rather hoping to skirt around that part of the tale," she called back.

"And why should you? 'Twas quite the cunning plan, and perhaps the most enjoyable exorcism I have ever performed. Well, at least until you struck me in that show of flailing about for the townsfolk's benefit."

"That was no more than you deserved for where you had your hands during your 'ministrations,' you lech. But the townsfolk were so overawed as he 'cast out' the demon that they decided right then and there the Lord of All had forgiven him for his indiscretions with the magistrate's wife and daughter, and let him depart with me in safety."

Maerten watched her with his lips pressed close together, trying his best not to burst out into laughter.

"Oh, just let it out. 'Twas not one of my proudest moments, I admit," she said. "But I was outnumbered and could not in good conscience stand by and let him be strung up just for being indiscriminate with whom he waved about his staff. Especially for the magistrate's wife and daughter. Let us just say if any minstrel were to sing songs of their beauty, they would be unquestionably farcical."

"For that matter, I think the magistrate had other threats to the uprightness of his wife and daughter than me alone, anyway," Hieronymus added. "I had a rather unfortunate rash for a week afterwards."

"Well, there is a thought I would like to do without," Elsabeth said.

"And you have traveled together ever since?" Maerten asked.

"Yes, someone has to be around to keep him out of trouble."

"As I recall, Tetty, 'twas your indiscretions that had us fleeing for our lives from the last village," Hieronymus said. His expression was unreadable as he watched the road in front of them through the gray curtain of the falling rain, but the indignation in his voice was evident.

"Now there is a tale or two I could stand to hear," Husson said.

"Then you can use your imagination, as I have no words for you on such a matter," she snapped back.

Husson just returned that greasy smile. "Oh, believe me, I already am. Now I actually have something to look forward to in camp tonight."

"I'll remember to keep my sword close, then."

They managed only a few miles more that day while the rains continued to pour down around them, and they set camp as best they could in the shelter of a birch thicket. The wet and cold did their dispositions no favors that night, little helped by the prospects of another cold meal. Husson spent much of the time after they stopped taking pulls from his flask and grumbling at every little thing; from the leaves Elsabeth had him pile on top of his soaked tarpaulin in a vain effort to keep the rain out, to the sodden ground beneath it.

Elsabeth was piling leaves atop her own shelter after tending to Felis, when a commotion from that end of the camp caught her attention.

"Boy! Where are you, boy?" Husson shouted. His words slurred together, and there was no mistaking the anger in his voice. Elsabeth paused in her work and looked over her shoulder. Husson swayed on his feet with his flask in hand.

"Wretched, useless boy. Come here! Now!" he called again.

Maerten appeared from deeper in the thicket with a large armful of leaves. "Yes, sir?" he said cautiously, and approached like a dog accustomed to a beating when called to heel.

"Where have you been, boy?"

"Gathering leaves like Mademoiselle Elsabeth said." Elsabeth frowned at what was shaping up before her, and she spied Hieronymus approaching from his shelter.

"What is this about?" he asked in a low voice.

"I am not sure, but I don't like the looks of it," she said. Elsabeth rose and wiped her hands clean on her thighs.

Husson took a drink from his flask and wiped his mouth on the back of his sleeve. "Why do you not have a fire going?"

Maerten shifted awkwardly. "There is not a dry place to put a fire, and all the wood is wet."

Husson strode forward and seized the boy by the collar. "Don't give me excuses, boy!" he hissed, and a sharp crack echoed across the thicket when his hand flew and struck Maerten across the face. The boy yelped and recoiled from the blow, and the leaves fell from his arms. This only seemed to enrage his guardian more. Elsabeth was on the move immediately and rushed across the camp. Husson's arm came about a second time, but his third blow was cut off when she placed herself between the two and seized his wrist.

"Enough!" she snapped. Husson snarled in rage and leveled a blow at her head in an effort to escape her grip, but in his current state she effortlessly twisted him into an arm bar and drove him face first into the ground. Her own temper flared, and she gave him a little harder pull on his arm than she really needed to restrain him. "I said enough!"

"Bitch! Take your hands off me!" he snarled, his voice muffled by the mud and leaves in his mouth.

Elsabeth released him and rocked easily back to her feet. Husson scrabbled against the slick mud beneath him. He immediately rounded on her and went for a rondel concealed beneath his cloak at his back, and rushed her with an awkward and unbalanced lunge. She casually deflected the blow safely past her, closed the distance, and threw him over her hip. He landed hard on his back, and the air rushed from his lungs with a sick grunt. Elsabeth put a booted foot down on his wrist.

"Now then, are you finished?" she asked. Elsabeth retrieved his knife and crouched over him with the tip at his throat.

Husson glared balefully up at her. "Get off me!"

"And I thought you have been fantasizing about having me on top of you all day." Elsabeth pressed the rondel against his throat, and Husson immediately froze. "Well," she said. She reached inside his doublet, relieved him of his flask, and slipped it into her own jacket. "I think you have had quite enough of this." She stabbed the rondel to its hilt into the ground next to his head and backed away from him.

Husson grumbled a string of rather creative curses and oaths under his breath as he retrieved his knife and returned to his feet.

"Now, apologize to the boy." she added.

"What?"

Elsabeth glowered at him. "You heard me."

Husson looked at Maerten, who had fallen in the scuffle and remained where he landed, with Hieronymus tending to the wicked bruise Husson's blows had left on his face. He turned his attention back to her and glared. "The boy is my ward and responsibility," he said. "What business is it of yours?"

"I am making it my business. Do you wish to argue further?" Even in his inebriated state Husson could not miss the hard edge and threat in her voice, and she did not need to lay her hand on her sword hilt; he merely bowed his head to Maerten.

"My apologies," he said without sincerity. Not expecting more, Elsabeth did not press the point further.

"If I were you, I would go to my shelter and sleep off that wine," she said. Husson started away. As if as an afterthought, she stopped him with a hand on his shoulder. "And if you should ever lay hand to the boy again, I'll cut it off and find out just how far up your ass I can stuff it."

Husson shook off her grip and stormed away with an exaggerated limp, and left the three of them alone.

Elsabeth watched him go for a moment, before kneeling beside Maerten and Hieronymus. She gingerly tipped his chin so she could inspect the bruise herself, while

Hieronymus went about preparing a salve. "Are you all right, love?"

He winced as her fingers gently probed the mark but gave her a small nod. "It hardly hurts at all. And besides, 'tis not the worst I have received. Husson has a fierce temper sometimes, especially when he has been drinking."

She fixed him with a hard look. "That ends. Now. Don't think for a moment I bluff or jest with what I have said. If he ever should touch you again in such a manner, he will be losing more than his pride."

Maerten shifted uncomfortably. "Thank you, but I don't wish to get you into trouble with him. He shan't let go his grudges lightly."

Hieronymus chuckled softly. "I would not worry overly much about that, my son. There is no one I know who holds to a grudge like my dear Tetty, here. Which I have learned to my endless regret."

"I hope you are right. I would not like to see you come to harm on my account."

Elsabeth offered Maerten a gentle pat on the shoulder, and let Hieronymus get back to work tending to the bruise across his cheek. "Hieronymus may like to argue to the contrary, but I truly can take care of myself."

OHECY WAS A SMALL VILLAGE JUST TO THE west of the road south from the Four Ways. It sat on the north side of a dirt path branching off the main road, on the edge of a small lake to its west, with fields and pastures cleared out of the woodland to its north and east. The woods to the south of the road were much denser than the more open woodland they had been traveling through, with dark shadows beneath the trees. Further west the road began to climb into a series of hills and ridges, and a steep, tree-lined bluff overlooked the western shore of the lake. Of the town itself, a mill stood on the banks of a stream draining the southern end of the lake, and the only other significant structure was a large communal hall at the center of a cluster of single-family dwellings, barns, and a few storage sheds. A low, rough wooden wall encircled the settlement, with gates on the south and north walls giving access to the road and fields, respectively.

The rains had reluctantly drifted off to the east, and the last day of their ride was relatively dry, though the road was a morass of mud. Their spirits lifted, and without his drink to exacerbate his foul disposition, Husson's company became more tolerable, though Elsabeth could not help but feel the dark looks he gave her whenever she drew near. But he gave them no further trouble and avoided Maerten altogether, which considerably brightened the boy's mood. Between that and the improving weather, Maerten quickly proved much more amicable, and frequently rode beside her, whiling away the long hours of travel listening to any story she would tell him of her travels.

By the time they reached the town it was late in the afternoon. The sky to the west was clear and golden with all the clouds slowly moving eastwards towards Boehm, and the shadows grew long as sunset approached. They were met on the road by a small group of men, most of age with Hieronymus or Husson, but one seemed to be within a summer of her, and there were two boys who looked to be about the same age as Maerten.

"Now Tetty," Hieronymus muttered as they drew nearer, "let us at least try to leave this place without angering the wives. They have a wall, so I little like our chances of escaping in a hurry."

She made a face at him. "Should I have you make the same promise about husbands and fathers? Pay attention to your own inclinations, love, and I shall see to mine."

Hieronymus grunted. "I am a man of the Wheel! I don't need you lecturing me on propriety."

Elsabeth just rolled her eyes and changed the subject. "Awful strange they would send out a welcoming committee. I wonder what this is about."

"Curious," he said with a nod of agreement. "I would almost say they were expecting us."

They pulled their horses up short of the gathering ahead of them and dismounted. "Keep an eye on the horses," she said. Elsabeth handed Felis' reins over to the friar, and waved Maerten over.

"Yes, Mademoiselle?" he asked, with a wary look at the faces watching them from further up the road.

"It looks as if they are waiting for us. This is your quest, love, so let us go and say hello."

He frowned and gave an uneasy look to Hieronymus and Husson waiting behind with the horses. Husson just glowered back at them and continued to fume quietly at her usurping his control over the boy. "Should we not all greet them together?"

"It always pays to be cautious, love," she said. "'Tis better we have someone to cover us from behind if things turn ugly."

She swept the tail of her coat aside to clear the hilts of her sword, and she led him the rest of the way along the road to meet with the group awaiting them. She saw no signs of weapons among them, and they all kept in a tight group, almost more curious about the newcomers than showing any sign of wariness themselves. They certainly made no attempt to encircle them.

"Do you expect trouble?" Maerten whispered.

Elsabeth quirked a grin. "When you are in it as much as I am, you come to always expect it. It keeps me alive."

They reached the group waiting for them. The leader, an older man perhaps a few years older than Hieronymus, with a rough but broad and pleasant face, silvering hair the consistency of straw, and a short silver beard shot through around his lip with streaks of brown betraying its former color, stepped forward to meet them. His skin was weathered and his hands were gnarled from long years working in the sun, and he dressed in simple homespun. He leaned on a wooden cane, but a closer look provided no further indication he was armed.

Elsabeth gave Maerten a surreptitious push forward, putting him out in front of her and making it clear that he was the one whom their challengers should address (unnecessarily, though, as aside from a few looks at her sword, the attention of the party was fixed on the boy). Maerten inclined his head politely to the group barring their path further down the road.

"Good day to you," he said, his voice somewhat uneasy.

The leader of the group returned the gesture. "Good day to you, young master."

"Could you please tell me if this is Checy up the road yonder?" he asked. Elsabeth smiled inwardly. *Well, it almost seems like the boy has done this before. Good lad, that should keep them guessing how much you really know.*

"Aye, it is," the man said. His voice was cracked with age, but there was no hint of malice or deception Elsabeth could hear. He spoke in the dialect of Navarrese common among the folk they had met in this part of the country.

Maerten let an excited smile slip through, which he hurried to mask again. Elsabeth watched the gathering closely, and from the small grins on the faces of the locals she guessed Maerten's expression had not been missed.

"Wonderful!" he said, unable to keep his excitement out of his voice as well as he did with his features. "Who is the magistrate of this village? I wish to arrange for shelter for the night, for myself and my companions."

The elder man leaned on his cane and regarded him with some amusement. "Well, I suppose 'tis me you wish to speak with, as we have no magistrate. We are too small, it seems, for the local lord to trouble with us overly much, so we are largely left to ourselves. We receive visitors from time to time, so there is room in the common house for guests."

Maerten smiled agreeably. "Very good! We are, of course, willing to pay for lodgings, and for news of the area."

The elder raised an eyebrow. "Are you indeed? Is there something particular you have come to such an out of the way place for?"

Elsabeth leaned on her sword and scrutinized the old man carefully. From his expression and tone of voice at that question, it sounded as if he knew more about their visit than he let on. *Careful, love, these fellows are no simpletons.*

"Perhaps. I am seeking someone, and I was told to meet him here," Maerten said.

He smiled. "I see. You have come seeking Sinopus, then?"

"Sinopus?" Maerten asked, trying his best to hide the excitement of being given a name to go with his rumors.

The old man lowered his voice conspiratorially. "The Wizard." He laughed at the discomfited expression on Maerten's face. "Do forgive an old man for taking some enjoyment at your expense. Of course you have come to call on him! Why do you think we came to meet you? He told us himself that you would be coming soon."

Elsabeth frowned, but Maerten's face was filled with wonder. "He did?" he said, and turned to Elsabeth. "Did you hear that? He knew that we were coming!"

"Extraordinary," she said, not nearly as ecstatic as the boy.

"Come! Come!" The old man insisted, and turned a moment to the men around him. "Go on, then! See to their horses, the poor things look positively miserable from their journey, and the weather has been dreadful!" The townsfolk muttered their acknowledgments and saw to the task. Hieronymus and Husson stiffened warily at their approach, but Elsabeth waved them down, and they allowed the men to take their horses and lead them up the road. Meanwhile, she and Maerten fell into step with the old man.

"My name is Talbot," he said, "and I am master of this village, so far as it goes. I built the first house here some thirty years ago, with my wife and sons, so the others who came after have taken to looking to me to speak for them."

"Rather strange that the local lord has not troubled with you before now," Elsabeth said.

"Ah, she speaks! I must admit you gave us quite a shock with that blade at your side, Mademoiselle. But the truth of the matter is, these lands were once in the dominion of the Ducs of Rouen. But the last of the old Ducs were exterminated fighting the Coventrish well over a generation ago, so when they were driven out again there was no one to take their place. After that, the old Duchy was never reestablished, and the King chose to break up the land among vassals of his own. The nearest is the Comte de Eze, to the West, at what was once the capital.

"I suppose you might consider him our Lord, but we are a small village and produce little more than we need for ourselves, so his Grace does not often bother with us."

They reached the village gate, and he led them inside. The walls were low, just a palisade of tree trunks without a walkway, best suited for keeping out riffraff and outlaws after dark and would not so much as delay a determined assault. The grounds inside were grown with grass, but clearly defined paths had been worn in the lawn and were now a slick morass from the recent rains. The population was mostly made up of families who either worked the plots outside the walls to the north and east or raised animals in the pastures. Like Talbot, they dressed in simple homespun. Elsabeth noticed right away there was no chapel here.

"And what does the Church think of your neighbor?" she asked.

Talbot shrugged. "That I can hardly begin to answer. We are not even large enough that they see fit to send us a priest of our own, and the nearest chapel is at a town a few days further west of here. I suppose they have too many concerns of their own to trouble about him."

He led them to the communal hall, a rather large wood-framed building with a thatched roof in the center of the village. A few of the villagers gathered round it and engaged in local business among themselves, but some watched their arrival with curiosity. Hieronymus and Husson hurried along to catch up with them.

"Well, here we are!" he said, then called up to a man and woman about Husson's age standing near the door to the building. "Colin! Ysabel! Do take our visitors in hand!" Talbot turned back to them. "If you have indeed come to see Sinopus, we will take you to him tomorrow, as it is too late now to visit him. For now, my son and daughter will see to it that you are made comfortable."

Talbot inclined his head politely again, then strolled off. Elsabeth watched him go with a frown, then followed after Maerten as the boy rushed into the common house.

LSABETH STOOD IN AN EMPTY AREA BEHIND the common house. The sky above and to the west was clear and dusted with a net of silver stars, though in the east she could still see the black smudge of the storm continuing onwards into Boehm. In its wake it left behind the fresh scent of summer rain on the grass and among the trees, and now that they had an opportunity to dry themselves and their gear after trudging through the mud and muck, they could actually appreciate it. Though the heat of summer promised to return on the morrow, tonight it was still cool, with a gentle wind out of the west pushing the rear guard of the storm away.

She held her sword in her gloved hands, dressed only in woolen hose and her undershirt, and her copper hair was drawn back in a loose ponytail. Elsabeth raised her sword to her shoulder and into *Vom Tag*, and started through a slow series of cuts, letting each one flow into the next. Some fell along a line across her body from shoulder to hip, or with a twitch of her hands flipped the point through a quick rising slice, and then through a level cut at eye-height. She slowly began to pick up speed, until she lost herself in battle against an imaginary opponent, every move short and precise, eschewing the theatrical flourishes of the tournament fighters in favor of the quickest and most direct cuts and defenses.

Her appearance, of course, had caused quite a stir amongst the villagers upon their arrival in Checy. Now, many stopped in their evening labors to watch, intrigued by the sight of her long hair rippling behind her like a banner while she worked through her drills, and the graceful movements of her lithe figure darting through an infinite series of attacks, evasions, and counters. If there were looks of disapproval she ignored them, accustomed as she was to them. All that existed for her was the feel of the red leather covering the waisted two-handed grip of her sword, and the weight of the slender Boehman steel blade as it flowed with brutal elegance through her cuts.

Hieronymus, taking full advantage of the villagers' hospitality and generosity with their ale, had been well deep into his cups when she stepped outside. She felt Husson watching her. He leaned against the outside wall of the common house and glowered at her back, and, she had no doubt, leered at her figure as all manner of impure thoughts passed through his head.

Then there was Maerten, who spent much of dinner questioning the locals closely about the man they called Sinopus, enraptured by each tale they told of the miracles he worked. It was all rather mundane nonsense to her ears: potions and powders of the sort local midwives and healers might use, and nothing that would interest even the basest of minstrels to spin tales of his power, but Maerten listened, enraptured. It was certainly enough to not even plant a seed of skepticism in the minds of the townsfolk, who paid him well for his services in goods; the best of their sheep or cattle, a generous supply of produce from the fields, or the finest of the ale or wine they brewed. And, of course, those wealthy travelers coming to see the truth of the rumor for themselves paid even more handsomely with gifts of gold or silver coin.

Elsabeth finished a complex pattern dropping in and out of half-sword, striking with her guard and pommel, stiff thrusts followed by powerful cleaving blows, and finally ended with a spring out of distance from her imaginary opponent and settled into *Pflug*. Then she relaxed her guard and mopped the sweat beading on her brow with the back of her gloved hand, and started back towards the bench where she had left her jacket, doublet, and scabbard, and a cup and pitcher of small beer.

Maerten sat at the bench and watched her in awe after finally tearing himself away from the stories intended to whet his appetite for the visit to Sinopus. Upon reaching him, she slid her sword into its scabbard, doffed her gloves, and took a long drink from her cup.

"Every time I see Soest it makes me think of an ox: Big, dumb, and crude," Husson said from where he was watching her exercise. "Yet, I think I am not giving enough credit to the ox."

Elsabeth rolled her neck to stretch out the muscles of her shoulders. "Da Lucca is only worthwhile for entertainment, and even then, only of the very basest sort. Even those foolish tournament showmen look upon him as an artistically deficient jester at best."

Maerten frowned at them. "I don't understand why you speak so about one another. Is there really such a difference?"

She laughed and took another drink. "There are three sorts of fighters, love," she said. "You have your soldiers, of course. Such fellows are well-trained in fighting together, and if you were to go into battle that discipline is certainly what you wish to have at your side. You also have fellows such as Russdorffer and da Lucca, who are more dancers than fighters. Oh, the crowds certainly love them, for they offer a great spectacle with their pomp and flash, but though such a show is fine when entertaining drunkards from the lists, if one's life depends on that bit of steel in one's hand, such excessive movement greatly works against them."

Elsabeth drained her cup and refilled it from the pitcher. "And what of the third sort?" Maerten asked.

She set the pitcher aside and swirled her cup for a moment before taking another drink. "The third sort are the warriors: students of teachers such as Hieronymus's dear Leonardus, and my own master, Paulus von Soest. True, simpletons find our art rather aesthetically displeasing because we eschew the overwrought dramatics of the tournament fighters, but this is because they teach that the whole purpose of our arms is to safeguard our lives as efficiently as can be." Elsabeth smirked over the lip of her cup. "That we dispense with their heroes in short order in the tournaments only intensifies the fools' dislike of us."

Maerten smiled. "So, you are one of these warriors." He made it a statement of fact.

"Of course."

"Have you won many tournaments, then?"

Elsabeth sighed. "Regretfully not. Unfortunately, I find it rather troublesome to even enter my name in the lists at all."

"Why is that?"

"Well, I am not quite sure if you have noticed, love, but I happen to be a woman." She chuckled when Maerten blushed in response. "I am the only woman Master Paulus ever taught, in fact. I suppose I could have become a master myself by now, had I been born with something other than what I have 'twixt my thighs, but the Schwertbrüder would not test me. In large part because no one wished to acknowledge a woman could be their equal with the sword, and Master Paulus could not do so himself, as I was his own student. The Grand Master was very insistent on holding to that point, though there was nothing explicitly against it in their bylaws, and I was left something of their dirty little secret." Elsabeth drained her cup and thumped it down on the bench next to her.

"'Tis much the same with the tournaments. Though most of the knights and masters of arms who compete would not even consider it possible for a woman to best them, there remains enough doubt — particularly as I have made no secret of with whom I studied — that they dared not risk the humiliation should I do so. So, my attempts to enroll are usually ignored or tossed aside."

Husson grunted. "That Soest would even lower himself to teaching her at all says all you need to know about the man, boy. I am rather amazed he was allowed to keep his school."

Elsabeth turned her eyes on the man and gave him a steely-edged glare. "If you wish to continue that line of slander against his memory, you and I will be heading towards a rather fatal disagreement. Master Paulus was the greatest swordsman and teacher I have ever known, and the arrangement was made by my father, so the Grand Master had little recourse but allow it."

Maerten frowned at her. "His memory?"

She sighed, and instead of refilling her cup, retrieved Husson's flask from inside her jacket. Elsabeth pulled the stopper, took a long drink, and made a face. The wine tasted strongly of vinegar and was thoroughly unpleasant, though was certainly potent enough.

"Hey!" Husson snapped. "That is mine, and cost me a good *sou*."

"If you want it back, come and take it, if you can. Though for the life of me I cannot imagine why you would even bother. Good wine my ass, you overpaid for it."

She took another drink in an effort to drown the bitter memories welling up and returned her attention to Maerten with a sigh. "Master Paulus was badly wounded in a quarrel perhaps seven years ago. He only just found the strength to return to the schola, and he died there." Elsabeth stared at the ground for a moment, then took another drink. "I must, with regret, confess the dispute was over me."

"What do you mean?"

"There were some things said at my expense, to which Master Paulus took offense. Though his argument was stronger, that of his adversaries had the advantage of numbers. Four of them, all together. He slew one, but he did not have the ground to contend with the others all at once."

"The ground?"

"There are different ways to fight depending on whether you are fighting one or many. The idea is to position yourself so you can force them to fight you one at a time. Doorways and narrow hallways in particular are good for this; furniture works in a pinch. That nonsense you see entertainers perform, where they show one man encircled by foes and he fights his way free? Well, that is just a good way to end up dead, unless your adversaries are utterly incompetent. Unfortunately for Master Paulus, they already had him outflanked before the first blow."

Maerten nodded. From his expression it seemed he did not quite understand what she meant, but he did not press her further. "What happened after?"

Elsabeth took a long drink. "I found them sharing a drink at the local tavern, and I slew them all right then and there."

He blinked at her. "All three of them?"

She nodded. "All three of them. I was not much older than you are now, but even if there were a hundred, I would not have let his death go unpunished." Elsabeth stared at the ground for a moment as the memory washed over her, and she recalled the anguished rage burning in the pit of her stomach when she set out in search of vengeance.

"I wish I could say I found satisfaction in avenging him, but in the end, I was without him and without a home. I had to leave Soest that night and have been on the road ever since."

Elsabeth set aside Husson's flask and picked up her sword. For a moment she rubbed her finger across the escutcheon — *Quarterly 1ˢᵗ and 4ᵗʰ Azure, on a bend Or three bears erect Sable Quarterly 2ⁿᵈ and 3ʳᵈ Gules, two longswords in saltire proper in chief a gauntlet Or* — set into the leather between the belt straps. Then she drew it, and studied her reflection in the polished Boehman steel. The prominent center ridge ran the length of its slender hollow-ground blade, and the edges tapered slightly for a good portion of its length before curving gracefully into a formidable awl-like point.

"All I have left of him is this. 'Twas his own sword, and when he died I took it with me and used it on his killers. Many of his other students would greatly desire to have it, but I will never give it up.

"You see, love, your sword is a part of you, and so long as I carry it, there is a part of him that is still with me." She slid the sword back into its scabbard and studied it for a long moment. "In turn, it has also become a part of me."

Husson grunted derisively. "Humph. Foolish sentimentality. A sword is just a tool."

"Hardly. A sword has a mind and will of its own. You don't wield it; you and the sword wield each other."

Maerten blinked at her. "But 'tis not just steel?"

"Oh, of course," she said. "But consider this: When you swing a sword there is weight behind it that gives it momentum, and that momentum determines where the sword will go. If you ignore that, you will be fighting your own blade as much as you fight your opponent. You must work with it, guide it, and redirect it, but never break it. You must feel what the sword wishes to do to properly control it. Even those twirling fops like Russdorffer and da Lucca recognize that."

"Could you teach me?"

Elsabeth blinked in surprise at his question, and even Husson was taken aback. "Now that is just too much to bear," the elder man snarled. "The boy is in my charge, and damned if I'll allow you to fill his head with Soest's boorish philosophy."

She glared over her shoulder at him. "I think the boy is showing quite a bit of wisdom in his choice, and 'tis his own decision to make."

Maerten fidgeted nervously. "I really don't wish to cause you any trouble," he said, "if Husson is not agreeable."

Elsabeth took him by his hand and pulled him to his feet. "Oh, don't worry about him. I neither need nor care for his approval. You are certainly old enough to decide for yourself." She leaned in and lowered her voice conspiratorially. "Besides, I rather enjoy annoying him."

Maerten laughed as she led him to the middle of the common area where she had been working, and left Husson to fume impotently for a moment before he stormed off to sulk in the common house.

HE NEXT MORNING DAWNED HOT AND humid. The sun was just beginning to rise above the rim of the horizon in the east when they were awoken by Colin and Ysabel, and there were no longer any signs of the storm clouds in the distance.

Talbot arrived as they were finishing their light breakfast, with three other villagers in tow. He found them seated at a table in the communal hall nibbling on the last of their meal and nursing their small beers.

"They have questions to ask of Sinopus as well, so they will show you the way," he said of the three men accompanying him. "He dwells on the far side of the lake. Unfortunately, there is no landing there for boats, so you will have to make the trip overland."

Elsabeth gazed into her nearly empty cup while she considered his words. "That will take much of the day. What if he decides he is disagreeable to having visitors by the time we get there?" she asked

"Sinopus has never yet refused anyone who has petitioned him," Talbot said with assurance.

"That does not mean he never will."

"But he is expecting me," Maerten said, no less assured than Talbot. "Surely he would not turn us away?"

Elsabeth sighed. "When do they intend to depart?"

"They just await your party," Talbot said. "We will prepare provisions for the day for you. You will need to leave your horses behind. The trail, I am afraid, is too difficult for the poor things to manage."

"Oh, of course, that would only make it too easy."

"Now, Tetty, be polite," Hieronymus said, waving a sausage at her in admonishment that he promptly stuffed into his mouth.

Elsabeth rolled her eyes. "Well, a hard walk would be good for you, at least. Will you be able to keep up, or have you enjoyed too much of their hospitality? Or should I say their ale?"

Hieronymus choked indignantly on his sausage and glared. "My dear, I was campaigning before you were even an itch in your father's codpiece. Don't be concerned about me being unable to keep the pace."

"Oh, good, I was afraid this would end up like our little trip through the Frueles."

Maerten did his best to stifle a laugh. "What happened in the Frueles?"

Elsabeth smirked at him and tossed back the last of her small beer with one swallow. "We barely made it up the first ridge when he caught sight of the next and tried to turn right back round again. And then he did nothing but huff and complain the whole march."

"If you are finished with your reminiscences, we should go," Husson grumbled as he finished his own drink. "The sooner we can be off, the sooner we can find this Sinopus. And the sooner you can be paid, and I can be free of you."

Elsabeth pouted. "And you were so eager for my company when we set out."

"That was before I learned what a troublesome harpy you are."

Hieronymus chuckled. "My son, I have been living with that regret for the past four years. I am sure you can manage a day or two more."

"So long as she walks ahead of me this time, where if I must contend with her tongue then at least the scenery will be more enjoyable."

Maerten frowned at her from his place at the table. "You and Brother Hieronymus will truly part ways with us, then?"

"That was the arrangement," she said, trying her best to ignore the familiar stab of guilt in her gut at the disappointment in his face. Hieronymus eyed her closely, but neither Maerten nor Husson seemed to take note of her troubled expression. Elsabeth quickly offered him a conciliatory smile to put her mind off the memory threatening to worm its way back to the forefront of her thoughts. "Don't worry, love, I imagine we will remain here a day or so more after we visit your wizard to restock our provisions and see about other work to be had before we move on."

"Well, unless you have a mind for farm work, I am afraid there is not much to be found here, miss," Talbot said. "Though, I suppose we might beg your companion to lend his ear for a spell, since we seldom have the chance to speak with a priest."

Elsabeth chuckled. "Oh, I rather think you would prefer to pass on the sorts of indulgences Hieronymus trades in, at least if you have any daughters."

Hieronymus glared and Maerten stifled another laugh, but Talbot disregarded the comment. "For the sort of work I imagine you would be looking for, you are best off looking around Eze."

"We will keep that in mind, thank you," she said.

They spent perhaps an hour more preparing for the march to Sinopus's dwelling, gathering what gear they would need for the day from their baggage and leaving the rest behind. Hieronymus was already grumbling about the heat when they stepped from the common house, and the air was close and stifling, filled with the singing of birds and the buzzing of insects. The wind had shifted in the night and was now coming out of the south, denying them a welcome gust off the lake west of the village.

With no other words between them besides Hieronymus's muttered oaths about a stiff wind from the Dark One's nethers, they set out along the westward road, led by a tall fellow named Galleren with several days' growth of beard. He was about Husson's age and owned the mill along the stream draining the lake. Another, a few years younger, was called Andry. He was a short but broad-shouldered man with shaggy hair, who kept goats on the pastureland outside the walls. The last was a farmer named Durant, perhaps a half dozen years Elsabeth's elder, with a neatly trimmed beard. All of them dressed in simple woolen trousers and doublets, heavy leather boots, and pattens for the mud. They carried packs or satchels, and Galleren wore a broad-brimmed hat with a low, rounded crown not unlike hers.

The road crossed over the water just downstream of the mill by means of a simple wooden bridge. Though the lake itself was clear, here the water was murky from the mud churned up by the wheel of the mill, or as it swirled round the wooden posts supporting the bridge. Shortly after crossing the woods closed in around them again and cut them off from the wind, and with it their only relief from the oppressive heat of the late summer's morning.

A short distance from the bridge, Galleren turned aside and started down a faint and narrow track leading deeper into the woods. It might have been heavily used in the past, but now it was fading as the woodland encroached to reclaim it. Behind Galleren went Andry, followed closely by Durant. Elsabeth sent Maerten on ahead of her, with Hieronymus following behind. Husson was left to bring up the rear, at which he huffed in irritation, but otherwise without too much of a complaint.

'Tis too bloody hot to put up with his mouth today. If he were to start on me, I would surely cut out his tongue and be done with it.

Much as she feared, it took the greater part of the day to navigate the trail. It was choked by roots and overgrown by brush, and at times all but disappeared under a blanket of old leaves cast off over many turnings of the seasons.

Branches reached for them like gnarled and clawed fingers, and despite the heat of the day, Elsabeth was grateful for her longcoat, which saved her from the worst of the scratching and grasping. They walked in silence, too focused on the trail to find much interest in idle conversation.

At times, she caught a glimpse through the trees of sunlight sparkling on the surface of the lake, taunting them with brief visions of its cool waters and the open air outside. The trail soon began to ascend, and the march only became more difficult. They climbed up a steep rise overlooking the lake and village to the east. Maerten slipped once or twice, and if not for her catching him he might have slid all the way back down the trail again. Hieronymus started grumbling and steadily grew louder, Husson stumbled on his bad leg, and finally even she could take no more and called for Galleren to stop.

"We are nearly to the top of the trail," he said in protest.

Elsabeth doffed her hat and mopped the sweat beading on her brow with her sleeve. "And the top of the trail will still be there waiting for us," she said. "I think we can spare a few moments to rest. If this wizard of yours truly knows we are coming, then I am sure he will understand if we stop for a spell. The boy has nearly fallen several times already, and I would rather we not trouble this Sinopus to mend a broken leg."

"I am all right," Maerten said breathlessly, but his voice rang of false assurance. "The trail is not so hard."

She gave him a smile and a pat on the shoulder. "Oh, I am sure 'tis not. But believe me, should you slip and fall, you will find the way down quite a bit faster than the way up. Besides, the good Brother could stand a moment off his feet. I know that my ears could benefit from a break from his carrying on, and I must admit my pattens are killing me."

"And if I had breath in my lungs, I would have a suitably indignant retort for you, Tetty," Hieronymus wheezed. Instead, he found a fallen log along the edge of the trail, plopped himself down heavily upon it, and hung his head wearily.

"Nearly to the top," as it turned out after they resumed their ascent, meant perhaps another half an hour of climbing before the trail leveled off. The bluff visible from Checy fell away sharply towards the lake below on their right, and they were afforded a spectacular view eastward across the lake.

Galleren led them on, and the way eased considerably. The trail angled westwards away from the brink of the bluff and back under the cover of the trees for a short way, before opening up onto a clearing nestled between the arms of another rise. A modest stone hut supported by timber beams with a tiled roof stood between the arms of the hill as it stretched westward from the end of the ridge. A low stone wall enclosed the entrance to the fold, and access to the space within was provided by means of an open archway. A large bell hung in a low tower next to the entrance.

"This is the dwelling place of the Wizard," Galleren said as they approached the wall. Wisps of white smoke curled from a chimney at one end of the building, and windows gazed out from the eastern face. A lawn of green grass filled the enclosure, and a garden of fragrant herbs occupied a well-tended bed on the south side of the yard.

In the middle of the lawn stood a rough-hewn slab of stone fashioned much like an altar, and beside it a pool of clear water. Cages with birds of a variety of colors were spaced irregularly about the space and filled the air with song. "We must announce ourselves, and wait," he added, indicating the bell.

Elsabeth glanced at Hieronymus, who merely shrugged with bemusement. Husson regarded the garden with disinterest, but Maerten's face was alive with wonder at the sight. The birds, at least, were of sorts Elsabeth was unfamiliar with, and foreign to this region. Some of the herbs growing in the garden possessed an odd aroma. Nonetheless, there was a wholesomeness to the air that seemed to ease the strenuous effort of the climb up the hill.

"Well," she mused, eyeing their surroundings carefully, alert for any signs of trickery, "I suppose we should announce ourselves then."

"Let me!" Maerten exclaimed, practically bouncing on the balls of his feet like an eager puppy.

Though his enthusiasm did nothing for her skepticism, it at least eased her lingering irritation over the heat and climb. Elsabeth smiled and nodded to the bell. "Go on. This is your quest, after all."

Maerten clapped his hands, stepped forward, and rang the bell. It resonated across the top of the bluff, and the birds within the garden immediately fell silent. The peal hung in the air for a few moments, and then slowly died away again, leaving the hilltop as silent as when they arrived.

"Now we wait," Galleren said.

"How long?" Elsabeth asked, and stared expectantly at the door to the hut.

"As long as it amuses him, I suppose," Andry said. "He is a rather peculiar fellow. I once waited almost half a day before he appeared."

Elsabeth grunted. "Well, I am glad he finds it amusing to keep people waiting, but we did not come all this way to stand around for his convenience."

"Please, Mademoiselle," Galleren said, "this is the way of it."

Hieronymus touched her gently on the arm. "Come now, girl, 'tis just a man assured of his own importance choosing to remind us that he is in control here. 'Twill hardly be the first time either of us has contended with such a preening fool."

She merely sighed in response and leaned against the archway.

IT WAS NEARLY TWO HOURS BEFORE SHE heard the door to the Wizard's hut creak open. Elsabeth rose from where she was sitting against the wall. She brushed the dust and detritus off of her backside, and joined the others waiting at the archway to watch the appearance of Sinopus.

At first, she saw nothing but the black opening of the doorway, until a striking and exotic young woman emerged. She wore her black hair piled elaborately atop her head, and her painted lips stood out cherry-red against her light olive skin. However, it was her dark, almond-shaped eyes that most clearly marked her as foreign. Her long, pleated, purple skirt brushed the ground. Above her skirt she wore a short, wrap-around pink jacket with voluminous, bell-like sleeves. Both skirt and jacket were made of satin and embroidered throughout with silken thread. A silk sash cinched the jacket and skirt tightly to her narrow waist. Aside from ornaments of jade and gold in her hair, she wore little jewelry of note.

The woman stepped to one side of the door, and a second woman, so alike in appearance and dress to the first that Elsabeth found it difficult to tell them apart, followed and stood on the opposite side of the opening. The women waited there in silence, like soldiers standing sentry, and for a few minutes more everyone who was gathered at the archway watched the black doorway yawn open on the eastern wall of the hut. Then, as Elsabeth's patience was beginning to wear thin, a third and final figure emerged, and the silence of their three companions from Checy took on a reverent air.

In his youth he might have been a tall man. Now he stood bent with age and leaned on an elaborately carved staff as he stepped from the darkness of his hut. Every minstrel's fancy Elsabeth ever heard suddenly sprang to life at the sight of him.

Whence came his companions was far beyond her reckoning, but Sinopus's garb unquestionably hailed from beyond the Free City-States and the sea, in the sun-soaked deserts of the western Izmiri Empire, though he himself was fair-skinned and blue-eyed, and not of the sort of men she had seen among the Izmiri traders who reached Boehm or Coventry. His white hair was thinning, and his long white beard trailed to the center of his chest. His cheeks beneath his beard were gaunt and sunken, and his nose was prominent and hooked.

He dressed in a long button-down robe that reached to his ankles beneath an open coat of similar length with billowing sleeves. Both robe and coat were woven from brilliantly colored and patterned silk (gold and blue, respectively), and his shoes were made from deep blue velvet that was richly embroidered. A white sheepskin kalpak with a turned-up brim sat atop his head, a multitude of amulets hung from his neck and clinked together whenever he turned, and a wide red and gold silk sash tied about his waist beneath the outer jacket completed his garb.

"Well, he certainly looks the part," Hieronymus muttered at her shoulder as he joined her to watch the old man emerge. The two women stepped up to either side, took him by the arms, and supported him as he shuffled across the lawn to the altar at the center of his garden.

"Looks, yes," she murmured back, and leaned her shoulder against the arch, "though it all could just be for show."

He grunted and fell silent while the rest of their companions gathered around the archway and waited. Maerten watched in awestruck wonder at the sight of the Wizard, and Elsabeth allowed herself a tight smile. Husson just folded his arms across his chest and leaned against the opposite side of the archway to watch the procession. Whether or not he actually believed the stories he had never really said, and whatever he thought of the spectacle he seemed disinclined to speak it now.

Sinopus reached the altar and passed his staff to the woman on his right hand, who accepted it with a reverent, stiff-waisted bow, before she turned her attention to the gathering.

"My master bids you welcome," she said in Navarrese colored by a peculiar, unfamiliar accent.

"Let those who come to petition Sinopus the Great come forward," the other said, with the same accent.

"Beginning with you," the first woman said, and leveled a finger at Galleren. The miller doffed his hat and bowed his head as he entered the garden.

As Galleren drew nearer, Sinopus waved a hand over his altar, murmured something in a strange tongue Elsabeth could not understand, and suddenly the top of the altar burst into brilliant golden flames. As the fire roared to life, Elsabeth jumped back in astonishment. Her heart leapt up into her throat, and her hand reflexively went for her sword. Hieronymus was similarly startled beside her and made the sign of the Wheel. Husson's reaction was no less alarmed than her own. Only Maerten remained where he stood, his mouth agape with wonder at what he had just witnessed.

"Did you see?" he asked, and pointed emphatically. Maerten seized her by the arm of her jacket, tearing her hand free of her sword-hilt. "The stories are true!"

"Calm yourself, love," she said in a low voice, and put a hand on his shoulder to stop his enthusiastic bouncing. "As impressive as I must admit that was, I have seen displays not unlike this, if not so spectacular, from jugglers playing to fair-goers many times."

"But surely—"

"Silence!" one of the women called. Elsabeth was unable to venture a guess which one of them had spoken.

She patted Maerten on the shoulder, and then folded her arms under her breast again. He restrained his impatience with great effort. With their interruption addressed, Sinopus turned his attention on Galleren.

"Speak, and be heard," the Wizard said. Unlike the women at his side his Navarrese was clean and without accent. Despite his age, his voice was strong and clear, and carried across the bluff. "Why have you come?"

Galleren bowed his head. "I am Galleren of the village below. My wife has fallen ill, and I come seeking your aid."

"Describe for me the nature of her malady."

"'Tis an illness of the stomach, your Magnificence," he said. "She has been unable to keep food down and has great pain in her belly. Her skin tingles, and she feels a numbness in her face and limbs."

Hieronymus leaned in. "Sounds like monkshood, or I am no Olivian," he murmured. "Poor creature." Elsabeth frowned and nodded, needing no lecture on the deadly effects of such a poison.

Sinopus made a show of gazing into his fire. "Your wife has been poisoned," he concluded, almost speaking over Hieronymus's own diagnosis. "You run the village mill," he added, making it a statement of fact. "Tell me, have you had vermin in the mill this summer?"

"There was an infestation of rats, yes. My sons and I treated them."

"You placed bait poisoned with ground monkshood."

Galleren hesitated a moment before he responded, and twisted his hat in his hands sheepishly as he spoke. "Yes, we did. My wife prepared the bait before we laid it out."

"Your wife mistakenly ingested some herself. Fortunately, it was a trace only from her hands after handling the bait, otherwise she would already be dead." The last was added without a trace of empathy, almost as if the Wizard was bored in delivering his conclusion. "I will prepare for you a treatment of foxglove, which shall purge the poison from her body."

Galleren bowed deeply at the waist. "Thank you, Magnificent One! Thank you!"

Sinopus waved him off. "Yes, yes. Follow the instructions I shall give before you depart, and she will recover fully."

Hieronymus folded his arms across his gut and leaned his staff against his shoulder. "Foxglove as a remedy? That is a new one," he remarked in a low voice.

"What was the name of that fellow from Ysa whose wife slipped foxglove into his wine?" Elsabeth asked. "'Twould have been rather a clever way to do away with him since they had no other herbalist to expose her had you not been there."

He nodded, but fell into silence as one of the Wizard's assistants called Andry forward. Galleren stepped aside with his hat bunched impatiently in his hands, allowing the other to approach with a bowed head. Sinopus disinterestedly motioned for the goatherd to speak.

"I, too, come from the village, your Magnificence," he said. "In the last three weeks I have lost four of my herd: a buck, two of my best does, and a kid have all vanished."

Sinopus sighed irritably. "This is why you trouble me?" he asked.

"My goats are my livelihood," he said. "Without them I have no milk or meat to sell, or food for my family. The buck is not so great a loss, but the does were my most productive. We have searched but found no sign they escaped in the night, or that they were taken by animals. My sons have scoured the woods for a day's distance from the village in all directions, and we have neither sight nor sound of them. If they left a trail, 'twas washed away in the rains."

The Wizard listened carefully as Andry spoke, then waved his hand above the fire blazing on the altar and murmured in the same strange tongue as before. The flames instantly and energetically responded to his commands, and flared brightly and with a loud *whoosh*. The flickering tongues abruptly changed from golden to green. Everyone gathered, except for the Wizard and his two companions, jumped back reflexively.

"I would say he is rather enjoying his little display," Elsabeth muttered, and spit the Wizard on an irritated glare.

If Sinopus heard her he ignored the remark, and merely made a show of gazing into the fire as the green flames bathed his face with an eerie light. "There is a family dwelling in the woods two days north of your village. They stole into the town and took the animals. Seek them beyond the north end of the lake."

Andry bowed his head. "Thank you! I will search for them!"

The Wizard, bored with the exchange, waved him away, and his assistants summoned Durant forward. "You have come to me before," Sinopus declared.

"I have, your Magnificence," he said, and lowered his head respectfully in greeting.

"Why then do you return? Do your crops not grow?"

"They do, Magnificence, better than I had hoped! But therein I am troubled. My fields are now so fruitful that I fear come harvest time much of it will be put to waste. There is too much to prepare for storage before it all begins to rot, and the rest of the village has work enough of their own at harvest to aid me and my family."

Sinopus fixed the farmer with as annoyed a scowl as Elsabeth had ever seen, and his voice took on a hard edge. "You came to me for aid, and now you come to give complaint over the results of my assistance?"

"No, your Magnificence!" Durant stammered, a note of panic in his words as he practically stumbled over himself to soothe the Wizard's injured pride. "I came only to seek counsel on what I should do! The size of the crop should give the village plenty to spare over the winter, and I cannot bear the thought of it going to waste!"

The Wizard sighed in annoyance, waved his hand once more over the fire, and murmured his words of power. With another sudden flare the flames changed color again, this time to a pale blue-violet. Elsabeth folded her arms across her chest and gazed into them, but whatever Sinopus saw — if anything — was hidden from her.

"The family which took the goatherd's animals is desperate. Their meager fields are failing, and they will have a poor harvest. But they have strong backs: a man, a woman, and three tall sons. In payment for the goats they have taken and for a share of the surplus that will otherwise go to waste, they will aid in your harvest."

Andry strode forward a pace in protest. "But Magnificence, 'twas my animals that were taken, and I who am owed for the theft!"

Sinopus looked up from his fire and glared at the goatherd, and his protest faltered under the Wizard's eyes. "They will repay their debt at harvest."

Andry shivered noticeably and bowed his head. "Yes, your Magnificence!" he said, and hastily retreated, seeking a safe place away from Sinopus's gaze. He need not have bothered, for the Wizard turned his glare on Durant.

"Do you object to my counsel on this matter?"

"No, Magnificence!" Durant said hastily, and bowed graciously. "Thank you!"

"Then you are done here. You have brought payment?"

Galleren nodded. "Yes, Magnificence," he said, and in turn each of the three villagers opened their packs and satchels and presented their offerings. There was nothing particularly special Elsabeth could see about the Wizard's price. Galleren offered him a sack of flour large enough to feed a family for a month, from Andry two large wheels of goat cheese, and Durant produced a sack of cherries. The Wizard regarded each in turn and nodded in satisfaction.

"I accept your offering," he said, and murmured in the ear of one of his companions, before the other started to lead him away.

"The great Sinopus shall now prepare the treatment for your wife," the woman who remained behind said to Galleren. He bowed so deeply Elsabeth thought he might fall over on his face.

Maerten shifted anxiously beside her and wrung his hands as the Wizard departed.

"What about me?" he whispered, and his frustration set off a pang of sympathy in Elsabeth's gut. "He did not ask about me."

Elsabeth laid a hand on his shoulder. "Easy, love, this is his little performance, so let him play it out. I am sure this is all some sort of dramatics for our benefit."

He glared at her irritably. "You still don't believe? Even after what we have seen here today?"

Hieronymus grunted. "I will confess 'twas quite the spectacle, my son," he said, as Andry and Durant retreated from the inner garden and made their way past. Husson watched the wizard's companion with a hungry gleam in his eye, and Elsabeth found a bit of relief in his attentions turning elsewhere for the moment. "It certainly had the look of darker powers."

"But you don't believe," Maerten repeated.

"Faith is my stock and trade, my son, and quite understandably I have given little study to the occult myself, though I suspect the Master of my order could even teach this fellow a thing or two. I certainly believe that there are other powers at work in the world beyond the Lord of All's." Hieronymus planted the end of his staff on the ground and leaned his weight against it. "This is beyond my expertise to judge its nature, but he does possess a degree of knowledge and wisdom, however he came by it."

Elsabeth folded her arms across her chest. "From this vantage I suspect he might have no trouble spying the household who robbed the goatherd's flock even without the need for scrying, or whatever purpose his little show served."

"But what about the flames?" Maerten insisted, pointing emphatically at the altar, where blue-violent tongues of fire continued to lick at the sky.

She sighed. "If 'twas just a clever trick, I cannot see how he managed it, though I was never that good at seeing through jugglers' deceits. Are you certain you still wish to go through with this? Sometimes the truth is hardly worth the trouble, and that bauble of yours could buy you a fairly decent bit of living for a time."

Maerten twisted his lip and stepped away from her defensively. "I cannot believe you would say such a thing!" he snapped. "I am so close to having questions I have asked all my life answered, and I shall see it through!"

Elsabeth sighed and pinched her nose. "I understand you think this to be important, but we still don't even know if this wizard can tell you anything, if he is so inclined. Powders, potions, smoke, and flames look impressive, but say very little."

"You speak as would my mother, if I knew who she was."

Hieronymus stifled a laugh, and she shot the friar a murderous look in response.

"I speak as one with a long history of disappointment," Elsabeth retorted.

"Mostly in the beds of suitors not up to your appetite, I imagine," Hieronymus murmured, earning him a sharp punch to the shoulder that he shook off with an amused chuckle.

"Fancies and dreams are wonderful things," she said instead, "but minstrels' tales lose their luster when you learn the truth behind them." She leaned against the archway and gazed levelly at him.

"I once spent an evening enamored with a fellow who spun grand tales of his adventures, until it chanced he spoke of his exploits in the Free City-States. He was challenged by a knight traveling out of Lucca when it came to the tale he was telling of protecting a village from an outlaw band. The knight revealed that when the battle commenced, the fellow actually spent it cowering with the children in a barn and making quite the mess in his hose."

Maerten eyed her dubiously. "So, what did you do, then?"

Hieronymus broke in before she could finish the story herself. "She dumped her ale over the storyteller's head, and I did not see her again until she stumbled from the knight's tent outside the town walls the next day. Never let it be said my dear Tetty cannot bounce back from a disappointment."

Elsabeth glared daggers at the friar, who took a great deal of amusement at the coloring of her cheeks. "And had the man's account of himself not been exposed?" Maerten asked.

"Then 'twould very likely have been his spear she spent the night working, rather than a knight's lance. All in all, I think she rather came out ahead, in her end."

She planted her fists on her hips and stared Hieronymus down, but he showed no more sign of being intimidated by her ire than before. "One more word from you, and I'll see if you can walk on water — from the top of the bluff. I suspect you would sink right to the bottom if the Checy locals don't mistake you for a whale, first."

"Oh hush, Tetty," Hieronymus said, not for the moment assigning her threat any sincerity. "If you intend to speak to the boy of truths and disappointments you can hardly spin falsehoods yourself."

"I would rather like to hear more of it, in fact," Husson said from across the archway, tearing his attention away from the Wizard's remaining companion to give her a greasy smile.

"I rather liked you better when you were eyeing me for a place to put a knife," Elsabeth snapped in return.

"Oh, I still am, but there is something else I would like to stick you with first."

"If I sit myself upon another lance before this trip is done, 'twill not be yours, and that is a truth of which you can be assured."

Before Husson could offer a retort, the door to the hut opened, and Sinopus reappeared. The Wizard handed a small cloth bag to one of his assistants, and she in turn gave it over to Galleren. "Infuse this as a tea, and make her drink it," he said, "It will counteract the poison. In the future, I advise greater care when baiting your mill."

Galleren bowed again. "Thank you, your Magnificence, thank you!" he said, his graciousness overwhelming to Elsabeth's ears.

Sinopus just waved the man off. "You are done here. Be gone and return to your village." And with that, he turned to start back into his hut.

Maerten's jaw dropped, and for a moment was unable to find his voice as he watched the Wizard depart. The hurt and disappointment in his eyes were more than Elsabeth could bear, and whatever the truth of the matter, she could not see him denied the opportunity to ask his question.

"What about the boy?" she called at Sinopus's back, and the Wizard stopped to glare at her over his shoulder.

"I said you are done here," he said.

She scowled at him and strode forward a pace. "Just a bloody moment! While I don't know what sort of trickery all this has been," Elsabeth snapped, and waved vaguely at the altar and the flickering violet flames, "we have spent a hard five days in bloody awful weather on the road to get here, and the boy has had an even longer journey."

"That is not my concern, come back tomorrow."

"Easy, Tetty," Hieronymus muttered at her flaring temper, but she ignored his subtle warning, and the flash of anger in the Wizard's eyes when she took a step through the archway and into his garden.

"Like bloody hell we will!" she snapped. "He has talked of nothing but this moment for days, the least you can do is humor him before brushing us all off."

Sinopus murmured in his strange tongue, and waved his hand over the fire. Elsabeth caught, or thought she caught, a subtle flick of his wrist, but whatever she might have seen was lost when a ball of flame appeared in the wizard's hand, and she froze in astonishment at the sight. He barked out a curse in the same language and flung the fireball in her direction. It struck the ground almost at her feet, and Elsabeth only narrowly managed to dive back through the archway before a wall of fire flared to life across the entrance to the garden.

Galleren, Andry, and Durant fled in a panic down the trail leading back to Checy. Husson ducked back from the archway and cursed in alarm, slapping at his arms and cloak in fear of an ember setting him alight, and Maerten cowered in fright behind him. Hieronymus's retreat was managed with greater dignity, but he made a holy sign and muttered a prayer to the Lord of All nonetheless. Elsabeth rolled back to her feet as soon as she struck the ground, and her sword rasped as it flashed from her scabbard. The barrier of fire sputtered and died again almost as quickly as it had ignited, and the stunned silence was broken only by the Wizard's cackling laughter hanging in the air.

"You have fire, woman," Sinopus said, and she was not quite certain if it was said in admiration or mockery. "But mine is hotter."

Elsabeth willed her heart back out of her throat and down into her chest where it belonged, and glared back at him. She kept her sword point lowered and her body relaxed, but ready to spring into motion at need. "And you have steel in your spine. Do I need to test how it matches against mine? Let him be heard."

Sinopus laughed again, this time full of mirth and amusement, and he studied her carefully. "So ready to fight for a boy you scarcely know? Intriguing. Very well, then, come forward," he said, and beckoned to Maerten.

Maerten peaked out from behind Husson at the summons, and swallowed visibly as he warily started forward. He eyed the archway with distrust, as if it might burst into flames again at any moment. The Wizard took delight in his caution, while his assistants watched dispassionately. "Come, boy, have no fear. If I desired you dead, you would not be standing there now."

Elsabeth nodded her head at Maerten, silently prompting him to continue. She casually returned her sword to its scabbard, then stooped to retrieve her hat from the ground whence it had fallen in her flight from the garden.

Hieronymus stepped up beside her and watched the proceedings warily. "Well, that was exciting," he murmured. "You and I must one day sit down and have a long talk over your manner of making friends; preferably before it gets us killed."

"I rather would like to not have to make the bloody trip up again just because the man has the whim to be contrary," she said.

They fell into silence once Maerten reached the altar, and he gazed in wonder and no small bit of fear at the Wizard's display of power. Sinopus just watched him closely. "Tell me, then. What is so important that your companion is willing to risk my wrath to force me to hear it?"

Maerten swallowed nervously, and slowly reached inside his doublet to produce his medallion. "I am an orphan, your Magnificence," he said quietly. "Husson has been my guardian for as long as I can remember, but he is not my father. All he could tell me is that when he found me, this was round my neck. I had hoped you might tell me its meaning, and whence I came."

"It is a divination you seek," Sinopus said, as a statement of fact.

"I suppose," Maerten said hesitantly. Sinopus motioned at the medallion in an unspoken command, and Maerten reluctantly pulled the chain over his head and handed it over to the Wizard.

Sinopus studied it closely. He murmured a few words in his peculiar tongue and waved his hands over it. "It is old," he said, his voice distant and his eyes going out of focus, as if looking into a far-away place or time. "Very old."

Elsabeth watched him closely, looking for some manner of trickery, but having no luck of it. What Hieronymus thought of the matter he kept hidden; he had fallen into his minister's face, which he used most when taking confession, and desired to hide his amusement or disgust at the sins of the laity. Husson merely watched with bored indifference.

Sinopus stopped what he was doing abruptly. "I can read no more at this time," he said wearily. "The spell of divining I must call upon is difficult and time-consuming, and cannot be performed here."

"It sounds expensive," Elsabeth muttered, just loud enough to be sure her voice could be heard. The sharp glare of the Wizard quickly told her it carried as far as she hoped.

Maerten looked to her briefly, alarmed by her impertinence, and then hastily addressed the Wizard. "I have brought you payment, of course! I would not have come all this way otherwise."

Sinopus sniffed and looked down his nose at Elsabeth. "I am afraid even as lovely as they are, her charms hardly make up for her tongue."

Hieronymus snorted in his attempt to hold back his laughter, while Husson made no such effort and guffawed loudly. He leaned one hand against the archway and slapped his knee with the other. Elsabeth felt her own face heat indignantly.

"I am no man's payment," she growled, and laid one hand to the hilt of her sword in the event someone chose to argue the point.

"That is true enough," Hieronymus said, and wiped away a tear escaping his eye over the effort of restraining his mirth. "I would say 'punishment' would be a more apt description."

Elsabeth glared hellfire at him, but her expression only robbed him of his control, and he fell into a roaring fit of laughter that earned him an irritated slap up the back of his head which only made him laugh harder.

"Are you quite finished?" she asked. She folded her arms across her chest and stretched so she was towering over the rotund friar. Hieronymus mastered himself with an effort and wiped the tears of mirth from his face.

"Ah, forgive me, Tetty. I have not had a laugh such as that since the time I found you hanging tangled in a bed sheet while trying to climb out of that merchant's house in Bintel before his wife found you."

A smug grin spread across Sinopus's features at the results of his gibe. He motioned to the gathering. "Come, let us continue inside," he said.

One of the women (Elsabeth could still not tell them apart) quickly went to work retrieving the offerings left by their departed companions, and the other supported Sinopus and helped him retreat inside his hut. Elsabeth eyed his back doubtfully as she considered how crowded the interior would be, but nonetheless followed with the rest of the party as the Wizard led them inside.

Y MEANS OF A CLEVER TRICK OF
perspective the Wizard's hut was not
nearly so small as its exterior implied, and
extended a fair ways into the hillside
behind it. The interior comprised one long, open chamber
with a sleeping area at the far end, and a kitchen nearest the
door. Odds, ends, junk, contraptions, and other
paraphernalia — many of them things Elsabeth could not
name — of Sinopus's profession filled much of the space,
with a small round table and four chairs in the center of the
kitchen.

Pots, pans, skewers, knives, and spoons hung on the
wall to their left over the hearth as they entered from the
garden. To their right were shelves laden with clay pots, jars,
plates, and cups of a haphazard collection of colors and
styles, and several large barrels, one of which smelled
strongly of ale. The fresh scent of meadowsweet lent the
wizard's hut a wholesome and earthy air, mingled with many
more smells of unfamiliar herbs and spices.

A curtain could be drawn across the hut to separate off
the sleeping area, which was dominated by a single large bed

in the middle of the right wall (Elsabeth did not see separate beds or mats for the wizard's two attendants) and a large storage chest at its foot. The rest was a cluttered mess of his tools and equipment. There was a large telescope and an armillary sphere of the sort she had heard described by adventurers returning from the wars in Izmir tucked away in one corner. Pushed up against the wall opposite his bed was a shelf laden with an impressive and diverse variety of books, scrolls, and bound sheaves of vellum. Another door in the far wall led deeper into the hillside.

There was little other decoration of note, aside from what Elsabeth suspected was the payment of visitors come from beyond Checy.

Sinopus paused for a moment upon entry, and addressed the woman tasked with bringing the offerings of their erstwhile companions into the hut. "Ch'u Niang," he said. The woman set Andry's wheels of cheese on the table and turned to face him with a bow and her hands clasped in front of her.

"Yes, Great One?" she asked, and waited for his instructions.

"Once you have brought the payments inside, see to our guests' comfort. The matter between the boy, his guardian, and I must be addressed in private."

She bowed again. "Yes, Great One." Ch'u Niang then brushed past them to continue bringing in the rest of the offerings.

Maerten frowned uneasily. "Can they not come with me?" he asked with a hesitant look at Hieronymus and Elsabeth. "They are my companions."

"No!" Sinopus barked. "The Lord of All is unwelcome in my sanctuary, and the presence of His servant will disrupt the lines of power within."

"But what about Mademoiselle Elsabeth?"

The wizard regarded her contemptuously. "She is polluted by lesser men, and I have not the time or desire to properly purify her."

Hieronymus snickered, and Elsabeth met Sinopus's contempt with an incensed glower of her own. "While my virtue has been insulted far more creatively and by better men than you, Wizard, I am beginning to tire of it," she said.

"Now, now, Tetty," Hieronymus said, and laid a hand on her arm as if in fear she might do something rash. "I am sure whatever heathen spirits empower him are merely particular about the company they keep, which is more than I can say of you."

She turned her annoyance on him and shook his hand off. "I wonder what they would have to say about you, considering the unseemly characters with whom I have seen you associate."

Hieronymus gave her a wounded look and leaned on his staff. "Still your lying tongue, harpy! You know full well my only concern is for the souls of those poor unfortunates!"

"Yes, I am sure that when the Lord of All observes your ministrations, he sees nothing to appall him. Regardless, I don't like this idea of Maerten going off alone with only that dancing fool to protect him," she added with a nod towards Husson.

"If you wish to settle this—" Husson began, and started towards her until Maerten stopped him with a hand to his arm.

"'Twill be all right, I am certain," Maerten said, as calmly as he could manage. Nonetheless, there was a nervous hitch in his voice. "If this is what I must do to get the answers I seek, then I'll not be afraid."

Elsabeth sighed and hung her shoulders in defeat. "Go on then, love, this is your adventure after all." She eyed the Wizard. "However, if anything should happen I don't like, I'll test whether your magic can keep me from splitting open your head."

"Have no fears for the boy," Sinopus said, with an admirable amount of restraint over her threat. "No harm shall come to him while in my keeping."

Elsabeth just fixed him with a scowl and folded her arms under her breast. The Wizard lead Maerten and Husson across the chamber and through the door at the far end. She shook her head at the door and sighed. "I don't like this in the least," she muttered.

Hieronymus grunted his agreement, leaned his staff against the table, and took a seat. "Nor I. Unfortunately, I would say we are rather at his mercy. As you said yourself, 'tis certainly his show."

She unbuckled her sword from her belt and propped it against the table, then dropped heavily into one of the chairs with her back to the nearest wall. "What do you think?"

"'Tis rather difficult to venture a guess. His display was certainly quite impressive, though I see nothing miraculous about his counsel." Hieronymus took a deep breath. "The air is certainly wholesome, but I smell nothing I have not seen discussed in every manuscript on herbalism I have read in my time."

Elsabeth nodded. "There is always that display with the fire, though. Oh, I have seen many cunning tricks before, but this, at least, puts them all to shame. If 'tis truly a fraud 'tis at least quite an impressive one."

The door leading out into the garden opened again, and Ch'u Niang entered with the sack of flour thrown over her shoulder. She let it drop next to the barrels pushed against the wall, then swiftly departed to retrieve Durant's offered bag of cherries.

"I suppose we might have offered to help while we were waiting," Hieronymus mused, though Elsabeth suspected his thoughts were, in truth, drifting to the barrel of ale tucked away next to the shelves, and imagining what the woman hid beneath her jacket.

Elsabeth regarded him with a smirk. "Are you so losing faith in the Lord of All to provide you with willing conquests you may actually be looking to use manual labor instead? Lord knows the effort would do you some good."

"Now, Tetty, I am merely being polite!"

"Of course you are, though I imagine Sinopus is unlikely to accept you doing his attendants' chores as part of the payment he desires for whatever drivel he has to say about that medallion."

"Well, at least you need not worry about paying him from your back. This may in fact be the first time I have seen your many blessings from the Lord so casually tossed aside."

"Oh, go jump in the lake."

Ch'u Niang appeared through the door at that moment and closed it behind her, then added the sack of cherries to the rest of the goods. She then bowed to the two of them. "If there is anything you require, please speak, and I shall attend to you."

Hieronymus smiled pleasantly at the woman. "I could stand a drink, myself," he said. "If 'twould not be too much trouble."

Elsabeth rolled her eyes. "I hope you are well-stocked. Once he starts that barrel will be dry by the end of the night."

The woman inclined her head to Hieronymus and went about filling a clay tankard for him. "We are more than well-supplied; the Master sees to it."

"I am sure he does," Elsabeth said. "But in that case, one for me, as well."

Ch'u Niang set a tankard on the table for Hieronymus and filled another for her. The friar took a long, slow draught, and nearly downed the whole tankard in one swallow. "Hmm, not bad," he said. "It reminds me of a brew I sampled once in my intemperate youth, when I was serving under the Baron of Godra after my studies with the great Leonardus."

The Wizard's attendant set a tankard in front of her, and Elsabeth took a drink herself. She quietly conceded the brew was quite excellent. "That is amusing," Elsabeth quipped, "as I somehow cannot imagine you having ever been temperate. Or a youth, for that matter."

"As a matter of fact," he said around another draught of ale and mostly ignoring the gibe, "'twas when I was little older than you are now, my dear Tetty. We were on a campaign suppressing some recalcitrant *ritter* or another, and had encamped for the night outside a little village named Failtz. I was just departing from an encounter with a lovely little golden-haired lass, when I chanced upon three quite inebriated fellows of the Olivian order. Well, they had plenty of ale to go around, and seeing as I had come fresh to the contest, I thought 'twould be no small matter at all to join the revelry. Much to my surprise, I found myself being carried back to camp by my new comrades."

Elsabeth rolled her eyes and took another drink from her own tankard. "And that is when you decided to devote your life to the Lord of All."

"Oh, no, of course not. I was a veritable devil myself in those days," he said. "But when I found my true calling, I certainly remembered them. And their ale." Hieronymus eyed Ch'u Niang closely, and Elsabeth watched as something turned behind his eyes. "I imagine another of my brothers must have come this way not long past."

"We have not been visited by one such as you before," Ch'u Niang said, her expression unreadable. "The Master is a skilled brewer by his own hand."

Hieronymus merely grunted and drained his tankard with a last swallow. "Well then, I must give my compliments on the fineness of his ale. If you would be so kind as to refill that for me, my child?"

Ch'u Niang bowed and did as he asked. Whatever Hieronymus was thinking Elsabeth could not guess, so she sat and nursed her drink. "What can you tell us about Sinopus?" she asked instead.

"It is not for me to discuss the Master's personal affairs," the woman said, and handed Hieronymus his refilled tankard. He smiled contentedly and tilted his head back for another long draught.

"I am merely curious as to why he would be dwelling in such an out of the way place as this, rather than serving as some great lord's conjurer."

Ch'u Niang fixed Elsabeth with her dark eyes, and her cherry lips twisted into a disapproving scowl. "Because the Master desires to be more than a slave to petty lords in a gilded cage."

"And I am sure to avoid too close scrutiny," Hieronymus observed into his tankard, "from the Church least of all."

She turned her glare on the friar. "The Master has nothing but distaste for servants of the Broken Prophet. Men sent by your bishops to spread the word of your God violated the hospitality granted to them by the *Huángdi*, and burned my village to the ground when we would not embrace the Wheel."

Elsabeth blinked in confusion. "Hoongdi?" she said in butchery of the word, clearly one from the woman's native tongue.

"*Huángdi*," Ch'u Niang corrected. "Master of all Chang'an."

Hieronymus considered his tankard. "I had heard stories of missions sent into the Great East after the success of a few merchants. No word ever came of them."

"The traders were welcomed, and behaved with greater respect and honor than did your men of the Wheel. The former were paid well for their goods and met with great interest over their tales of the West. The latter, the *Huángdi* had executed wherever they were found within the bounds of Chang'an once they showed their true faces."

The friar took another drink. "Barbarism," he grumbled.

Ch'u Niang remained composed and refused to rise to his bait. She instead smiled wickedly. "Yes, and we repaid theirs in kind."

"And how did you come to be in the service of Sinopus?" Elsabeth asked, hoping to steer the conversation towards something potentially more informative than a debate on the overzealousness of missions into the East.

"Six years ago, my sister and I survived the sacking of our village when all the others were massacred. The Master saved us before we, too, could be put to the sword, and so we follow him."

She raised an eyebrow. "Saved you?"

"He appeared among them with a flash, like lightning, and they were all struck dead on the spot."

"So he came with the missionaries?"

Ch'u Niang scowled in disgust at that suggestion. "Of course he did not! I cannot say whence he came, but he appeared out of the West. Perhaps he traveled with the merchant caravans, or perhaps he wandered alone. However he came to be there, his timing was fortuitous for my sister and me. I am happy to serve him, and will continue to do so until he should release me."

Hieronymus took another drink and set his tankard down on the table. "Has he ever spoken of how he comes by all his knowledge?"

"Never!" she said sharply. "And it is not my place to question him on such matters. If he should desire to pass on his wisdom, it is his place to do so. I am but to serve him."

Elsabeth considered that. "In what manner, I wonder."

"In whatever manner he requires of me."

She smirked into her tankard. "Oh, I imagine so. You chose the wrong calling," she added with a grin at Hieronymus.

He chuckled back. "So it would seem."

"Do you mock the Master?" Ch'u Niang asked, a hint of warning in her voice.

"Love, we mock nearly everything," Elsabeth said.

"I remind you that you are guests in the Master's home, and I advise you to respect his hospitality."

"In all seriousness, my child," Hieronymus interjected around a mouthful of ale, "I am quite intrigued by your master's knowledge, particularly his skill in herb-lore. Why, I was just telling my dear Tetty even in all my studies I had never heard of foxglove used as anything but a deadly poison."

"I find it doubtful he would wish to impart his secrets on you, Man of the Wheel," she said dismissively.

"A pity, then, if he intends to hold it to himself when it might be of benefit to many."

Elsabeth let out a short laugh. "Though 'tis certainly of benefit to him to keep it secret. Unless I miss my guess, everything in this hut was donated as payment for his services."

Ch'u Niang spitted her with her dark eyes and was about to issue a retort, when the door at the far end of the hut swung open and Sinopus emerged, supported on the arm of Ch'u Niang's sister. He carried a large leather-bound manuscript tucked under his other arm. Maerten followed behind him with a dazed expression that put a lump in Elsabeth's throat. Last came Husson, no less stunned.

"Arise and give homage!" Sinopus said in a loud voice. "For the Duc of Rouen has returned!"

IERONYMUS'S DRINK WAS FORGOTTEN IN the aftermath of Sinopus's pronouncement. Elsabeth lowered her tankard, and could only stare in stunned silence at Maerten shifting nervously and red-faced behind the Wizard. It took her several long moments before she finally managed to find her voice.

"What."

Sinopus shook off his attendant and strode forward purposefully. He beckoned Maerten to stand beside him.

"I had my suspicions, but have now concluded with certainty: The medallion he wears has been passed down through the line for six centuries, protected by an enchantment so it shall never leave the possession of one with the right to carry it. It marks him as the rightful heir to the Ducs of Rouen."

Elsabeth blinked a few times in a vain effort to process what the Wizard was telling her. Then she let out an exasperated groan, and wearily pinched the bridge of her nose. "Oh, God, Hieronymus, I told you this was a bloody awful idea from the start."

Sinopus hobbled up to the table and laid his manuscript down flat, opened to a page somewhere in the middle. Elsabeth was unfamiliar with the tongue and script in which it was written, and the ink was faded and browned. The parchment itself was cracked and aged, as was the leather binding and cover, but otherwise it was well cared for. On the illuminated page to which the Wizard opened it was a painting of the medallion, reproduced in perfect detail. As with the script around it, the colors were fading, but still clearly legible.

Hieronymus frowned at the image. "They said in Checy the line was exterminated fighting the Coventrish."

"The male line was extinguished, yes," Sinopus said. "But there is rumor that when the Coventrish stormed the castle at Eze and the Duc and his sons were slain in its defense, his daughter was spirited away by a loyal knight at the Duc's command. It is also said that when the Duc was slain, neither he nor his sons were in possession of the hereditary arms and armor of Rouen."

Elsabeth drained the last of her ale and thumped the tankard down on the table. "I think I need another one of those," she murmured, and Ch'u Niang inclined her head and went about refilling her drink. "And what, I wonder, became of them?" Elsabeth asked the Wizard.

"The Duc's daughter vanished into the countryside with the knight, never to be seen again. Of the arms and armor of the Duc, that is not so mysterious. They were taken from Eze and entrusted to Estienne, Baron du Auch. Auch itself later fell and was razed by the Coventrish, but the arms and armor were not found. That is where I advise you to begin."

She stared at Sinopus without comprehension. "Begin what?"

"For the boy to reclaim his birthright, he will need these tokens."

Elsabeth gawked at him. "This must be a jest."

Maerten stepped around the Wizard and clasped his hands in front of him. "I came here to learn who I am," he said. "How can I stop now that I know the truth?"

Elsabeth mopped her face. "This is the sort of thing that belongs in stories and songs, love. It does not happen in real life. What will happen if you pop up making such a claim is a hanging, if you are lucky."

"I would listen to her, my son," Hieronymus said around a swallow of ale. "I have seen my share of pretenders in my day, and it never ends well for the claimant."

"If what Sinopus says is true, then I am no pretender, but the rightful heir!"

"And you have only your bauble and the word of this man to go by," Elsabeth said. "You cannot with any sincerity believe that the King of Navarre would merrily reinstate a peerage he clearly had no desire to maintain in the first place."

"Of course not!" Maerten said. "That is why we must go to Auch!"

She buried her face in the palm of her hand. "And just why is that?"

"If the arms and armor of my grandfather are there, I must find them."

"The arms were stored in a vault beneath the castle," Sinopus said. "When the Coventrish came they never found it, though the whole castle was thrown down in the fighting. Nor were the arms and armor of the Ducs among the treasures spirited away by the Baron du Auch when he retreated."

"Hieronymus and I have no intent of wandering the countryside looking for a treasure that may or may not exist, much less commit treason against the King of Navarre."

Maerten's face fell, and Elsabeth vainly tried to drown the hollowness in her stomach at his despair with a long draught of ale. "You would not come with me?"

"We already had this discussion, love. We would be moving on once this matter is finished."

"But 'tis not finished!" he said, and his frustration was growing palpable.

"We accepted only to bring you this far. We never agreed to help foment rebellion against the Comte de Eze and the King."

"But you must come with me!" Maerten looked between her and Hieronymus with pleading in his eyes, and Hieronymus glanced sidelong at her. Elsabeth tried to hide her own distress with her tankard, and she felt the eyes of the Wizard on her, as if they might burn a hole clear through her.

"I am sorry, my son," Hieronymus said. "But as Tetty said, once we return to Checy we have other business to see to."

Elsabeth took another drink to avoid meeting the boy's gaze, but out of the edge of her vision she could see the tears welling in his eyes. He departed abruptly and made for the door out to the gardens. Husson gave her a withering glare as he hobbled out the door after him, but the tension remained palpable.

"The hour grows late," Sinopus said, more to fill the silence than anything else. "Your party may camp here for the night, and Ch'u Niang and Hsiu Mei shall prepare a meal for you."

Elsabeth merely nodded in response and drained the last of her ale with one long swallow.

ELSABETH SAT AT THE EDGE OF THE BLUFF AND gazed out across the lake. The moon, mirrored on the surface below, was full and hung above the horizon in the east. On the far shore she could just make out the cook fires and lights of Checy, and further around to the north a single point of light, where she suspected the farm Sinopus mentioned to Andry and Durant might be found. The sky overhead was black but dusted with twinkling stars like millions of chips of diamond sparkling in the night, and a warm late-summer evening's breeze stirred the tops of the trees and rippled the reflection of the sky on the water.

She took a long drink from the last of Husson's wine, too deep into it to care about its harsh flavor. Her sword lay in the grass beside her, but her coat, hat, and doublet were left behind in the camp, and she sat naked in her undershirt and hose. Elsabeth sighed heavily.

The solitude of the bluff was broken by the sound of someone shuffling through the grass behind her, but Elsabeth did not bother to greet the intruder. Instead, she just kept gazing out eastward across the lake, not entirely sure what it was she was looking for.

"You have the look of one who grieves," Sinopus said, and for the first time Elsabeth turned to find him standing over her and leaning heavily on his staff. They were alone now. Hieronymus, Maerten, and Husson's voices could be heard in their camp back nearer the gate to Sinopus's garden, where the Wizard's two attendants were seeing to their needs for the evening.

"And you seem to have less trouble walking than you like to make it appear," she replied, and took another drink of wine. "If you came all this way out here just to try prying answers from me on my life, you would have had better luck asking them of Hieronymus. A few tankards of ale and some time with one of your assistants, and you would have all you need to know." She downed another swallow of wine. "The man cannot resist drink or women, much less both together."

"I do not desire answers from him, though he certainly expected quite a few from me."

Elsabeth chuckled. "Prying into your secrets, was he?"

Sinopus smiled tightly. "Your companion is quite inquisitive for a man of the Wheel. I will confess, I find it refreshing after my past dealings with the Church."

"Hieronymus is hardly a typical priest."

"And you are hardly a typical woman," the Wizard said. He stepped up next to her, planted his staff in the turf, and gazed out across the lake.

"I thought I made myself clear that I am not a part of the boy's fee?"

"Quite clear, and you need not worry, I have no need for your companionship. In fact, I cannot imagine abiding it for any length of time."

Elsabeth blinked in surprise. "Wait, what? Why not?" She blinked again at her own words. "That is to say—"

"Oh, I understand your meaning quite clearly," he said, cutting her off gently but firmly. "You are quite the prideful creature; certain you can sway anyone with your charms if it suits you. And perhaps you are right. But I see through it. You are hiding."

"Hiding from what?" she said irritably around another sip from the flask.

"I find it curious that you scarcely know the boy," Sinopus said, rather than answer her question, "and yet you have already grown so protective of him." He eyed her closely. "You have the aspect of the mother about you, yet he is not your son. There is much guilt driving this attachment."

She glared up at him and smothered the rising tide of remorse beneath the indignation over this line of questioning. "I warn you fairly, Wizard: That is ground you do not wish to tread. I suggest you step back from it before it crumbles from beneath you."

Sinopus's expression softened as he looked down on her. "I intend you no offense, I speak only the truth that I see. You are concerned for him."

Elsabeth shook the flask at him reproachfully. "You are killing him, if you insist on prying into my business with him," she snapped. "He came all this way just on the rumor of you, and now that you have filled his head with stories, he is determined to press on. He will go to Auch. And then he will be hanged. You are right, I am bloody concerned!"

"Yet you will not stand by his side."

"Because 'tis bloody madness!" She brought the flask to her lips again, but no more wine was forthcoming. Disappointed, she upended and shook it, and when it became clear through the fog in her head the flask was empty, threw it as far out over the bluff as she could. It disappeared without a sound into the darkness and trees below. "This is life, not a bloody minstrel's tale."

Sinopus shifted a bit on his feet. "Surely even you have seen and done things best befitting a tale by the fireside in your travels. I myself have traveled widely, and I have seen many things you would not believe. Life is strange and wondrous, and even in the wildest of stories there is often a hint of truth. Some tellers exaggerate them for their own ego, others to entertain, but always at the heart is the truth."

Elsabeth mopped her face in frustration, and idly wondered whether if she tossed the Wizard over the edge of the bluff after the flask, he might be able to fly away before striking the bottom. "You are telling Maerten he is the missing heir of a house exterminated a generation ago, based on rumor and hearsay, and the implausibility of his trinket not ending in the hands of outlaws or being sold."

"Such is the power of the enchantment upon it," Sinopus said. "In all the days of the Ducs of Rouen, it never failed to find its way into the hand of the rightful heir."

Elsabeth laughed caustically and shook her head. "Considering my experiences with the lengths a claimant might take to defend his assertions of late, I would think you could forgive me for wondering just how many of the Ducs used that tale to justify an illicit grab for power. And it certainly says nothing about whether anyone will actually accept it on its own merits now were someone to appear laying claim to a title that has not been filled in thirty-odd years."

"Do you have so little faith in the boy?"

"Faith in Maerten plays no part in my objection. He seems a good lad, but he is naïve and maybe a little too romantic for his own good. I know the danger of that combination, even without the stakes of court politics at work." Elsabeth heaved a sigh. "'Twas a lesson I learned at great cost to myself.

"Suppose for a moment that the arms are where you say they are. Let us even be enthusiastic and imagine that his claim is seen as genuine. It seems clear enough to me from what I have heard in Checy that the Comte de Eze would view any return of the Ducs as a threat to his own power. To say nothing of what the King might do. The Comte would accept no rival, and the King no one that would weaken his control over the region."

"And if he should try and come to a bad end, and you do nothing?"

"What I would do is have him go home to the miller's daughter," she said, "and use that bauble to provide a comfortable life for them. It may not be an exciting one, but 'twould be a life not likely to be cut short by the end of a rope."

Sinopus looked at her pointedly. "Unlike yours?"

Elsabeth glared up at him. "That is a choice I made."

"And is it not his choice to make as well?"

She wrapped her arms around her knees and hugged them against her chest. "I may risk my neck at times, but I don't seek out the block to lay my head down on it."

"Spoken as one who is always running from their choices." Elsabeth scowled at him, but there was no reproach in the wizard's voice. "So, you run from him in his need, as you have refused to face your other responsibilities in the past."

Elsabeth found her hand reaching for the hilt of her sword as her guilt and anger twisted together, and the burning desire to lop off the Wizard's head grew. Instead, she seized the scabbard, and rose unsteadily to her feet. "I warned you before," she snapped irritably, and leaned her sword against her shoulder. "Save your judgments for the ones who pay you, I did not come here for it. And if Maerten dies, 'tis because of the ideas you put in his head."

With that, she turned and started away.

"If he dies, it is because you were not there to safeguard him," Sinopus said as a parting shot to her back. Elsabeth stopped and turned. "That is what I have seen: If Maerten is to succeed and reclaim his rightful place, he needs you. Without you, he will fail."

Elsabeth hesitated a moment longer as the Wizard's eyes bored into hers. They accused nothing, but at the same time were filled with certainty. A thousand different thoughts and feelings festered in the pit of her stomach; memories and regrets, and one sorrow sharper than all the others cutting at the edge of her conscience. But no retort came to her lips, and instead she turned away from Sinopus's gaze and headed back to camp.

HIERONYMUS CHUCKLED IN CONTENTMENT AT the tankard gripped in one meaty fist, and leaned back against the wall encircling the Wizard's garden. A volume of parchment bound between poplar boards lay in his lap, and he held a stick of charcoal in his other hand. A warm late-summer evening's breeze hissed softly among the trees, and the wholesome scent of the herbs growing behind the wall filled the night air. Their campfire crackled merrily and bathed the clearing around the wizard's hut with golden light. It cast dancing shadows against the wall and illuminated the faces of Husson and Maerten seated on their bedrolls across from him.

Lord of All, bless the brewers for the gift of ale. May their malts be sweet, and their yeasts be fruitful!

He tossed his head back and swallowed a generous draught. It was a potent mumm ale, sweet and powerful, with a strong caramel flavor.

Hieronymus wiped his mouth on his sleeve, set his tankard down next to him, and picked up his stack of parchment. The letters he had written thus far doubled and swirled and wheeled about on the page, and the point of his charcoal stick (or was it points? They seemed to have multiplied within the last few hours) vexed him with its refusal to land where he wished it. Finally, after much effort and many grumbled oaths and curses about the Dark One leading his hand astray, the point found the line he sought, and with a grunt of satisfaction, he continued his writing.

Maerten watched him, his small beer cupped between his two hands, and as downcast an expression as Hieronymus could imagine on his features. Husson sat at ease nursing his own ale, and gazed disinterestedly into the fire, except for when one of the Wizard's lovely attendants appeared to refresh a drink or bring them food, at which point his eyes followed them hungrily. But the uncouth and inelegant lech restrained himself from issuing one of his vulgar propositions; Hieronymus suspected out of respect for the Wizard's display of power earlier that evening. Though he little liked the profane energies Sinopus called upon, Hieronymus at least acknowledged his delight at seeing Husson silenced.

He scratched out a few more lines of text until, feeling his mouth parched once more, he returned his attention to his ale.

As he relieved his thirst, Maerten finally gathered the desire to speak. "What is it you are doing, Brother?" he asked.

Hieronymus set his tankard down, swallowed the mouthful, belched quietly, and cleared his throat. "I am committing for posterity the herbological wisdom of our esteemed host," he said, and blinked to stop the swirling of the letters on the page when he resumed writing again.

"I thought you objected to his magic, why would you wish to write of it?"

"I have a purely intellectual interest in recording my observations. Though he is a right secretive bastard about the mystery of his heathen powers. But at the very least his herb-lore would be quite welcome among the hospitals."

"Is that where you will go once we return to Checy?"

Hieronymus glanced up from the page he was working on to eye Maerten and his two identical brothers jockeying for a seat next to the fire, while the rest of the clearing danced and spun around him. "That, I have yet to discuss with Tetty."

"But you shall resume traveling together," Maerten said, making it a statement of fact.

Hieronymus took another drink from his tankard. "Aye, we shall. Though from your tone it sounds as if you wish to make another arrangement."

Maerten clasped his hands and rocked uncomfortably as he stumbled over his words. "I don't wish you to think I aim to set you and Mademoiselle Elsabeth against one another, 'tis just that I need your help if I am to do this. You understand these matters far better than I, and I need your guidance."

He sighed. "My son, my knowledge of these matters is that 'tis best to stay out of them so long as I value my neck. Which I do, as I am quite attached to it. 'Tis in part why, after all my long years of service, I remain a humble Brother of the Olivians and have had no desire to climb the ladder of office in the church."

"I thought 'twas because none of your superiors could stomach the thought of you as a leader in your order," Elsabeth said, as she returned from wherever she had been hiding throughout the evening. She stumbled a bit as she rounded the fire on her way to her bedroll, and threw herself and her sword down upon it, burying her face in her arms. "I imagine friars turning white at the thought of 'Father Hieronymus.'"

"Actually, I imagine there are more than a few who would see fit to promote me if it meant shutting me away inside a monastery for the rest of my life. Sadly, I am much too fond of the open road and your pleasant company to ever accept."

"Lord, bless my luck. The Wizard expects us gone just after first light tomorrow," she added without removing her head from her arms. "I suggest we all get some sleep."

11

HEY WERE WOKEN JUST AS THE SUN crested the horizon in the east by Ch'u Niang. Or perhaps it was Hsiu Mei. Hieronymus could not quite tell them apart at such an early hour, particularly while still within the grips of the quantities of ale he had consumed the night before. A light breakfast of sausages and fried apple slices was brought out for them, but they saw no further sign of Sinopus that morning, and soon they were packing up camp for their return to Checy below.

The way down was much quicker and easier than the ascent, and they made good time with Elsabeth walking alone in the lead, well ahead of Hieronymus. He watched her back thoughtfully on the descent from the bluff while he walked alongside Maerten, with Husson bringing up the rear and grumbling about his leg. Something was deeply troubling his companion, but she had declined to speak on it during breakfast, and showed no more inclination of doing so while they descended the bluff. So, Hieronymus just trailed along behind her, supporting himself on his staff to ease his way along the path, which somehow seemed even steeper going down than it had been going up.

Maerten followed beside him with his head bowed dejectedly, and Hieronymus's heart ached to see the boy come so close to fulfilling his dream only to have it pulled away again by circumstance. But there was little to be done when kings came between one and one's destination except to seek another road and hope it would be a clearer one. Somehow, given the tone of the boy's conversation before they turned in for the night, he suspected the lad would not be so easily dissuaded, and he fervently hoped it would not lead him to a solitary dance at the end of a hangman's rope. What Husson thought of the matter Hieronymus was not quite certain, but the man certainly seemed quite put out by Elsabeth's refusal to go on with this whole folly. Given how little consideration he had shown the boy along the road thus far, Hieronymus found himself questioning this unexpected concern.

'Tis as if he sees the boy as a sudden stepping-stone for respectability. Well, the one blessing to come of shattering the poor lad's hopes is certainly keeping that one from riding along in his wake.

The day promised to be somewhat cooler than the one before. The sky far above was clear and blue, and birds sang merrily in the branches of the trees closing in about the trail. There was still no breeze to speak of finding its way among the pillars holding aloft the leafy hall, but even the small change in temperature did wonders. The woods felt not nearly as close as they had the day before. None of the others seemed much interested in conversation, so Hieronymus kept the time by happily murmuring a psalm to himself. There was no sign of their former guides along the trail, who evidently chose to flee for home during the

Wizard's brief display of anger, rather than return for their guests. Fortunately, now that he and Elsabeth knew the way, there was no further need for their guidance.

They paused for a quick bite of lunch around midday, little more than a bit of dried meat and cheese with hard bread baked for travel. Maerten plopped himself down on a stump next to Husson, who leaned against a tree tilting out over the path with its branches stretching to catch the light of the sun. Elsabeth stood somewhat apart from the group chewing on a bite of cheese and watched the path, and Hieronymus watched her quietly in turn while he took his own lunch. He frowned in concern at the slump of her shoulders and hang of her head, but nonetheless resisted the urge to approach her for the moment.

Not long after their break for lunch, the trail slowly and smoothly leveled off, and they were soon breaking out of the deeper woods and back onto the main road from Checy.

They turned east along the road and followed it back to the village. The lake appeared on their left, and the sun sparkled magnificently in the clear blue sky mirrored on its glassy surface. Beyond the lake they saw the distant black figures of the townsfolk working in their fields, and the mill and wall of Checy loomed up on the far shore. Elsabeth led them back across the bridge spanning the muddy stream draining the southern end, and before long they were back at the gate, none too soon for Hieronymus's weary feet. Talbot came out to meet them as they arrived and bowed deeply.

"Ah! You return at last!" he said in relief upon seeing them. "When Galleren, Andry, and Durant returned without you and spoke of the Wizard's anger we feared the worst."

"There was hardly reason for them to fear at all," Elsabeth said dismissively. "Just a show of light and smoke, and we were still standing at the end of it."

Talbot chuckled in amusement and leaned on his cane. "But you now see for yourself, they are no mere stories." He looked to Maerten. "Were your questions answered, my young friend?"

Maerten nodded. "They were indeed, and I and my guardian must soon depart. I hope to soon properly repay you for your hospitality."

"Of course, of course. But tonight, you shall be our guests once more. Now come, you must be weary from the walk back."

And with that, he beckoned the group back within the town walls. Maerten stepped around Elsabeth without sparing her a glance, and Husson followed. Elsabeth did not, however, and Hieronymus frowned between her and the boy as Maerten disappeared around the gate.

"All right, out with it, girl," he said, and stepped up beside her.

Elsabeth folded her arms across her breast and leaned her shoulder against the wall. "Out with what?" she asked in that familiar tone which suggested she would rather prefer to be left alone but did not seriously expect him to honor the unspoken request.

"Out with whatever thought you have been clinging to all day and allowing to fester in the pit of your cold yet shapely bosom," Hieronymus said, and jabbed a finger into the ball of her shoulder.

"You leave my bosom out of this," Elsabeth growled irritably.

"Ah hah! My keen ears detect that 'tis only your bosom you decline to speak of."

Elsabeth rolled her eyes, sighed, and leaned her head against the wall. "And mine lead me to suspect that 'tis the main thought running through your mind."

"As a man of God I do have an appreciation for perfection. But that is not what brings me to you now. So go on, then! Out with it!"

She turned and glared at him, but the expression was empty of her usual fire. "You know, with the lake near at hand I find myself wondering how well you swim, and if you should sink right to the bottom from all your weight, how long it might take them to pull your fat carcass out again."

Hieronymus pouted indignantly. "Now, Tetty, that was hardly called for! Something vexes you terribly, and here I am offering you my shoulder, and instead you see fit to issue threats and insults!" He threw his hands up in exaggerated exasperation. "Lord of All knows why I even bother with you!"

"Do you always need to carry on like this when I decline to give the answer you are prodding me for?"

"It generally works, does it not?"

Hieronymus grinned broadly. Elsabeth let out a strangled growl of annoyance in response and put her brow to the wall, but said nothing more.

"Now then," he said, and took advantage of the moment to reach out and pat her on the backside. Elsabeth stiffened indignantly and fixed him with a glare when his hand stopped and lingered on her bottom. "Out with it!"

"Love, you are picking a rather wrong time to be your insufferably lewd self," she said warningly. "Do remove your hand from my backside, or else I will cut it off!"

"Now Tetty, I am only trying to get to the bottom of whatever is troubling you!" Hieronymus gave her one last groping pat, but nonetheless removed his hand when he finished.

Elsabeth's green eyes flashed angrily. "Right now, 'tis a particularly impious friar who cannot keep his hands to himself. Now go and bugger off!"

"My word, you are on edge today." He folded his arms across his gut and regarded her thoughtfully. "I think you have taken this little venture more to heart than you have been willing to let on."

She turned on him and leaned her back against the wall, more, he suspected, out of a desire to safeguard her backside from his hands. "Oh, don't even start with me; this whole adventure was your idea to begin with."

Hieronymus conceded the point with a shrug. "Perhaps, but my interest has been solely a professional one. There is something more with how you look at the boy I am not quite certain what to make of."

Elsabeth scowled down at him. "I don't know what you are talking about."

He twisted his lip at her obstinacy. "Oh, don't bother denying it, girl, I have known you far too long. I am not saying 'tis anything akin to your mad fancy for Cuncz, which has you fondling that ring of his with who knows what manner of impure thoughts rampaging around your skull." Elsabeth opened her mouth as if to voice her protest over the observation, but he cut her off with a sharp wave of his hand. "And there is no good in denying that, either. Now, have some faith that this humble servant of the Wheel might ease whatever burden you are carrying, and tell me what the devil is wrong!"

She heaved an exaggerated sigh and rolled her eyes. "I hate it when you back me into a corner," Elsabeth said.

"Only because you like to run so long as you have open ground ahead of you."

She sighed and hung her head, and worked her jaw in frustration at his pestering for a few moments.

"What do you think we should do," she finally asked, and folded her arms beneath her breast once more. "Is it right of us to just walk away from him now?"

Hieronymus considered that for a moment. "We did what we were hired for, if that is what you are asking."

She pinched the bridge of her nose, and for the first time Hieronymus noted a measure of weariness he was unaccustomed to seeing in her. "And that is always what happens: We do what we agree upon, but never more, unless it serves our interests."

Hieronymus sighed and leaned heavily on his staff. "Elsabeth, my love, I have been on the road since long before the Lord saw fit to grace the world with your beauty. We live our lives this way because we must. We certainly have freedom, but it does not come without cost. Sometimes it means we are beholden to manipulative bastard lordlings. And at others it means we are quick to reach the end of our welcome and must depart with haste, as you have quite effectively demonstrated rather recently.

"Now, I sought out this little venture precisely to take your mind away from your unseemly obsession with the good Cuncz, and here I find you dwelling instead on the revelations of the magnificent Sinopus. I must confess to being rather perplexed why you should take this so near to your heart."

Elsabeth sighed. "I am merely concerned for him," she protested.

Hieronymus rolled his eyes. "Oh yes, that is plain to see, but the why of it is what nags at me. I find that I have grown rather fond of him, too, as he is certainly a good lad. Though his guardian I could perhaps do without, particularly so long as I must stand downwind of him. But you, my dear, in such a short time have grown remarkably attached. Something is troubling you far more than the needs of our arrangement."

She eyed him, and Hieronymus gazed back at her, searching her green eyes for some hint as to what brought on her sudden sullen mood. "Love, don't push me to the test on this."

He sighed. "Must I make this a proper confession?"

"No, you daren't," Elsabeth snapped. "I am warning you fairly: 'Tis none of your concern, so do not push me!"

Hieronymus raised his hands in surrender. "Very well! Very well! But if I may at least offer this advice: We have fulfilled our contract with him by taking him to the Wizard. He knew even before we set out from here that once that obligation was fulfilled we would likely be on our way again. We can part ways here with clear conscience, whatever your feelings towards the boy. Of course, there is nothing to say we cannot renegotiate."

Elsabeth let the back of her head thump against the wall behind her. "And are you even giving a thought to the fact that he is arguably intending to commit treason by pursuing this wizard's suggestion?"

"That is ultimately his decision to make, Tetty. All we can do is advise him for, or against, such a course."

She folded her arms across her chest. "I have spent all this time trying to argue against it. 'Tis foolhardy."

"To which I would agree, though he has certainly set his heart on it. I suspect nothing will prevent him from trying."

"Bugger," she murmured.

Hieronymus shifted his feet a bit and leaned heavily on his staff. "So that is our choice: we may consider our part in this madness concluded and be on our way, or we may continue alongside him. No prior agreement holds us to him, and there is only whatever is playing upon your conscience."

Elsabeth mopped her face. "I seem to recall saying I would blame you when this went wrong. Well, I fully blame you."

Hieronymus chuckled. Beyond the village wall he could smell the cook fires starting for the evening meal, and his belly began to rumble at the thought of supper. "Now, now, Tetty, this has hardly been a complete disaster. Missing dinner, however, would certainly be a tragedy without comparison. So, if you are quite finished feeling miserable for yourself, let us retire to the common house. If we are to be making a decision on where we shall go next, I would much rather do so on a full stomach and with a tankard of beer in hand."

And with that, he snapped up his staff and offered Elsabeth his arm. Elsabeth merely rolled her eyes, pushed off the wall, and turned into the open village gate with Hieronymus falling into step behind her.

12

IERONYMUS'S ATTENTION WAS QUICKLY taken by the village's ale — obliged by Ysabel placing a mug in his hand — almost upon entering. Elsabeth ignored their hosts and crossed the common room to the out of the way corner where the baggage they did not bring on the trek up to Sinopus's hut was stowed, and laid aside her sword, jacket, hat, and pack, and stepped out of her pattens. Maerten and Husson were both seated at the table, with a small beer for the former, and the latter taking pulls from a tankard of the local ale. Talbot departed after escorting Maerten and his guardian to the common house, leaving his son and daughter to finish tending their guests. The light of late afternoon streamed through the open windows and provided most of the illumination in the hall.

Elsabeth took a weary seat beside her pack and watched the boy for a moment, before Colin appeared with a bowl of water and a cloth held out for her with a bow.

"Supper will be ready shortly," he said. "Did the Wizard answer your questions?"

Elsabeth accepted the bowl from him and dipped her hands into the water. It was a bit cool for her liking, but wet, so she gratefully splashed it on her face to wash away the grime and sweat of the trip up the bluff.

"I had no questions to ask, this was the boy's quest. But the Wizard certainly had plenty to say regardless," she said.

Colin frowned at her. "Curious, I have never heard of him offering counsel to those who did not ask for it."

She managed a laugh. "Well, he certainly did in this case. But I would rather like not to talk about it." Elsabeth wiped her face dry on the towel and returned it and the bowl to Colin, who accepted it back with a slight incline of his head.

"Very well, but may I say that I hope you found whatever it is you sought?"

Elsabeth glared at Colin as he made his rounds with the washbowl.

Oh, what does he know about it. For that matter, what does the Wizard truly know about anything?

But though she tried to push aside Sinopus's observations, Elsabeth could not help but feel unsettled by how keenly he read her. She sighed and rocked easily back to her feet, and made her way to the table seeking a distraction her from such thoughts rather than any desire for company.

"Ah, Tetty! Come sit and share in this gift of ale!" Hieronymus said over his nearly empty tankard, already quite merry. Elsabeth dropped heavily into a chair beside him. He had chosen a place where she could put her back to the wall. "My compliments again to your house on the quality of its brew, and may the Lord bless it in perpetuity!" he added with a shout and a leer at Ysabel who had set down new tankards for him and Elsabeth.

Elsabeth took a long draught and studied Maerten closely. "So, where do you go now?" she asked over the rim of her own tankard.

Maerten glanced towards her with as glum and sullen an expression as she had ever seen while he dried his face on the towel offered by Colin. Once he finished, their host quickly followed his wife from the common hall to help prepare the evening meal, and left them for a time to talk in private.

"Sinopus said I must go to Auch," he said. "I don't know where else to go."

"I would say home to the miller's daughter, but I suppose that is not the counsel you would hear."

"With what would I return?" He absently touched the pendant tucked beneath his shirt. "This is all I have to offer, but 'tis of no value without the title to which it belongs. I will go to Auch, alone if I must. I cannot turn around now."

"And what do you do when you arrive, my son?" Hieronymus asked around a mouthful of ale.

"Find the vault, of course!"

Elsabeth sighed and mopped her brow. "Love, even assuming the Wizard's story can be believed and there was ever a treasure vault in the first place, how do you know 'twas not raided when Coventry sacked Auch, or emptied by the Baron du Auch himself when 'twas abandoned?"

"I..." Maerten began, but trailed off as he considered what she was saying. He sighed in resignation. "I don't, I suppose."

"All the more reason to at least have a look for ourselves," Husson said after a swallow of ale. "No harm I can see in that."

"Aside from a great deal of disappointment," she said, "and that I see as the most favorable outcome."

Husson gazed levelly at her. "But you shan't know for sure unless you go, shall you?"

She raised an eyebrow. "Are you yourself asking me to join this expedition? I thought you were anxious to be rid of me."

"The boy has taken a liking to you, though aside from the obvious reasons—" he made a show of letting his eyes wander what parts of her body could be seen above the table "—I cannot imagine why. You talk a might too much and too loudly." Husson flashed a greasy smile at her. "I would rather like to fill that mouth of yours with a little something to keep you silent."

Hieronymus choked on his ale at that, and Elsabeth returned a mocking smile. "The emphasis being upon 'little,'" she said. Husson glared indignantly, and Maerten's face colored when he pieced together the meaning of the exchange.

"Please, but Husson is right," Maerten said hastily to change the subject. "Surely there is no harm in having a look, is there?"

He looked up at her solemnly from his small beer, and Elsabeth was reminded of nothing less than a puppy begging a treat from its master. She sighed and took a long drink of her ale, more out of a desire to look away without being obvious about it than any real need to quench her thirst.

"I would double what we promised as payment, if you continue with me," Maerten added.

Hieronymus eyed him over the rim of his tankard. "Ten *sous?*"

He nodded and looked significantly at Husson. The elder man sighed and thumped his tankard down. "Now?" he asked. Maerten nodded again.

"They brought me this far. I would not even ask them to take us back north again first."

Husson rubbed his brow and grumbled something into his hand. "You have a lot to learn about negotiations, boy," he said irritably. He reached into his doublet, withdrew a small pouch, and dropped it on the table in front of her and the friar. It landed with a solid thud and a jingle.

"I would say he is a rather quick study," Hieronymus said, and reached to retrieve the pouch before Elsabeth could make a move to do so herself.

Instead, she had to satisfy herself with looking over the friar's shoulder when he opened the pouch and peered inside. The mingled light of the afternoon sun and lamps set out on the table glittered on the silver coins within, until he drew the pouch closed once more and gave her a subtle nod that was all the confirmation she needed that the pouch's contents matched the promised payment.

Elsabeth leaned back a bit in her chair and idly ran a finger around the lip of her tankard while she considered the offer. "He is quite right, of course. That was very cleverly played, love," she said, and Maerten smiled broadly. She picked up her tankard, took another drink, and sighed. "I suppose you would need to seek directions again."

Husson shook his head. "Auch I know of. It lies to the southwest of here, further along the road from the Four Ways, and then west along the northern edge of the Massís Miterre. The castle itself is on the road overlooking the Vert River."

"Then it sounds like you hardly need us to get there."

"As much as I would love to be rid of your mouth, as I hear it the country down there has grown rather wild and uncivilized since the wars with the Coventrish."

"Well, you would feel right at home, then."

He scowled at her but did not rise to the bait. Instead, he took another drink of his ale. "'Twould be safer to ride with at least some numbers. Highwaymen prefer to avoid strong companies."

"Not unreasonable," Hieronymus noted. "It does one little good to spend most of one's prize on leech craft and funeral arrangements."

Husson nodded his agreement.

Elsabeth considered Husson's words for a moment and swirled her tankard as something niggled at the back of her mind. "Have you traveled that area often, then?" she asked, and tossed back another mouthful of her drink.

"Only briefly, and in passing, a few summers before I found the boy," Husson said.

"One would expect the story of the Ducs de Rouen to have been quite the local legend. I wonder that you heard nothing of it before we met with this wizard."

Husson leaned forward over the table and glared at her. "As I said, I only came through briefly. The Coventrish made this area rather inhospitable to travelers, and I wanted no part of the wars, so I did not linger. Do you accuse me otherwise? Because we can take this argument out to the yard."

Elsabeth's eyes flashed a warning. "Please, you don't want to make any greater an embarrassment of yourself than you already have by acknowledging your study of da Lucca."

"If you don't—" Husson began as he rose to his feet, his chair skidding out from beneath him. He was silenced almost immediately by Maerten's hand on his arm when the boy hastily rose and put himself between them as best he could from across the table.

"Husson, Mademoiselle Elsabeth, please," he said, his voice full of pleading as he looked between them. "I don't want to see you at odds in this manner!"

Husson rounded on him but, remembering Elsabeth's warning on the road, restrained his hand. "Boy, if you think I'll sit here and take such insults, you and I shall be having words as well."

Fortunately, before the situation could escalate any further the doors to the common hall opened, and Colin and Ysabel returned bearing platters of baked fish and vegetables, and warmed bread with butter. Husson dropped back into his chair and masked his lost temper behind a drink from his tankard, and they all fell into silence as the couple laid out their supper. Talbot followed behind them and took a seat at the head of the table. "If you don't mind, I would join you for dinner tonight," he said.

Elsabeth smiled politely. "Not at all, we were merely discussing our plans for tomorrow."

"Ah, it seems I have arrived just in time, then!" he said, with a broad smile. "As I recall, before you departed to meet the Wizard, you and the good Brother suggested you might be looking for some work after you finished here."

She glanced at Hieronymus with a raised eyebrow, and the friar leaned forward, as much to eye the village elder as to grab a piece of bread for his supper. "Aye, we may. You mentioned the village might request my services," he said, "though I imagine you would have little need of my companion's. Well, so long as you wish to keep the peace with your wives." The last he added with an amused grin her in her direction.

Elsabeth glared at him over her tankard. "You will be needing of a priest yourself if you keep that up, love," she said. Hieronymus just chuckled at the futile warning and popped a large bite of bread into his mouth.

Food and drink were placed before Talbot, and he joined them as they began to eat. "Oh, of course," he said. "If you are agreeable to holding a service this evening we would be most appreciative, but I am speaking of another matter. A ways to the south there is an inn where the old road from Auch meets the main road. Galleren has a delivery to make, and we would be happy to pay you for your protection along the road, if you would be willing to travel with him."

Elsabeth regarded Hieronymus with silent surprise and more than a little suspicion, a sentiment he clearly shared when he met her look, but he said nothing and merely shrugged. When she glanced towards Maerten she saw nothing in his expression to suggest anything untoward as he nibbled on a bit of fish, while Husson seemed to be splitting his attention between his supper and trying to manage a peak down her shirt from across the table. She took a long drink of her ale and returned her attention to Talbot.

"Very well. By some coincidence, I believe we were going to be headed that direction, anyway," she said, and watched Maerten's face light up brighter than the lamps on the table from the corner of her eye.

"Wonderful!" Talbot said around a bite of baked vegetables. "I'll let Galleren know he will have the pleasure of your company once more!"

She chuckled as she set down her tankard and turned her attention to the plate in front of her. "Oh, I somehow think Galleren will hardly be the most enthusiastic about our company."

ELSABETH PERCHED ATOP THE TRESTLE table out back of the common hall, with her feet on the bench and her naked sword across her lap, and watched Hieronymus genuflecting in front of the residents of Checy. His voice carried across the village, and despite the tankard of ale in his hand and the generous amount he had imbibed during supper, the friar's words were clear and orderly while he led the villagers in the haphazardly assembled service. Maerten sat beside her and gazed wide-eyed at the deft turning of Hieronymus's words; he verbally danced through his oration with all the skill and precision of his oft-boasted training with Leonardus. Her lip curled in amusement, knowing full well that the friar was so completely smashed he would not remember a word of what he said come the morrow.

The evening was getting on and the sun was beginning to disappear behind the heights further west, though fading golden light still lit the horizon, while in the east the sky was deepening to a gloomy indigo. A few lamps hung from posts on the outside of the common house and other dwellings provided a little more light within the village. There was no wind to speak of, but the day was much cooler than the one before, and the night promised to be quite pleasant. A handful of residents milled about carrying out some task or other. Some joined the congregation once they finished, and others listened in while they worked. Andry, Durant, and several others arrived through the village gate, returning from their errand to the farm nestled away in the woods beyond the town. They did not speak of what transpired, but their quiet and amicable chatter as they parted for their own homes suggested a measure of success.

Elsabeth turned a somewhat flat, globose, and purplish-skinned apple in her hand. She brushed off a bit of dirt before taking a bite of its soft greenish flesh and took a moment to savor its sweet and aromatic flavor. A wooden bowl of them sat between her and Maerten, with a tankard of small beer for each of them, while on her other side lay a small leather case filled with neatly ordered files, stones, and bottles, and a few ragged strips of cloth. Elsabeth swallowed her bite of apple, set the fruit down next to her, and resumed working the edge of her sword with a whetstone from her kit.

"How long do you think he will be going on?" Maerten asked.

"How much has he had to drink so far?" she replied, never taking her eyes off the blade as she ran her stone the length of the edge. The fading sunlight flashed along the prominent midrib of the hollow-ground blade. "I once saw him go for five hours without a stop on a barrel of good Luccan wine."

Maerten blinked and looked at her in surprise. "That long?"

Elsabeth chuckled at the memory of exasperated townsfolk seeking for any excuse to escape the friar's grasp. "The congregation was desperate for him to stop, and I cannot tell you how relieved they were when he finally did."

Maerten took a sip of his beer and watched Hieronymus with a growing smirk of amusement. "What finally stopped him?"

"The bottom of the barrel. He was so screwed he fell asleep right in the middle of a parable — and on overindulgence at that, if you appreciate the irony — and ended up flat on his back, giving everyone a rather unwelcome look up his habit that I am sure most would sooner forget."

Maerten laughed aloud and hid his mouth behind his hand to stifle the sound before it could carry to the congregation of villagers listening with rapt attention to Hieronymus's surprisingly coherent sermon. "Goodness! What did you do?"

Elsabeth inspected the edge she was working with her thumb. "Well, you have seen the size of him. 'Twould take a good strong team of mules to haul him away without him to lend a hand, so we just threw a blanket over him and let him sleep it off." She chuckled softly. "I'll not say he was left undisturbed, but as I promised I would never tell how exactly he found himself when he finally woke again, I'll leave it at that."

Satisfied with her work on her blade, Elsabeth set aside the whetstone and turned her attention to her unfinished apple.

"It sounds like he was upset," Maerten said after a drink from his small beer.

She swallowed the bite of apple she was chewing. "Oh, that would be putting it mildly. He called upon all manner of divine retributions when he discovered the state he was in when he awoke. Not that anyone found it possible to take him seriously, but I certainly got an earful from him."

"Was it Brother Hieronymus who convinced you to change your mind about accompanying us to Auch?"

Elsabeth's stomach knotted itself involuntarily at the question. Old guilt threatened to well up on her, and she hastily took another bite of her apple to avoid making an immediate response.

"Hieronymus had nothing to do with that, though I would not be surprised if he were to try taking the credit," she said when she found her voice again. "We are always in need of a bit of extra coin, and as it happens, the locals have a job for us that will be taking us that direction, anyway."

Maerten eyed her doubtfully. "Then that is all it is to you? Work?"

Finding herself unable to look in his direction, she just took another bite of her apple. *What in the name of the Dark One is the matter with me? I am usually a much better liar than this.*

"'Tis the life I lead, love. All there ever is for me is the next job."

"You don't think of finding a place where you can stay and make a home, so that you need not wander anymore?"

That question struck her like a blow to the gut, and not even her apple was enough to distract her from the feelings threatening to force their way up from the pit where she had long ago carefully buried them. Elsabeth fought against the memories and regrets to keep them in check, and it took some moments before she finally sent them retreating back behind the wall she long ago built around them. "As I said, this is my life."

If Maerten noticed the sudden ache his line of inquiry caused he said nothing of it, and instead stared for a long moment into his beer as he attempted to put his own thoughts in order.

"This is the farthest and longest I have ever been away from home," he said solemnly. "'Tis not that I regret coming here, as I know now I was meant for something grander, but I do miss Husson's hut, the village, sneaking a kiss from the miller's daughter." He blushed a bit at that last one, which managed to draw a smile from her as she finished off her apple. "I suppose I am even a little frightened of what is to come."

Elsabeth took a last bite and with one carefully measured throw discarded her apple core into a nearby midden heap. "Most people are when they find their lives coming to such a crossroads," she said. She picked through her kit for a small glass bottle of oil and a rag, and went to work oiling the blade of her sword. "I have been there many times myself, once when I was even younger than you."

"Perhaps once we succeed, you would be willing to stay with me?"

She paused a moment in the midst of her work and glanced at him. "And what would I be doing?"

Maerten considered for a moment. "Well, perhaps you could open a school of your own," he said.

Elsabeth could not restrain a laugh at the offer. "I am sorry," she said, when she saw his face color in response, "but 'twould be rather more complicated a business than just hanging out my shingle for all to see."

He straightened indignantly. "When I become Duc, I would think if I were to order it, then 'twould be done."

She carefully checked the surface of her blade as she ran the oiled cloth along the flat. "You are getting rather ahead of yourself, love. That little trinket might call you the Duc, but at the moment 'twould be generous to call Husson your vassal, and Hieronymus and I are just mercenaries in your employ."

"I know," he said, and the brief trace of haughtiness in his tone faded away. "But there is no harm in planning."

"I rather wish Hieronymus would consider that before dragging me along on some of his mad schemes, but at least it keeps things exciting." Elsabeth turned her sword over and started to work its other flat. She caught a flicker of motion out of the corner of her eye as someone emerged from the common house. "Plans are wonderful things to have, but make sure you have another in the event things fail to turn out as you hoped, or else you might find yourself wandering the countryside with Husson for the rest of your life. I cannot imagine a more horrifying fate."

"Aside from being trapped with you for an eternity?" Husson grumbled. He limped up beside Maerten to watch Hieronymus's wild gesticulations, with his staff in one hand and a tankard in the other that Ysabel struggled to refill as it kept moving away from her every time the friar gestured. He spared Elsabeth a glance while she carefully ran her cloth the length of her sword, and flashed his leering smile at her. "When you finish with that, I have something for you to polish."

Elsabeth wrapped her oil cloth around one hand, laid her blade across it, and peered down the length of both flats for any further blemishes. She found none, and once satisfied with her cleaning she returned her sword to its scabbard and quickly wiped down the hilt and scabbard fittings. "Have you arranged our supplies for tomorrow?" she said without rising to his bait. "If we run out of food on this little scavenger hunt, you will be the first one we eat."

"Talbot says Galleren will carry enough to get us as far as the inn in exchange for this meaningless bit of work you volunteered me for. After that, we can purchase whatever we need there before we set back out again."

"Oh, what are you complaining about? The inn is on our road anyway, and 'tis not like you shan't be getting a share of the pay as well."

Husson folded his arms across his chest and glared at her as she packed up her kit. "For as little enthusiasm as you have for this expedition, you are certainly taking quite a bit of control over it."

She flashed him a mocking smile. "I just wish to make sure it gets done right. I would rather not get lost or starve to death on my way to being hanged."

Maerten frowned at her. "You are still worried?"

Elsabeth sighed. "Love, given my experiences, I think we will be counting ourselves fortunate to get to Auch and find nothing at all."

14

HE NEXT MORNING THEY WERE WOKEN by Colin and Ysabel before the dawning of the sun, and they ate a quick but hearty breakfast while Galleren and his sons loaded the wagon with perhaps a good two-dozen sacks of ground flour. More goods were piled inside along with the miller's delivery; four bushels of the purplish apples Elsabeth had sampled the night before, a half-dozen barrels of the local ale Hieronymus had found a taste for, several wheels of Andry's cheese, and more goods packed up in crates, sacks, and barrels Elsabeth could not name, alongside the supplies for their use along the road. Two burly cart horses were hitched to the wagon, while the villagers helped saddle Felis, Josephus, and Maerten's and Husson's Hackneys.

Faint rosy light was only just beginning to appear on the horizon to the east when they started off on the road once more, and left the low wooden wall of Checy behind them. Elsabeth rode up front alongside the cart horses with Maerten near at hand, and Hieronymus further back on the opposite side. Husson brought up the rear, an arrangement he briefly grumbled over but finally accepted without much further argument.

It took them perhaps two or three hours to reach the main road again, slowed as they were by Galleren's wagon, and by then the sun made its appearance and cast its golden light across Navarre. The weather remained pleasant, and a cool breeze gently shook the branches of the trees overhead. As they rode south the road was crossed here and there by small, clear streams gurgling in stony beds, spanned by fords or the occasional bridge of wood or stone. Insects buzzed and birds sang in the trees, but otherwise the ride was silent and peaceful, with little sign of human encroachment on the area.

Each day passed like the one before: They awoke just before dawn and broke their fast, before packing up camp and hitching the cart horses to the wagon. For several hours they rode at a leisurely pace before pausing briefly for lunch at around midday. After lunch they rode again until the sun reached the horizon in the west. Then they led the wagon just off the road, unhitched and picketed the horses, and set their camp for the night. They said nothing to Galleren of their plans after they parted company with him at the inn, and Elsabeth found some relief that Maerten needed little warning to hold his tongue about the Wizard's revelation.

"Words rashly spoken have a habit of spreading," she told him in a private moment before setting out from Checy. "Best we keep where we are headed and why between us 'till the time is right."

So, their nights in camp were instead spent mostly telling tall stories and, at least for Maerten and Galleren, much enjoyment was taken from stories of Elsabeth's and Hieronymus's previous travels. Husson interjected a few disdainful remarks at times, but otherwise ignored them or listened in silence, and with his wine gone they had no further trouble with him in camp.

The forest around them was bright and airy, and plentiful sunlight found its way down through breaks in the canopy overhead. The space between the trees was filled with the singing of birds. Elsabeth warily swept her eyes across the edge of the road, but she saw nothing but moss-covered tree trunks, with low scrub and brush sprouting from the layers of dead leaves littering the floor where shafts of sunlight reached all the way to the ground.

The remainder of their ride south from Checy proved to be uneventful in the end, and before long they neared the fork in the road, and the inn standing in its northwest corner. It was little more than a small timber-framed, two-level hut nestled into a clearing cut into the woods. Further west the road began to climb in earnest into the Massís Miterre; the upland region stretching away south and west and separating much of Navarre from its southern coast.

Upon seeing it, Elsabeth decided calling it an "inn" would, in fact, be rather generous. It certainly was not so prominent a stopover or landmark as the Four Ways further north, and was little more than a private residence opened to travelers along the road.

There was a stable with room for perhaps six or so horses, and a storehouse, but otherwise nothing to suggest any sort of self-sufficiency, and it seemed the inn relied wholly on goods traded or bartered from the surrounding countryside, or travelers stopping there for the night.

It was late in the day, and the sun was swiftly descending towards the top of the ridge as Galleren drew up his wagon. The master of the house, who called his sons out to take their horses to the stable and unload the goods, greeted them upon their arrival. Elsabeth slid lightly out of the saddle, and gave Felis' neck a gentle caress when one of the innkeeper's sons — a tall and strong fellow perhaps her age — led her away. She felt the curious looks wander over her, particularly the sword hanging at her hip, but she ignored it with the same familiarity with which she always endured such attention, and helped Maerten down from his Hackney so it could be put up for the night as well.

Maerten frowned at the inn as they gathered near the wagon. Elsabeth saw signs there might once have been a larger structure here in the past, mostly in the form of a few burnt timbers and piles of stone that had not yet been cleared away, but whatever stood for glory days for the establishment had long ago passed.

"This is it?" he asked.

Galleren nodded curtly. He unhitched his carthorses so they could join the rest of the animals in the stable. "This is it," he said. He returned to the back of his wagon, lowered the gate, and hopped up into the back. "You folks go on inside, you don't need to linger out here for me. Once I get my goods stowed and arrange payment with the innkeeper, I'll be along to join you and pay you for your company."

Maerten leaned against the wagon. "You will not need us to take you back to Checy?"

The miller shook his head as he made his inspection of his cargo. "Once I load up here I expect to pick up some folks headed back north that will do the job going home."

Elsabeth leaned her shoulder against the wagon and watched the miller work for a moment. "Besides, love," she said to Maerten, "we may not be headed back this way for some time, and I doubt he can wait for us. Try not to feel too down. More often than not, that is how it works in this life. Though I have been trying to lose that vagabond friar for a good four years now without much luck." The last she added with just enough of a rise in volume to be sure Hieronymus would not miss it.

"And every day, when I begin to question why I continue to follow you, harpy, I just take a look at the abundant charm the Lord saw fit to fill your hose with as I trail along in the chaos you leave in your wake," Hieronymus said grumpily from beside the wagon.

"And I'll be glad when all this is done with and I am rid of you both," Husson grumbled. He brushed past her towards the door of the inn.

Elsabeth snickered and followed after Husson with Maerten at her side and Hieronymus bringing up the rear.

An open space dominated the common room of the inn, with a stair in one corner leading up to the sleeping areas above. Downstairs were a few trestle tables running the length of the timber floors, with lamps set out to light the space within, and open windows that looked out onto the wood and let in the air and light. At the far end was a fireplace and hearth that also served as the kitchen area, and there the innkeeper's wife was hard at work preparing the evening meal. Shelves running the length of the walls held pots, pans, kettles, platters, bowls, tankards, cups, and all the utensils she needed for cooking for and serving the guests, with tools for tending the fire and extra firewood neatly organized next to the hearth. The rich fragrance of fresh and dried herbs, burning wood, and cooking food filled the interior, and lent the inn a comforting air promising rest to road-weary travelers. What it lacked in the rowdy grandeur of the Four Ways, it more than made up for with its quaint and rustic hominess.

"Dinner will be ready shortly," the innkeeper said as they entered. He was a tall man, and was probably quite imposing in his youth, but age had shrunk him in all directions but around his middle, and he now rivaled even Hieronymus's prodigious gut in girth. He dressed in simple homespun, though his clothes were in good repair and much cleaner than that of a man who needed to labor for a living. "You may take your belongings upstairs while you wait."

At that, he ushered them up the stairs and to the second level, which consisted of another open area at the near end with palettes laid out on the floor, a few storage trunks, and a door leading to the private living quarters of the innkeeper and his family. Elsabeth was offered a palette along the far wall which could be screened off to provide her with a measure of privacy, while the men were given their choice of where to make their beds from the remaining palettes. Grateful for the moment alone, Elsabeth shed her jacket, doublet, and pattens, changed into a fresh shirt from her pack, and threw herself down on her palette and gazed at the ceiling of exposed timber beams supporting the peaked and shingled roof for a time.

ER FIRST WARNING THAT SHE HAD FALLEN ASLEEP was an insistent rapping on the screen, and Maerten's repeated "Mademoiselle!" while he politely tried to get her attention. Elsabeth blinked against the subdued lamplight illuminating the upper level, and she wiped the sleep from her eyes. She sighed at the repetitive tapping on the privacy screen echoing in her temples.

"Mademoiselle, are you awake?" asked Maerten.

"Yes."

"Are you decent?"

Hieronymus barked out a sharp laugh. "Ha! My son, you will find one of the only real consistencies in my dear Tetty is her utter indecency."

Elsabeth sighed and made her way to the edge of the screen. She peeked around to see Maerten standing shyly with his back to her palette and shifting rather self-consciously over what she might be doing on her own now that she had a moment of privacy. She managed an amused smile at that.

"Oh, good Lord, love, you can turn around," she said, and leaned against the wall with her arms folded under her breast.

Maerten turned and inclined his head to her. "The master of the house has called us to supper."

She took a deep breath, and the fragrance of cooking food from below set her mouth to watering. "How long was I asleep?"

"Not more than an hour, I suppose," he said.

Elsabeth stepped around the screen and emerged to find Hieronymus bent over at his palette rummaging through his baggage. She quickly averted her eyes from the view of his backside sticking into the air. Husson was seated on one of the storage trunks, stripped to the waist and cleaning himself up from the ride with a washcloth and bowl of water provided by the innkeeper.

He flashed a greasy smile her way when he caught her looking in his direction. "See something you like?"

Elsabeth just rolled her eyes and turned to Hieronymus. "You two had best hurry up and finish, as I don't intend to wait on you before taking supper," Elsabeth said.

Hieronymus casually waved her off without looking up from what he was doing. "Go on, we will be along shortly. I trust you can handle our payment from the miller. And mind he does not file the corners off! If we are to be paid twice for one job I wish to know we are not being cheated again!"

Elsabeth planted her hands on her hips and glared indignantly at him. "You will never let me hear the end of that, will you? 'Twas one time, and he had me distracted!"

"Yes, distracted by the thought of bouncing in the most undignified manner upon the shawm of the first minstrel you came across, whom I am not unconvinced was in league with the charlatan from the outset!"

"Oh, don't even start with that, or need I remind you of the nunnery for whom we hunted down those fellows who mishandled the bawd, and how you were seduced into wasting half the promised fee before we were even paid?"

Hieronymus turned away from his bag and waved an indignant finger at her. "I still say you could have more than made it back with a good day's work if you had not been so stubborn."

Elsabeth made a sound of disgust in the back of her throat and threw her hands up in the air in defeat. "For God's sake ..." She turned her attention to Husson. "What say you to an exchange? I take the boy off your hands, and you take to traveling with him?" She jerked a thumb at the friar in exasperation. "The two of you belong together."

Elsabeth spun on her heel and stomped away for the stairs without waiting for a reply, and Maerten scrambled to follow.

"Mademoiselle," he said, as they entered the stairwell and passed out of earshot, "I must ask, if Brother Hieronymus so often speaks to you in such a manner, why travel with him?"

Elsabeth turned into the common room upon reaching the lower level, and stepped aside to allow Maerten to walk beside her. Galleren was already seated at one of the trestle tables, while the innkeeper's wife — a rather dowdy woman in a simple dress of russet wool, with wisps of graying hair peeking out from beneath a cap of white linen — filled his bowl with the stew over which she had been laboring. The miller accepted his supper with a polite nod, and waved Elsabeth over when he saw her emerge from the stairwell.

"Oh, I would not worry overly much about it," she said, and made her way to the table. "As often as there are times I would rather like to toss him off the nearest cliff, I think more often than not I would miss his companionship. He, at least, usually means such things in jest and with affection of sorts, and I have frequently heard far worse from others who say it with conviction.

"But that is a discussion for another time. Let us see about something to eat."

Elsabeth dropped onto the bench with her back to the wall, and Maerten slid in beside her. The innkeeper's wife dutifully returned with bowls of pottage — the night's meal appeared to consist mostly of cabbage, beans, carrots, and barley, with small pieces of cubed pork lending a bit of meat — for each of them, and dark rye bread with butter. The woman came around again with wooden tankards of ale from the supply Galleren had brought down from Checy, before she returned to the fire to continue minding the pot.

"Where are the good brother and your other companion?" the miller asked around a mouthful of bread.

Elsabeth cooled a spoonful of her stew before taking a bite. "They should be down soon," she said.

He set his piece of bread down, reached to his belt, and dropped a large leather purse on the table. "I think your companion would not mind that I give this to you, then."

Elsabeth set down her spoon and scooped up the pouch. "You might be surprised at that. Hieronymus is under the impression I cannot be trusted to handle our money, yet he is the one I have seen spend all of his share in one night on ale and someone to warm his bed."

"And you?"

She quirked a grin, "And I don't need to spend my own money for drink and a meal if I don't wish to."

Elsabeth undid the lacing wound around the mouth of the purse, and made no effort to disguise her actions as she poked through the coins within. The miller merely shrugged it off and returned his attention to his supper.

"I believe Talbot promised you the sum of sixty *deniers* for your trouble," Galleren said.

Elsabeth satisfied herself that the amount of coin — a mix of *sous* and *deniers* — matched what the miller claimed, tied the purse closed again, and tucked it away inside her shirt. "Yes, thank you."

Their conversation was interrupted by a loud bumping on the stairs as Hieronymus and Husson came down and turned into the common room. Hieronymus spotted them gathered at the table and made his way to join them with Husson following behind. The bench shifted beneath her as the friar dropped heavily beside her, leaving Husson to take a place next to the miller. A moment later the innkeeper's wife appeared to place a bowl of pottage, a piece of bread, and a tankard of ale in front of each of them. Hieronymus happily tipped back his drink and took a long draught almost as soon as it appeared before him.

"Now that we are here, where shall you go, if I might ask?" Galleren said around a bite of his pottage.

"Our business here is our own," Husson said sourly, and eyed the miller warily. "'Tis none of your concern."

"We actually do have questions about the area," Maerten interjected much more diplomatically. "Husson has only passed through this region briefly many years ago, and my other companions are unfamiliar with the land. Is there anything you can tell us?"

Elsabeth quirked a smile in his direction. *Good boy, we do need some information if we are to follow this little treasure hunt to its conclusion.*

Galleren regarded his stew thoughtfully a moment. "I confess I seldom come farther along the road than here, and only occasionally at that. The road has become rather wild since the Coventrish withdrew. Bandits have been a particular nuisance on the road the past few years, most of whom I suspect started off as deserters from one army or another during the wars."

Husson let out a grunt around a mouthful of stew. Elsabeth eyed him for a moment, but he showed no sign of being inclined to elaborate further on his thoughts.

"Not many folk come by this way these days," he continued, "Save for the odd treasure hunter or two, but they seldom stay long."

"Treasure hunter?" Maerten said with a frown.

Galleren grunted an acknowledgement. "Mostly stirred up by local gossip about the old castle away to the west, and the Baron du Auch."

"Tongues are wont to wag at the passing of armies," Hieronymus said around a swig of ale. "And grow from idle gossip into legend. 'Tis my experience that such tales are of little more value than a few coin in the pocket of a passing minstrel."

The miller nodded his agreement. "True enough, but some folk are certainly more easily stirred up than others about tales of easy wealth to be had."

It was Elsabeth's turn to grunt. She watched Galleren carefully for any sign of deceit, however, she noted nothing untoward in his features. "'Tis my experience that wealth lying round for anyone to find is seldom as easily gained as that. Or as cheaply," she said.

"In this case 'tis all just minstrel's fancy, as the good Brother says."

"I could do with a bit of minstrel's fancy after the ride," Maerten said. "'Tis been a while since any of us have had a real tale round a good meal, at least."

Elsabeth hid a smile behind her tankard. *Clever lad.*

The miller shrugged and considered the piece of bread in his hands while he chewed. "Well, there is not truly much to tell, but it goes back to after the Duc and his folk were wiped out. Supposedly, a substantial part of the family treasure was safely secreted away under the guard of the Baron du Auch in the aftermath.

"However not long after, the Baron was obliged to withdraw when Auch proved untenable after Eze fell, and the Coventrish razed the castle to the ground when they left. Most of the people fled, and I think that was when the old inn — at the time, as Richart tells it, it was a true and proper one. That was back when his father ran it — was raided and destroyed by foragers. A few made it a ways further up the road, but Checy was largely spared trouble.

"Auch itself was never really a strong position. Oh, it did a good job watching the Vert from its bluff, but from the north it was quite exposed, which is why it was abandoned during the wars, rather than defended. The story goes that when the Baron fled much of the treasure of Rouen was left behind, locked away in a vault deep beneath the castle. However, the old Baron himself died fighting the Coventrish not long after, and with him those who knew where the entrance was hidden."

"Surely the Coventrish would have stumbled across it after razing the castle," Hieronymus said, a note of suspicion in his voice.

"Which is why I am inclined to believe it never existed in the first place, and began as nothing more than a rumor to distract the Coventrish and buy time for du Auch to escape while they were busy hunting treasure. But as you have said, rumor has a way of growing in the telling, so every now and then a few enterprising folk come looking."

Galleren eyed them all suspiciously. "Now, I don't know what your business in these parts is, but if you have a mind to go poking around the ruins for yourself, I suggest you keep a wary eye. You are not likely to find much more than a quarrel in the back and knives in the dark if you are not on your guard."

Elsabeth nodded as a show of graciousness for the advice, and carefully hid her concern over this bit of news. "Thank you," she said. "We shall certainly keep that in mind."

15

THEY BID FAREWELL TO GALLEREN THE following morning and set out again, heading west from the inn. After a few miles the dirt track faded. Dense thickets encroached upon its edges on either side, and for long stretches the packed earth was replaced by short green grass. Enough traffic still passed along the westward road to keep the track distinct, but even now it was slowly giving way to wilderness as the ground began to climb into the northern foothills of the Massís Miterre. Tree-clad hills rose on their left and screened a maze of winding hollows and gullies from their view in that direction. The broad swath of forest marching away north towards Checy pressed in on their right.

Branches stretched across the road on both sides and formed a verdant hall with a ceiling of green, with occasional gaps allowing the sun to dapple the way ahead. Wildflowers popped up along the margins in these open areas. Birds sang from the cover of the deeper canopy, and at times a deer or rabbit bolted across the road.

Elsabeth scanned both sides of the road for any sign of danger lurking in the shadows beneath the trees, but the first few days out from the inn were quiet, broken only by birdsong and the incessant buzzing of insects. They spoke little, for they all felt as if human voices were unwelcome in this empty country, and Elsabeth little liked the thought of an errant word giving their presence away to the highwaymen who might prey on travelers on such lonely stretches.

At times they passed some reminder that folk did once dwell here, and the road saw heavy use from goods moving west along the hills. A few clearings set back into the woods betrayed the site of some old woodsman's hut, and they camped one night in the overgrown ruins and fallow fields of an old farm. None of them bothered to rummage through the refuse; anything of value had long been looted by the Coventrish and Navarese armies that had battled for control over the territory during the Wars, though Maerten remained optimistic that Auch would be different.

The road ran relatively straight with little turning aside as it followed the northern slopes of the hills stretching away southwards, climbing at a more leisurely pace than the heights frowning down on them. They were just drawing to within a day's march or so of Auch by Husson's reckoning, when Elsabeth noted a spur of the hills jutting out northward, spanning the path head.

The road climbed gently up onto a saddle between two heights on either side, both crowned with trees. The level of the forest floor rose on either side of them. The grade up into the trees was smooth and gentle on their right, though rose much more sharply on their left. Low underbrush obscured their view of the crest of the slope on that side. Further up ahead, just below the top of the saddle, she saw a sight that formed a ball of ice in her gut: Three figures, one in the center leaning on a tall spear, and those on either side of him carrying an old pick mattock and a large wood axe, respectively. The way further along the road was barred by a barricade of four old wheelbarrows loaded down with rocks and dirt. Elsabeth muttered a curse and looked to Hieronymus, who nodded curtly and loosened his sword in its scabbard.

"What is this?" Maerten asked in a low voice when he caught sight of the men and heard Elsabeth's low curse.

"Trouble," she said. "Be ready to run for it hard back the way we came."

"But—"

"Just do what I say!"

Elsabeth met Hieronymus's eyes and subtly indicated the slope on their left with her chin, and he nodded in understanding. *Rush the left and cover south of the road.* She then glanced over her shoulder at Husson trailing behind them, and he looked back at her. His dark eyes were alert to the danger and sweeping both edges of the road seeking for the threat that doubtlessly lurked behind the brush. A surreptitious waggle of her thumb told him all he needed to know of her plan. *Sweep around on the right and clear the north side of the road.*

The center is mine.

All of this took only moments, and as Elsabeth turned away from Husson they drew within a stone's throw of the roadblock and she pulled up her horse.

"Clear the road!" she called out to the man with the spear, whom she quickly identified as the leader of the group from the somewhat better condition of his garb. Otherwise, there was little of note to differentiate the three. All dressed in homespun hose, shirts, and doublets of a fashion typical of this part of Navarre. The spearman's doublet was particolored and might have at one time been the colors of some lord or another. Their hair was shaggy and their beards were unkempt, ranging from black to dirty blond, and they watched their approach with alert and eager eyes peering out from hard and weathered faces. All three leered at her in the sort of manner she found all too common, and more than a little discomfiting.

"Not quite yet, love!" he shouted back in rough Navarrese, touched by a hint of a Coventrish accent. "The road is closed, and there is a toll on the return trip. You all get down from those horses and throw down your purses and arms, and we will see about letting you pass." The spearman grinned broadly, and it was quickly evident proper care of his teeth was not high among his concerns. She felt his eyes, and those of his companions, wander her body. "Well, I'll see about letting them pass. You, I think, I'll keep a bit longer."

Oh, of course you will. Elsabeth eyed both sides of the road but could still see nothing there. Nonetheless she thought she felt unseen eyes watching them from the undergrowth, hidden by the top of the slope as the ground climbed away from the road. "I'll give you a better offer," she said. "Clear the way now, and I let you keep your shriveled little cock between your legs rather than cutting it off and shoving it up your own arse."

The bandit glared. "For that one I cut out your tongue when we finish with you! We have you outmanned and surrounded. This is your last chance, love!"

Elsabeth speared him with her fiercest glare. "No, love, 'tis yours!" For a moment the spearman blanched at her tone, but pride quickly got the better of him in the face of his men. He started to raise his spear overhead in what she suspected was part of the signal to his hidden comrades, but Elsabeth was faster.

"Go!" she called before their adversary could give voice to his own command, and dug her heels hard into Felis' flanks. The rasp of steel broke the peace of the woods as she, Husson, and Hieronymus drew their swords, and as her long blade flashed clear of her scabbard and out from beneath her jacket, the three men at the barricade fell back in alarm. Felis bellowed as training took command, and with no further urging on her part the old jennet charged the blockade. Elsabeth felt the wind stream against her cheeks and set her hair to flapping behind her like a banner of molten copper, and the thunder of hooves roared in her ears. Felis covered the length of the road in the space of a few heartbeats, and she gently directed her charge to ride down the man on the left.

The outlaws tried to dive out of the way, but Elsabeth was on her adversaries before they could clear a path. She reached out and swept her sword in a broad rising cut at the leader of the band, and she heard the distinct ring of steel tearing through flesh and felt her sword jerk in her hand. Blood sprayed in a rising crimson arc into the air and glistened brilliantly in the afternoon sunlight falling on the road. At almost the same moment she cut down the spearman, Felis surged beneath her and vaulted into the air to clear the wheelbarrow barricade blocking the road. Her front hooves connected with the skull of the second man as she leapt, and knocked him sprawling to the dirt, where he lay without moving.

ON ELSABETH'S SIGNAL HIERONYMUS KICKED Josephus and turned towards the slope rising away from the road to the southwest. The old Hackney snorted his disapproval of the sudden movement, but bounded up the slope. His sword rang as it cleared his scabbard, and he let loose as fierce a cry as he could manage. Something whistled past him on either side. Another bolt hissed from the trees ahead of him, but within moments Josephus was up and diving through the foliage.

He found himself in the middle of a line of four men concealed in the foliage atop the slope, all dressed alike to men down on the road, with here and there a hat or cap, all armed with crossbows. As he emerged among them the nearest man on the right — so close Josephus nearly trampled him beneath his sharp hooves — yelped in panic and tried to snatch the axe leaning against the tree he was using for cover, but a falling backhand from Hieronymus's sword bit into his shoulder and drove him to the ground before he reached it. A second rushed him with his axe raised from his left. Hieronymus spun his horse with precision and skill born of long experience, and used the movement to tear his sword free of the first outlaw and wheel it through a rising cut that split the second fellow's belly open from groin to throat.

Hieronymus abandoned the reins with his free hand, and quickly snatched his buckler from his belt. None too soon; another bolt whistled in from his right. The shot rang off his shield, and Hieronymus urged Josephus forward in a sudden charge. Though slowed by the undergrowth he was upon the shooter before the fellow could ready another bolt, and a quick stroke of the friar's sword sprayed blood across the foliage.

The fourth took one look at his comrades lying dead among the trees and took off in a stumbling run deeper into the woods. He threw aside his crossbow and every other weapon he had in the panic of his flight, and soon vanished into the foliage.

"The Lord blesses those who exercise the wisdom of discretion, my son!" he shouted at the man's back. Hieronymus chuckled, returned his sword to his scabbard, and hung his buckler from his belt. He offered Josephus a pat on the side of his powerful neck. "There is a good lad. Well done!"

Josephus snorted indignantly and shook his head.

USSON CHARGED HIS HACKNEY UP THE embankment on the other side of the road, while the friar plunged into the woods on the left. He circled back around to the right to find an easier slope for his horse to climb, and ducked under a hail of crossbow bolts that buzzed from the foliage like a swarm of angry bees from their hive. From the corner of his eye he saw Maerten flying back eastward, and by some miracle none of the quarrels found their mark.

But then he was up the embankment and among the trees, and could see nothing more of the road. Husson emerged at the eastern end of a line of four men loading and loosing their crossbows as quickly as they could, filling the air with a constant hail of missiles.

The moment he crashed through the brush they were aware of him, and turned in a panic in his direction. Husson gave a cry, deftly flipped his sword to his left hand, and urged his horse forward. The animal balked at the notion of riding into the line of bodies and tried to shy away from them. Husson fought to keep it on line in his charge, and swiftly cut down the first he reached.

The scent was almost too much for his horse. It staggered and bucked in fright, and Husson only just managed to reach his second target. Another rising slash split the man's face in two, and this time the gore was more than the horse could bear.

It reared and screamed at the smell and batted the air with its hooves. Husson snarled a curse, and fought with the reins and kicked its flanks to nudge it back into the charge. But now it was too late, and the moment of surprise was gone. He heard the snap of a roller release, the twang of a cord and prongs, and the whine of the bolt speeding through the air. Then his left shoulder exploded in pain, the sky wheeled overhead, and he felt himself topple backwards out of the saddle. His horse squealed in panic and bolted, and the ground rushed up to greet him as he fell. His last conscious thought before everything went black was the sound of steel tearing flesh and two agonized screams.

And then he knew nothing more.

IERONYMUS!" ELSABETH CALLED AS SHE scrambled down from her horse and hurried to where Husson lay unmoving on his side in the undergrowth. The feathered end of the bolt protruded from his left shoulder just below his collar bone, though he showed no other sign of injury. She slid her sword back into its scabbard and crouched over their companion's still form. At least some of her urgency faded when she found him still breathing, if unconscious.

"Hieronymus get your fat arse up here!" she called again when the friar did not immediately materialize at hand.

"Just a moment, just a moment!" came his grumbling reply. "Would that the Lord teach his impetuous daughter some patience and serenity!"

Elsabeth rolled Husson so he was flat on his back and placed her hand over the wound to stem the flow of blood. "Oh, save your prayers for later, love. I know how little you care for the exertion, but run if you have to!"

A few moments later she heard a loud crash off to her right, and the friar stumbled through the undergrowth and dragged himself up with a grumbled cursed mixed between prayers of contrition under his breath. "All right, all right, here I am, Tetty. Now what was so damnably important you could not ..." he trailed off into stunned silence when his eyes fixed on Husson. "Lord have mercy! Is he ...?"

"He is alive, though I have yet to decide whether to be relieved or annoyed the insufferable bastard is still with us. The bolt is in his shoulder. I think it missed anything particularly vital, but I remember the scolding you gave me the last time I tried to pull an arrow from someone."

Hieronymus trundled forward through the brush supported by his staff until he could crouch beside the man, as well, and brushed her away from the bolt. "Well, I am glad at least some of my wisdom is finding its way into that thick head of yours."

"Right. Well, you and your wisdom deal with him," she said. She pushed herself back to her feet and brushed her hands off on her knees. "Now that I have made sure no one sticks a knife in him while he is lying helpless, I saw his horse bolt and run to the east. I best go and fetch it and Maerten before either get lost for good."

"Your compassion for those in need touches my heart, Tetty."

Elsabeth returned to Felis, calmly nosing among the brush and seemingly oblivious to the nearby carnage, and led her away. "Oh, shush. If you need me for anything now 'twill be to move him, and you can do that well enough without me. But we will need that horse."

Hieronymus just waved her away. "Go on. I think he is coming around, now, anyway."

She swung herself up into the saddle and turned Felis back for the road. "Keep a sharp eye out. I don't know if these fellows were part of a larger band or not, but if so, I would like to be moving on before their reinforcements arrive."

With that, she nudged Felis in the flanks, and turned her back to the road.

OOD LAD! UP WE GO! LEAN ON ME AND WE shall have you comfortable soon," Hieronymus said, as he threaded Husson's arm across his shoulders, and lifted him from the ground.

"Oh shut your mouth already," their surly companion grumbled. "I am no child or invalid, and can manage myself."

Nonetheless, he staggered and settled much of his weight on Hieronymus. The friar grunted and felt his knees buckle under the unaccustomed load, but he murmured a quiet prayer to the Lord of All to give him strength to manage the burden (and the wherewithal to endure the man's stench, which was unbearable in such close proximity), and together they started back to the road.

Hieronymus guided him to a small clear area just on the side of the road near at hand, where the sun fell brightly on a bed of wildflowers and soft grass. Josephus, picketed deeper into the clearing, snorted disdainfully at the sight of his companion. He eased Husson down into the grass and propped his back against one of the trees at the edge of the road. Then he knelt beside his charge and considered the wound.

Husson clutched at the base of the bolt protruding from his shoulder and panted heavily. "Well? How does it look, then?"

"'Twill be in the hands of the Lord of All, my son. Fortunately for you, my hands are now the Lord's hands," Hieronymus said.

He knelt where he could better examine Husson's shoulder. "Now then," he murmured, and took hold of the fabric of Husson's doublet and the shirt beneath. Hieronymus tore them both open to fully expose his shoulder and the wound with it. He was a fit enough fellow with strong shoulders, and here and there Hieronymus saw a trace of old scars crisscrossing his chest, the tale of many old duels and sparring matches in the man's past.

"Here now!" Husson snarled. "That shirt cost me a pretty penny."

Hieronymus grunted. "And you greatly overpaid for it. But for now, 'tis more important I see what I am doing." He gently probed the wound with his finger and gauged the length of the exposed shaft of the bolt. Husson bit back a curse of pain at the touch.

"Watch what you are doing!" he snapped.

"My son, I spent ten years studying with the finest surgeons in Boehm after accepting my calling among the Olivians," Hieronymus said indignantly, and in response none-too-gently pulled Husson away from the tree so he could feel the man's back along the shoulder blade, seeking for the point of the bolt. Husson let out a strangled yelp at the sudden movement. "So cease your mewling and have faith in my hands!"

Hieronymus found no trace of the bolt penetrating all the way through his shoulder, and he judged from the length of the exposed shaft the quarrel stopped well short of his shoulder blade. He released their unpleasant companion and let him collapse roughly against the tree again, drawing another snarl of complaint from him.

"Be careful you damn fool!" Husson growled.

"Stay put," Hieronymus said. "I need to have a look at one of the bolts these fellows used and retrieve a few things from my baggage."

Husson grunted. "And where do you think I'll be going, anyway?"

Hieronymus ignored him. With an effort he levered himself back to his feet and stepped out into the road. Fortunately, finding one of the spent quarrels proved to be a simple task. A few stuck out of the road, and he retrieved one that looked to not be buried too deeply into the dirt. He turned it in his hands and studied it for a long moment. It was the typical sort of quarrel used for hunting, with a short shaft of poplar and leather flights. However, what concerned him most was the head; it was a broad iron point, barbed like a swallow's tail at the back. Hieronymus twisted his lip into a disgusted scowl at the sight of it. He checked a few of the others lying about, and they were all of the same make.

Well, this will make extracting it unpleasant, but there is nothing for it.

Hieronymus tapped the bolt against his hand as he waddled past Husson to Josephus tied up in the back of their clearing. The old Hackney snorted and stamped at his approach, not at all liking the look of the barbed missile in his hands, or the smell of blood on his robes.

"Here now, my lad, 'tis just me," he said, and gave the old Hackney a gentle pat on the neck. "No need for that! 'This has been a hard day for us all now, so don't you be adding to it!"

Josephus merely snorted again irritably in response.

Hieronymus retrieved one of his bags and returned to Husson's side. He knelt once more and fumbled with the strings holding it closed. Within was a leather case and, buried at the very bottom, a stoppered glass bottle filled with a clear golden liquid.

"What is that?" Husson asked.

"Something I make a point to keep on hand for just such occasions, acquired at some expense from a monastery hospital outside of Waldeck some time back."

The other's eyes widened in surprise. "*Aqua vitae?*"

Hieronymus glanced at him sharply. "You know of it?"

Husson grunted. "I have heard enough songs of what you priests actually use it for."

"Yes, well, educated sorts are wont to find more recreational uses for such concoctions. I am not sure if you know this, but monastery life is decidedly boring, and lacking in a certain sort of pleasurable company."

Hieronymus looked past him and smiled at Elsabeth as she returned with Maerten. Husson's Hackney was tied to her saddle.

"The poor thing managed to run a good several miles back east before we finally ran her down," Elsabeth said as she swung down from the saddle. "I can't say I can blame her, considering how unaccustomed she must be to a fight. I don't think we were followed here, so this lot must have had this stretch of the road staked out."

Maerten dismounted behind her, and when his eyes fell upon his wounded guardian his face blanched, and he forgot entirely about the battle.

"Husson!" he cried in alarm, and rushed across the distance between them, his expression a mix of worry and fright at the sight of the bolt protruding from the elder man's shoulder. "What happened?"

"What does it look like?" Husson snapped irritably. "I have been stuck and unhorsed. My head is spinning, and my shoulder is on fire, and that damnable harpy took my wine!"

"Well, I am sorry!" Maerten said. "I am no more accustomed to this than your horse!"

"If we can dispense with all this bickering for the moment and focus on the task at hand," Hieronymus said, and glowered between the other three to forestall any further arguing, "I'll need a fire going."

"Come on, love," Elsabeth said, and led the horses deeper into the glade. "When he is in this mood 'tis best to just do as he says."

While Elsabeth and Maerten did as he asked, Hieronymus unstoppered the bottle of *aqua vitae*, and poured a careful measure into a cup from his bag.

"Drink," he said, and forced the cup into Husson's good hand.

Husson grunted. "At last, an order from a priest I will gladly follow!"

He tossed his head back and downed it in one swallow.

Hieronymus flipped open the leather case from his baggage and laid it out flat on the ground in front of him. Their wounded companion eyed the rows of iron implements neatly tucked away into the pouches and compartments with suspicion, and no small amount of trepidation. A collection of forceps, tooth-pullers, trephines, cauters, fleams, lancets, arrow and medicinal spoons, smaller blades of varying sizes, one rather large and wickedly curved knife sharpened along both edges, and a compact but heavy saw were arrayed in orderly fashion within.

Hieronymus held the sample bolt with one hand and picked through his collection of arrow spoons. He pulled two or three from their compartment in his kit, matched them to the head, and grunted in satisfaction once he produced one of the proper size. He carefully returned the others to their places in the case and selected a small blade, which he laid beside him.

"Now then," Hieronymus said as cheerfully as he could, "All I need do is follow the shaft of the bolt to the head with the spoon and extract it."

Husson's eyes widened, and his face paled while Hieronymus casually described the procedure. "I think," he said, and his voice was ragged from pain, "I would rather keep the head right where it is, so put away those instruments of torture and trouble me no more!"

"Nonsense, my son. If I leave the bolt where it is, an abscess will form and pus will inundate the wound, and you will lose the use of the arm."

"I would rather leave it in the hands of God than in your murderous devices!"

Hieronymus huffed indignantly. "But you are in the hands of the Lord, my son, for he has provided me with the knowledge and skill to tend to you."

"And I call into question your state of grace, Brother, for I have seen the indulgences you trade in. Or have you forgotten your ministrations with that girl at the Four Ways?"

"I'll have you know my business with that poor child was merely to take upon myself the burden of her sins."

"Oh, I am sure she burdened you with something."

Before Hieronymus could issue a suitable retort, Maerten returned, and flicked his eyes between him and Husson. "I have a fire going, Brother," he said, and sure enough Hieronymus could smell the fragrance of burning wood.

"Excellent! And well timed," he said, and turned away from Husson to regard his tools. He selected a cauter of appropriate size, handed it to the boy, and indicated the blade. "Put that end in the fire and come back here. I'll call for it when I am ready."

"Yes, Brother," he said, and hurried off to do as he was told.

After a few moments Maerten returned and waited for his instructions. Elsabeth busied herself at the back of the camp with the horses; Felis had weathered the day's action like the old warhorse she was, but Maerten's Hackney was no less distressed than his guardian's.

"Come here, my boy," Hieronymus said. Husson glared at his ward, and Maerten shied his head away, unsure where exactly to be looking. "Hold him tightly, but mind the shaft that you don't move or jar it. He will want to move, so you must keep him fast!"

Maerten did as he asked, and Husson cried out when the boy's hand found purchase on his shoulder near to where the bolt protruded from his shoulder. "Unhand me!" he said. "Inflict your cruel art on someone else! I said let me go!"

"By God hold him still!" Hieronymus snapped irritably. He picked up his arrow spoon and leaned over Husson's shoulder. Their comrade kicked and thrashed, but Maerten managed to get a firmer hold on him, and practically climbed atop his guardian to put all his weight on his shoulders. Hieronymus slammed one meaty fist down in annoyance on Husson's near leg. "Now stop that at once or I shall sit upon it!"

Husson stilled his flailing, and glared hellfire at him.

"Good," Hieronymus said. "Now then, do try and remain still!"

Hieronymus took his arrow spoon in his off-hand and picked up the small surgical blade with the other. The flesh of Husson's shoulder had closed around the shaft of the bolt, and the wound was not quite wide enough to fit his tool along the shaft. He gently parted the edges of the tear in Husson's flesh, and with a quick flick of his knife slightly widened the puncture. Husson screamed as the blade sliced into his flesh, and it took all Maerten's strength to hold him still while Hieronymus worked.

With the bolt-wound opened further the blood was able to flow much more freely, and poured forth in a great torrent. Hieronymus wiped it away with one of the ragged strips torn from Husson's shirt to keep his view clear, and carefully slipped his finger into the hole made by the passage of the missile. He ignored Husson's agonized snarls and writhing as he followed the path of the shaft to the bolt head. He murmured a soft prayer to the Lord to guide his hands and to ease the poor churl's suffering while he worked, and grunted in satisfaction when the end of his finger reached the barbs at the end of the head.

"The Lord is with you, my son, for the shaft and head are still attached, and the head did not penetrate down to the bone!" Hieronymus said

He delicately removed his finger from the wound. Husson had no words of gratitude, and merely gasped, moaned, and growled. His breathing was ragged and sweat beaded on his brow. Hieronymus just wiped his finger clean upon the ragged remains of Husson's shirt and mopped up the flow of blood which followed the withdrawal of his finger.

Hieronymus laid aside his blade, took his arrow spoon back in hand, and placed the tip into the opening in Husson's shoulder. With the same care as before, he followed the shaft of the bolt deeper and deeper into the wound. Every movement of the iron tool drew a fresh groan or cry of agony from his charge, and Husson sporadically thrashed and kicked against the hands holding him. Each time Husson moved Hieronymus paused in fear of jarring the bolt and separating it from the head, but finally reached the end of the tear left by the passage of the missile. It took a few moments of fishing around a bit with the spoon before he successfully hooked its end around the point of the bolt, (during which time Husson made every effort to tear away from Maerten's grip and rip the spoon from Hieronymus's hand) but finally Hieronymus felt it find purchase.

"Hold him tightly, my son," Hieronymus said, "for he will surely want to move now."

And with that he began to pull on both spoon and shaft together, and the bolt slowly withdrew from Husson's shoulder. He cried out in agony and writhed against the arms holding him. Hieronymus needed several long minutes of pulling, and much of his strength, until finally the bolt popped free of the wound with a spurt of blood. He chuckled in satisfaction as he parted the bolt head from his arrow spoon. "Well done, my son!" he said, turning to Maerten. "Be a good lad and fetch my cauter, if you will."

"Yes, Brother," Maerten said, and spared Husson a look as the latter lay panting and sweating from his ordeal. Husson just glowered back at him weakly.

"We are almost finished, my son," Hieronymus said. "Your faith in the Lord of All has been well-placed."

"When you are finished, I'll send you to him directly," Husson said, and his voiced wavered from enduring the pain of the surgery. "I am sure he will have words to speak with you about your manner of medicine."

"Come now! Do you know how fortunate you are to have me to tend you, rather than one of those rank amateur barber-surgeons? I devoted a part of my wanderings after taking my vows to attending university, and you shan't find a finer surgeon outside of Carcassonne."

"You should have studied longer," Husson grumbled wearily.

Once again, Maerten's return forestalled any retort from Hieronymus. He held the cauter with its hot end upright, and it was glowing red from the fire. Husson's eyes immediately opened wide as saucers, and he desperately scrambled in an effort to escape.

"Thank you, my son!" Hieronymus said, and carefully accepted the cauter. "You will want to hold him good and tight; this will rather sting a bit."

"Now wait half a moment!" Husson cried as Maerten seized him, and he strained against them in his effort to escape. "You keep that away from me!"

"Oh stop your complaining, you have already passed the worst of it. Now be still and let this miracle of the Lord of All seal your wound and keep you from bleeding all over the damned ground!"

And with that, Hieronymus jabbed the end of the cauter into the wound with no real delicacy. Husson's screams shook the trees standing over the road and drowned out the sizzling of muscle burning under the heated iron as black smoke rose from the wound. Maerten struggled to hold him down while Hieronymus worked his way around the entirety of the wound, and the stench of burned flesh filled the air. He needed only a few moments to finish, and leaned the cauter upright and away from anything flammable before wiping the last of the blood from Husson's shoulder. The man panted and moaned in agony.

"There we are, as good as the day the Lord made you!" Hieronymus said, and clapped him heartily on the shoulder, drawing another anguished — and more than a little enraged — snarl from their companion.

Maerten leaned over Husson and looked over Hieronymus's handiwork for a moment, before his guardian seized him by the doublet and put his face in his. "What are you looking at, boy?" he growled between his teeth. "Get away from me!" Husson then released him with a rough shove, and the boy fell backwards onto his rear.

"Go on," Hieronymus said sympathetically. "Our brave lad will doubtless like some time to himself." Maerten stood and started away, but Hieronymus called him back, and carefully turned over his cauter. "Douse that in some water and bring it back to me when you are finished."

"Yes, Brother," Maerten said, and hurried off, more out of a desire to escape the wrathful glare of his guardian than any haste to carry out Hieronymus's wish.

Hieronymus poured out another measure of *aqua vitae*, and Husson reached out for it with a trembling hand. But before he could lay hold of it, Hieronymus tilted back his head and downed it in one swallow himself.

"Ah, I needed that!"

ELSABETH WRINKLED HER NOSE AGAINST the stench of seared flesh hanging thickly in the air, and cupped Felis' face between her hands. Her horse's nostrils flared, and she pawed at the earth restlessly. Elsabeth sighed.

"I know, love, 'tis not a pleasant smell," she said. "And the man can howl like the Dark One himself was fucking him up the arse, can't he?"

Felis snorted. Maerten's and Husson's Hackneys danced and reared while the latter carried on, but tethered as they were to Felis neither made an effort to bolt. Josephus endured the clamor with his usual irritable indifference, and nipped at Husson's horse (Elsabeth noted he showed no more liking for the horse than he did the rider) when he was jostled away from some dainty of interest he was nosing through among the wildflowers sprouting up in the little glade.

"Well, 'tis all over for the present. So no more to worry about for tonight." Elsabeth patted Felis on the neck, and the old jennet nuzzled her cheek with a velvety muzzle.

Elsabeth giggled as she stepped away and turned back into the camp proper. Maerten dejectedly poked at the fire nearby, while Hieronymus fussed with Husson propped against the tree. Elsabeth stood and watched Maerten for a long moment. He quietly continued stirring the embers and gave no notice to her scrutiny.

"How is your guardian?" she said, after a few moments of empty silence broken only by the crackle of the fire and the bickering of Hieronymus and Husson.

Maerten shifted and his face paled a bit. "Brother Hieronymus was able to remove the bolt."

She nodded and quirked a grin, more out of a desire to lift the boy's sullen mood than any humor she herself found in the situation. "I knew I kept the drunken lech around for something. If Hieronymus has done half the job I know him to be capable of, he should recover nicely."

Elsabeth then made her way over to the tree. There she found Husson lying stripped to the waist, while Hieronymus fought against his fidgeting so he could bind his shoulder in linen. The whiff of burned flesh still hung heavily in the air.

"How is he?" she asked upon drawing nearer. Husson flashed his greasy smile at her, and made no attempt to disguise his eyes wandering her body from head to toe and back again.

"Come to minister to me in my need?" Husson said, his words slurring together. "I got an ache you might be able to do something with."

Elsabeth rolled her eyes. She said nothing.

"Well, I have tended to him with all my skill," Hieronymus said. "Whether he lives or dies is all in the hands of God, now, though I'll keep a close watch on his humors."

She nodded idly. "Can he ride? I wish to put as much distance between us and this place before we camp for the night as possible. I saw no signs of trouble while I was tracking down his horse, but I can't say if it might come from the other direction."

Hieronymus finally managed to cinch the linen bindings, and sat back on his heels and mopped his brow. He poured out another measure of *aqua vitae* from the glass flask he thought was safely hidden away at the bottom of his bags (but which Elsabeth knew right where to find at need) with a trace of irritation on his fat face. "The man is so drunk right now he cannot even stand, much less stay in the saddle, though I suppose we could tie him to the poor beast."

Husson laughed. "Oh, I can still ride." He eyed Elsabeth and slapped the ground next to him. "Come here love and bend over, and I'll show you how well I can ride."

Elsabeth snatched the cup from Hieronymus when he tried to pass it to Husson and drained it herself. It burned all the way down. "'Twill have to do," she said to Hieronymus. Husson seemed to take no notice of her dismissal of his proposition, and just giggled to himself drunkenly. "The further we can get from this place the better. I would rather not find out these fellows had friends. Finish up here. I'll have a look at the roadblock to see if we can ride around it. If not, I may need you and Maerten to help me move it."

He heaved an exaggerated sigh. "Have you no consideration for a poor, tired old man, Tetty?"

She handed him back the empty cup. "This from the man I have seen jump right from a day on the road to raiding every tavern and nunnery in the first town we come across?"

Husson chuckled. "Now that is a tale I could do with, Brother. I still am not sure 'tis not where you truly met this one," he said, and reached up to strike her across the bottom on her way past.

Elsabeth jumped at the stroke and glared indignantly at him. "How much has he had to drink, anyway?"

"Enough to stop his complaining and keep him quiet for a time," Hieronymus said irritably. "The man has done nothing but moan and bleat from the moment he came to again."

"And enough that he thinks of himself as the court jester as well, 'twould seem," she said. "I may actually prefer him as a surly bastard than a merry fool."

Husson chuckled. "I knew you would come round, love," he said. "Now why not take a rest and come ride on my stallion?" And with that he grabbed himself in a most obscene manner, which sent her away before she could act on the urge to draw her rondel and give Hieronymus more work to do.

"I think you seared the wrong hole," Elsabeth said over her shoulder. "Next time, start with his mouth."

"Don't tempt me!" Hieronymus called to her back. She walked away with a laugh under her breath and a shake of her head.

Elsabeth left the tree and made her way to the wheelbarrows blocking the road. Stone and dirt were piled high in their beds, and they were hooked together with a good, heavy chain that would make it impossible to move one without needing to move the others as well. She leaned on her sword at her hip and considered the lead cart carefully.

The outlaws clearly did not want anyone breaking through; the axels on all were jammed, with wedges driven into the joint between the axel and the frame of the barrow to prevent its wheel from turning, and the chain linking all the carts together ran through the spokes. The chain would either need to be broken, or all the carts moved together. A tall order for a woman, a boy, and a fat, old friar.

She straightened again and considered the woods closing in on the road on either side. On their left the hills continued to soar up quite steeply, and there would be no taking the horses round to that side. But on the right the ground was more forgiving, and there was an open space between the trees they might be able to lead them through on foot before rejoining the road at the far side.

Satisfied they would not be left to deal with the carts themselves, Elsabeth turned and made her way back to camp.

HIERONYMUS SPARED ONLY A FEW BRIEF WORDS over the bodies of the slain outlaws, and with Maerten's help he laid them in as dignified a manner as could be just off the side of the road. But they wasted no time in burying them, or even making a proper cairn from the rocks and dirt loaded in the wheelbarrows (for which there was not enough to cover even half of them).

In the end it took them about an hour to lead the horses through the woods on the north side of the barricade and back onto the road. The way ahead was narrow and uneven, and Josephus in particular protested the path.

But soon they set off again. With Husson unable to ride himself they sat him on Maerten's horse, with Maerten riding behind him to hold him in the saddle. Fortunately, Husson was so deep into the *aqua vitae* Hieronymus gave him to keep him silent, he largely dozed and gave them no more trouble that night. They tied his Hackney to Felis' saddle, and in this fashion they resumed their journey west along the road.

They rode for several hours to put as much distance between them and the site of the skirmish as they could, and continued along even after the sun fell behind the trees in the west and night enfolded the woods. Enough starlight found its way down through the canopy to light the road, so they pressed on a bit longer than they might have otherwise, before finally setting camp.

Their supper was a rather cheerless affair, as no one wanted the light of a fire to give them away to anyone that might be lurking in the woods, particularly if the outlaw band they encountered had friends waiting for their comrades' return. Fortunately, the night was pleasant and they had no need of the warmth, though Hieronymus gave them all a drink from his secret flask.

None of them were much inclined towards conversation that night, but Maerten particularly remained quiet and troubled throughout the evening. The boy wandered off a short distance after Hieronymus went to turn in for the night, and threw himself down on a small patch of grass to stare up into the stars. Elsabeth sat with her back against a tree and watched him for a time. She felt the dull ache in her belly threaten to sharpen and begin poking at her once more, and sighed heavily.

Bugger. How did I let Hieronymus talk me into this madness, anyway?

She pushed herself back onto her feet and looked about the camp. Husson lay sprawled on his back and continued to snore deeply with a light blanket thrown across him. His sword and other belongings lay carefully piled up alongside him. Elsabeth grabbed his sword, tucked it under her arm, and stopped by her bedroll to retrieve her own weapon. She leaned it against her shoulder as she made her way across camp to the clearing where Maerten sat and gazed up at the sky.

"Are you doing alright?" Elsabeth asked, and smoothly lowered herself to the grass beside him. She folded her legs beneath her and laid the swords next to her. "You have been rather quiet tonight."

Maerten sat upright and hugged his knees against his chest. His face colored slightly in embarrassment.

"I have never actually been in a fight before today, though I suppose I made a poor accounting for myself fleeing while the rest of you fought," he said quietly. "'Tis not that I have never seen people die before, but..." Maerten trailed off and wrung his hands as he tried to put his thoughts in order. "Not like this. 'Twas an awful lot like watching my village's butcher at work. But seeing it being done to men..."

Elsabeth nodded distantly. Maerten's discomfort stirred up faded memories she had not considered in many years. "'Tis not a pleasant thing to see."

"How do you forget? I close my eyes, and I see that lead fellow's face as clearly as if he were standing here now."

"You don't," she said simply, and sighed at the disappointment in his features at the dashed hopes for peace of mind. "If you want comfort, love, talk to Hieronymus. Though I imagine if you tried that now you would find him rather grumpy, as he is a right cantankerous bastard when he is woken early. The best I can offer is that it gets easier. Whether that is a good or bad thing is something for the philosophers to discuss. Me? I am too busy living one day to the next."

Elsabeth unfolded her legs and stretched out with her hands folded behind her head to lie in the grass and stare up at the stars. The night sky was clear and dusted with countless points of silver light winking down on them from above.

"When I was maybe two or three years younger than you, Master Paulus permitted me to witness my first duel. They fought unarmored, and 'twas not a pretty sight at the end; much as you described, 'twas not unlike seeing a butcher at work. But Master Paulus said to me 'twas important to be able to look into the face of death, because when I carry a sword that is something I must be prepared for.

"Even then, I was still not wholly ready the first time I raised my sword and spilled blood in anger. 'Twas my fifteenth summer, and he was a drunken fool named Matthias Bock who could neither keep his hands to himself nor comprehend the meaning of 'no.' I still remember the man's face as clearly as that day." She sighed and considered the memory; the violence in his eyes, his lips twisted in indignant rage at the tankard she'd smashed over his head, and the blood spilling round the blade spearing through his big mouth. "The faces which followed after his blur together. But that first one will always be clear to me."

"Why continue fighting, then?"

"Because I am fond of breathing," Elsabeth said matter-of-factly. "And because a few spans of steel is the best means I have to preserve my virtue on the road. Well, 'twould be had I any virtue left to preserve, but at least it ensures that the only way into my bed is by invitation."

Elsabeth smirked and found Maerten's face turning brilliant crimson at her frank commentary. She sobered a bit as she looked up at the stars again.

"The truth is, love, this is a bloody, brutal, dirty business," she said. "You need to put any thought of minstrel's stories about honor, shining armor, and standards waving nobly in the breeze from your mind. Oh, the tournament fighters like da Lucca love to conjure up that laughably misplaced sense of romanticism, but remember your first business once your sword is drawn is life or death. The first time you strike a man down stays with you, and it should, because that is what reminds you why you must keep your sword sharp and your skills sharper. Otherwise, you will become just another face lost in the fog of your adversary's memory."

Maerten considered that and nodded glumly. "I suppose I understand your meaning," he said. "Though I would hope I never need know it for myself."

"As would I, love. But better you be prepared in the event you must." Elsabeth rocked herself back up, levered herself off the ground, and pulled Maerten to his feet with her. "Which, seeing as we have a moment to ourselves, we ought to take advantage of the quiet to do so." She stooped, picked up Husson's sword, and slipped it into Maerten's hands.

He frowned uncertainly. "This is Husson's sword."

"So it is." Elsabeth reclaimed her own sword and stepped back from him a few paces as he drew it. "I think he will not miss it much this evening."

Maerten hesitated a moment. "I don't think he will like knowing I have handled it."

Elsabeth smiled and winked. "Then 'twill be our little secret. Besides, you have done enough mere stomping around, 'tis past time you had some practice with something in your hands. Now, remember what I said about how to place your feet," she added, and stepped forward to kick them where she wanted them. "Like so: shoulder-width apart, and whichever foot is your sword side trailing. Bend your knees a bit, keep your weight centered over the balls of your feet, or slightly forward. This is even more important when you have the sword in your hands. Now, we start with the most basic of guards ..."

ASTLE AUCH WOULD HAVE BEEN A formidable fortress when it was intact.

It stood at the brink of a bluff, high in the hills of the Massís Miterre, and south of the road running west along the ridges to a meeting with the north and south way leading to Eze. It was reached by a narrow track that wound through the troughs between several naked hills on either side, and passed through stone barrier walls spanning the gap by means of a fortified gate. There were five altogether, and the hills on either side were steep enough that an assault up their flanks in force would be nearly impossible, making the gates the easiest means to approach the castle.

However, these walls were all broken and thrown down. Little remained of the gates themselves but twisted and rusting wreckage, so the party passed through without difficulty.

They followed the path as it zig-zagged among the hills, through each of the old gatehouses once crowned with battlements but now open to the sky. The road was overgrown with grass and trailing vines. Lichen gnawed at the stonework, and more vines sent searching green fingers into the fine cracks and joints between the heavy granite blocks, slowly tearing whatever the Coventrish had left standing apart. Solemn silence hung over the road, broken only by the muffled tread of their horses and rattle of their gear, and the occasional piping of birds.

Finally, they came to the castle itself, standing atop a rise stretching southward from the last of the hills to the precipice of the bluff overlooking the blue-green waters of the Vert River winding through a gorge carved out of the heights as it flowed westward. Its outer wall had once stood some twenty feet high and enclosed a wide bailey filled with barracks, workshops, smithies, stables, storehouses, and armories. The gatehouse was massive and heavily reinforced, flanked by large crenelated towers, and arrow loops stared out in all directions like sightless black eyes. More towers had fortified the span of the wall as it curved from one end of the bluff back to the other in a broad arc, each end anchored by another tower build onto the slopes of the bluff itself.

Or at least, that is what it had been at its height. Now the outer wall was in a terrible state of repair. Whole segments between its towers lay in ruin. The buildings within the outer bailey had been torched, and everywhere were signs of the terrible final assault that broke Auch's control of the crossroads and river. All that remained now of the outer fortifications were a few shattered remnants of the wall and towers rising from the grass like the bleached bones of some tremendous beast of legend.

Elsabeth pulled them up short as they rounded a corner from the last of the five gates leading up from the main road and stared up at the ruin. A sickening feeling settled over her, mirrored on Maerten's face as he sat beside her on his Hackney. Husson and Hieronymus remained silent, and the only sound was the mournful moaning of the wind swirling through the old stonework.

"So here we are at last," she said. "Castle Auch. The Coventrish certainly were thorough in their work."

"Is this really all that is left?" Maerten said, his voice very small, and awed by the destruction before him.

Elsabeth considered the ruin. The wall separating the outer bailey from the inner grounds was in little better condition than the outer wall, but she could see nothing of the keep itself from their vantage.

"It seems that way, though I can't say that I expected otherwise. This place has been a ruin for a generation. Weather, wildlife, and scavengers will have picked almost anything of value clean by now."

"But the vault ..."

Elsabeth sighed. There was still a shred of hope clinging to Maerten's features, and for all her misgivings she could not bring herself to dash them now that they were so close to their destination.

"If 'tis still there, it must be well-hidden. Every now and then some new treasure can still be found in places like this, in some unexplored cranny or other that has been missed, but I shan't say I expect overly much, and I don't spend much time looting old ruins as there are more profitable ways to make a living."

"Well. The vault shan't find itself," Maerten said. "So I see no reason to just sit here staring at it from afar, and not have a look for ourselves."

Elsabeth smiled in spite of herself at Maerten's undiluted enthusiasm for the venture.

"All right," she said. "But let us set a camp first. We can have a closer look after that is in order."

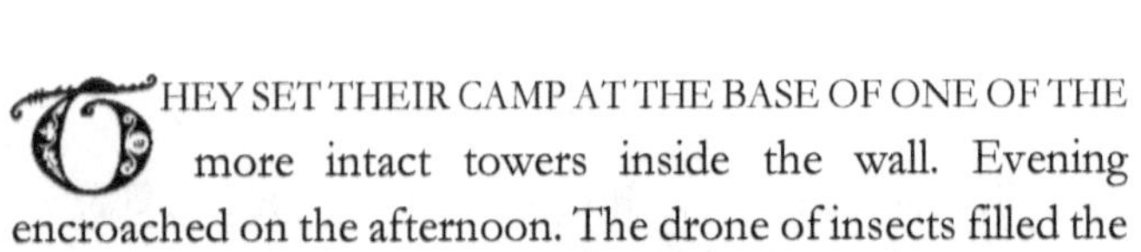

THEY SET THEIR CAMP AT THE BASE OF ONE OF THE more intact towers inside the wall. Evening encroached on the afternoon. The drone of insects filled the air as the sun began its descent into the west, with shadows deepening in the gaps between the hills, and the first stars appearing overhead.

Elsabeth stood away from the camp and scrutinized the inner wall; little more now than a few crumbled sections of white stone and collapsed towers. At some places along the base of the surviving stonework were ugly black scorch marks where the walls had been fired. Once it might have been even more formidable than the outer wall, for the ground rose sharply for a good ten feet, and the inner wall was built at the brink of this natural embankment. A causeway led up to the inner gatehouse — the only part of the structure still standing relatively intact — and the road disappeared through the arched opening. The old iron portcullis lay twisted and rusting on the ground, and the heavy timber gates were splintered and scattered on either side of the causeway, slowly moldering away under a dense layer of fungus.

The outer bailey where they set their camp was heavily overgrown with grass, weeds, and wildflowers, and some pioneering bush or shrub. Vines dug into the crumbling stone walls and pried them apart as nature slowly reclaimed the site. Here and there were great pits torn up in the grass from enterprising looters who had come to the castle in hopes of scoring some bit of treasure not carted off safely by the Navarrese before Auch fell, or seized by the Coventrish in the aftermath.

Husson stepped up beside her and leaned on the sword hanging at his hip. She glanced sidelong at him and edged a little farther away. If he noticed he said nothing, and if there was any consolation from the skirmish it was that the man's disposition had become more tolerable. However, a strange light was in his eyes as he gazed up at the ruins that Elsabeth might almost have described as enmity. But there was something more there clouding his gaze; a pall of bitter memory not unlike what she at times spied in her own reflection when her mind drifted back to the training hall at Soest.

Whatever Husson was looking at now was not the tumbled and broken ruin standing before them.

"Well?" she finally said, when it was clear he would not be forthcoming with his thoughts.

"Well, what?" Husson replied, almost too hastily. He blinked and shook his head.

"Well, where do you think we should look? 'Tis a fair bit of ground to cover, though there is little enough intact that I imagine it shan't take long to do a thorough search."

"How should I know? As I said I only came through once in passing, and that was years ago." Again, his response came almost too sharp and quick for her liking, and her finer hairs bristled.

Elsabeth folded her arms across her chest and hugged her upper arms tightly. A strong breeze rolled up the river beyond the castle out of the west, and tugged at the tail of her coat. "I merely want to expedite the search. I don't like the idea of remaining here longer than we must. These heights are too exposed to view from below, and after that fight the other day who knows if there might be anyone else about."

Husson speared her with an annoyed glare. "You and the friar are welcome to leave at any time, if you don't like it, and good riddance! The boy and I can manage on our own."

"Please, I would hate to see naught between Maerten and a highwayman but your sword-arm, even before you took a quarrel to the shoulder. I would rather it be done right the first time."

Husson's face reddened, but he choked back the retort forming on his lips. Elsabeth supposed he had turned his mind to more important matters than where he might stick a knife.

"I would suggest we start where folks have not been tearing up the grounds," he said, and considered the bailey around them.

Elsabeth grunted, not finding his grasp of the obvious particularly impressive at the moment, for she had already come to the same conclusion herself. *I may as well let him have that little bit of a victory. Perhaps he will be a bit more bearable for feeling useful.*

"And I suspect we might as well disregard the outer bailey," she said. "And in fact, the inner as well. If there was ever a vault, 'twas likely beneath the castle itself. 'Twould be more secure there, and less out in the open."

Husson considered. "We'll have no choice but go into the ruin, then. 'Twill be considerably more dangerous."

"Well, you are always welcome to remain at the camp while the rest of us do all the work."

"I don't need nursemaiding, woman. I can carry my share, bolt or not. And I'll not have you abscond with the treasure and leave me and the boy behind."

Elsabeth turned on him, and her eyes flashed in warning.

"Hieronymus and I may be doing this for coin, but when we make an agreement we hold to it. And I certainly shan't be stealing from him!" She waved vaguely back towards the camp, where Hieronymus and Maerten conversed quietly with one another. "So, I suggest you put that thought right out of your mind."

Without waiting for a reply, she turned and stomped back towards the camp.

"I AM AFRAID 'TWILL BE A COLD SUPPER FOR US tonight," Hieronymus said, while he laid out his bedroll next to his pack and saddle bags. Elsabeth and Husson stood away from the camp studying the lay of the ground. "Even under cover a fire could be seen from the road. Especially from these heights."

"Do you think there might be trouble?" Maerten asked from the horses. He scratched Felis behind an ear. She nickered softly and nuzzled his hand in appreciation. Josephus bore his presence with more patience than he granted Husson, but bucked his head away if ever Maerten tried to reach out and pet him.

"'Tis best to be on our guard, at least," Hieronymus said. He opened their food bag and rummaged around for a few moments, before coming up with a loaf of hard bread provided by the innkeeper's wife before their departure. There was also a small supply of fresh fruits and vegetables to supplement their dried stores. "We don't know if those rascals we fought on the road were alone or not, and we'll certainly be vulnerable once we scatter amongst the bones of this place."

Maerten gave Felis a last scratch, then went about hanging the animals' feedbags. "You have done this before?"

Hieronymus broke off a piece of bread and chewed on it thoughtfully. "Tetty and I have done our share of treasure-hunting, though I can't say we have ever come upon a score such as this."

With the horses contentedly working on their fodder, Maerten turned his attention to laying out his own bedroll, and dropped wearily onto it once he finished. Hieronymus broke off another piece of bread and tossed it to him.

"I confess I have little experience in such matters as these. Husson normally decides what we are to do." The boy laughed at that thought. "I imagine it must be frustrating him tremendously to suddenly be following someone else."

"All our lives are spent in following another," Hieronymus said, with a look skyward, "so I see little difference in what voice the Lord of All chooses to issue his direction."

Maerten considered that for a moment. "What does He say about the path you and Mademoiselle Elsabeth will follow once we have finished here?"

"What do you mean by that?"

"Have you given thought to what you will do, or where you shall go once our contract is completed?"

"More likely than not, we shall resume our wanderings, for that is the calling of my Order, and I can hardly imagine Tetty settling down quietly somewhere. That girl lives for stirring up trouble wherever she goes. Why do you ask?"

Maerten hesitated a moment, and chewed on his piece of bread as he tried to put his thoughts in order. Hieronymus gave him time to do so, though a fair bit of suspicion over the line of questioning tugged at him.

"Even once I reclaim my family's arms and armor, I will be alone," he said quietly. "'Tis just Husson and me to reclaim my birthright. I fear that we two shan't be enough to even make a beginning of it. But you and Mademoiselle Elsabeth are well-traveled, and you have experience in matters that I am lacking."

"Are you asking to extend the contract, then?"

"I mean that, I would like to make you a part of my court, for I'll surely need one if I am to be viewed with legitimacy."

Hieronymus laughed aloud at the brazenness of the request, and Maerten's face colored brightly. "Forgive me, my son!" he said once he mastered his outburst. "You caught me unawares, and that was certainly a bold statement to make. So, now you desire us to support your rebellion against the King of Navarre."

Maerten stammered for a moment, clearly flustered by the accusation, before finding his voice again. "I don't see that it is a rebellion! I am merely wishing to reclaim my family's land and title."

"My son, I am not sure what Tetty would say ..." He trailed off at the sheepish expression on the boy's face as those words left his mouth. "What?"

"I already asked her," he confessed, and his face colored even more brightly than before.

"I see, and what did she say?"

"She declined."

Hieronymus nodded and gestured his agreement with Elsabeth's sentiment. "And there we have it. God would find it rather unacceptable should I swear myself again to the service of another mortal lord, as one cannot at once serve two masters. As for Elsabeth, as the trail of broken hearts and angry wives she leaves in her wake would attest, she is not the sort to swear herself to any one man."

Maerten blushed fiercely at that. "'Twas not what I meant to imply when I asked her."

"Oh, of course not! Though 'twould not change the facts. I am sorry, my son, but as much as we have enjoyed your company — though I cannot say the same for your guardian — once we are finished here, we will be long past our time to move on again."

The boy deflated noticeably and hung his shoulders with a nod of defeated acceptance. "I understand, Brother."

"Now, cheer up, my lad. And have faith that the Lord of All is watching, and whatever happens is all a part of His plan. All that is left to us is to make our own and pray for His benefaction in seeing it to fruition."

19

HE INNER BAILEY WAS IN LITTLE BETTER condition than the outer. Trenches and pits dug by years of treasure-hunters and looters scored what had once been a neatly ordered lawn of green grass quartered by walkways of white stone (most of which had long ago been carted away for construction material elsewhere, leaving only a few cracked and broken blocks). Some of these were now overgrown by weeds and bracken choking the oldest holes gouged into the earth.

Barracks, workshops, and stables once crowded to the inside of the enceinte. However, little now remained of them but their foundations, or the skeletal wooden framework collapsing into rotten ruin. Everywhere were signs of fire that time had not yet scoured from the white bones of the remaining stonework.

And frowning down upon them was the ruin of the keep itself, slowly falling into shadow as the sun descended.

It alone of all the fastness of Auch was the only largely intact structure, a testament to the solidness of its thick stone walls, and reinforced framework. The roof had collapsed, as had the eastern wall, and the crenelated tower that once fortified the northeastern corner lay in crumbled ruins. But otherwise, apart from the ugly black scorchmarks, its outer structure had withstood the fury of the final Coventrish assault.

Maerten looked upon its silent edifice with a troubled expression on his features, and Elsabeth frowned at him in turn. Husson and Hieronymus said nothing

"So this is it, then," he said, his voice hushed as if speaking were an intrusion upon the ghosts drifting among the collapsed masonry. "This is what I have come for."

"Well, unless you were looking to rebuild a castle I would say not," Elsabeth replied. "But at least this is where your wizard said we were to search." She considered the many holes scattered around the bailey. "Though so many others have been here before us, I can't imagine they have left much for us to find."

Maerten clenched his jaw into a determined set and squared his shoulders. "Sinopus said it would be here. I shan't despair yet."

She allowed a smile to tug at the corners of her lips in spite of herself. "I am sure you shan't."

Hieronymus leaned on his staff and considered the ruin. "What do you think?"

"It all seems solid enough from the outside, Elsabeth noted, "though the fire surely destroyed much of the timber, and more than likely weakened the stone in places. I don't think we ought to all pile inside together. For one, we ought to set a lookout here in case of trouble."

"Hm, I agree." He struck the ground with the end of his staff. "Well, I am too old to be clambering around inside such a precarious wreck as this, so I, at least, shall remain here."

Elsabeth turned and spit him with an annoyed glare. "So you drag me into this whole affair, yet shan't do any of the real work now that we get here? And don't give me any of that business about your age or girth! Remember that adventure in the mines of Bamberg? I am still amazed the catwalks supported you."

Hieronymus's face heated in indignation. "'Tis not like I had much choice! Someone had to go and fetch you after you lost yourself in the lower levels."

"I was not lost! I merely dropped my torch while dealing with the leader of those ruffians that absconded with the foreman's daughter."

"At any rate, I already called it." Hieronymus smirked. "And I think it best the boy remains here, as well."

Marten bristled. "'Tis my birthright, and I ought to be the one to claim it."

"Hmph, now that is hardly thinking like a man of your station. Wherever this vault may be, 'tis certainly far below, and 'twould be perilous for you to risk your own neck when you have others to command to do the work in your place."

Now Husson turned his ire on the friar. "I am not the boy's servant, Brother," he snapped, and started towards him menacingly. "And I am certainly not yours to command."

Elsabeth reached out and seized him firmly by his shoulder. Husson snarled in pain when her fingers found the wound, and she dug her nails into it.

"You are right now," she said. "As little as I like the thought of wandering about in the dark with you trying to paw at particulars of my anatomy when I can't see you, I agree 'tis best that Maerten remain here where 'tis at least marginally safer.

Husson shook her off and nursed his shoulder with one hand. "Bitch! I should cut your hand off for that!"

"Tch, right now I doubt you could even lift your sword above your shoulder, so save your strength. If we are to be groping around in the dark, let us just be on with it."

Maerten wrung his hands anxiously and looked between her and Husson. The latter rolled his shoulder and glared murder at her, but said nothing more.

"Are you sure I should remain here? I can help carry anything you come across."

Elsabeth smiled and laid a hand on his shoulder. "Easy, love. We can manage it. You stay here and keep Hieronymus company. And make sure he does not wander off."

She turned and considered the collapsed eastern wall. Little was visible in the darkness beyond.

"We'll need some light," she murmured. "Maerten, fetch a lamp from the baggage, would you?"

Maerten hurried back to their camp in the outer bailey to do as she instructed, and soon returned with a small brass lantern. Its four sides of sheet brass were perforated to allow light through, and there was a ring to serve as a carry handle or allow it to be hung. Though even a light as small as this could be seen from a long way from such a height, she stooped over it and lit it, shielding it with her body as best she could. It cast a small circle of golden, flickering light around her, but nonetheless rolled back the deepening shadows, and the darkness clinging to the inside of the ruin before them.

Elsabeth gave one last look over her shoulder and flashed a reassuring smile at Maerten, who stood anxiously shifting his weight from one foot to the other. Then she stepped inside, with Husson behind her.

Much like the exterior of the keep, the interior was largely ruined. Rubble blocked many passages, much of it from stone collapsing from the upper levels when the floors and support beams had burned away. What little remained of the furnishings were utterly ruined; tables were smashed and charred, and nothing remained of the artwork, tapestries, or other adornments. The plaster that once sealed the stone walls had crumbled away, and all that remained of the flooring was bare flagstones.

They made their way deeper into the keep, following what few passages remained open. With all the corridors looking so much alike, it took Elsabeth little time to lose track of where she was. However, the further they went, the more it seemed that Husson seemed to be taking the lead over their course, and bearing unerringly for a particular part of the keep. She frowned as he led her through a few chambers and cross-halls with assurance. He continued to hobble on his bad leg, but there was an eagerness in his step she had never before noted.

Though she could not place her exact location, she still retained enough sense of direction to know he was cutting a meandering path through the keep, roughly towards the northwestern tower. At times he backtracked when they came upon a passage choked with rubble, or skirted a place where the floor beneath them had collapsed entirely or the walls on either side proved too unstable to risk passing, but otherwise he seemed assured of his direction.

Soon they reached the intersection between what Elsabeth guessed were the north and west walls. The outside wall cut at an angle across the corner. Some debris — a large, upturned bookshelf, charred wooden beams, and some crumbled stonework — was piled up in front of it, but upon closer inspection Elsabeth spied a door set in the middle of it.

"Help me with this," he said, and put his good shoulder against the bookshelf. Elsabeth set her lantern on the ground and joined him, and together they were able to topple it over. Old wood clattered to the ground, and the rest of the pile collapsed. Together they moved the larger beams away, and soon had the doorway cleared.

Husson tested the door, but its handle would not turn. He muttered something under his breath. Elsabeth frowned in suspicion.

"What is it?" she asked. She retrieved her lantern from the floor and held it up in an attempt to study Husson's face.

"This door leads into the base of the northwest tower," he said. "I suspect there will be a stairwell down."

Elsabeth grabbed his arm when he turned to put his shoulder into the door and spun him around.

"All right, and then where after that?"

"If there is a vault, it shan't be up here, now, will it?"

She narrowed her eyes with suspicion. "No, but don't you find it odd to come across a locked door in the middle of a ruin that has not been touched by looters over however many years this place has been empty?"

"That debris would deter a lot of treasure-hunters," he said matter-of-factly. "Almost anyone coming through here would be looking for whatever could be made off with in a hurry."

"That debris seemed more like a barricade, to me. And I think you underestimate just how determined looters can be."

Husson flashed her a wicked smile. "Speaking from experience on that one?"

"I am just saying I don't like this."

Husson shrugged, took hold of the door handle again, and struck it with his good shoulder. "Don't like it, then. But you can either go back — and give up any claim to the spoils — or keep going. 'Tis your choice."

He did not wait for her to respond, and after several forceful blows, shouldered the door open. The latch gave way, but there was no squeal of rust on the hinges; in fact, it opened quite smoothly once the lock broke. Husson immediately passed through, and Elsabeth stared after him for a moment before following. Something gnawed at her belly, and she took hold of her sword-hilt in one hand, while lifting the lantern aloft with the other as she stepped across the threshold yawning black and unwelcoming before her.

She found herself on the landing of the northwest tower. There were two flights of steps: One leading upwards to the next level, which was choked by debris, and a clear passage leading down into darkness below.

"Come on, this way," he said, and started down without waiting to make sure she was following him. Elsabeth hurried after, lifting the lantern to light the way ahead as best she could, and carefully made her way down the staircase as it spiraled into the darkness beneath the keep. Husson, his back silhouetted in the dim circle of flickering light, showed no sign of slowing, or gave any indication he would allow her to question him further.

The staircase descended deep into the bedrock, and the carefully fitted block walls soon gave way to natural stone. They reached a landing with a door leading to one of the basements, but Husson passed it by and continued down another set of stairs spiraling deeper into the tunnel delved into the rock. Elsabeth might have been impressed by the feat of engineering required for such a thing, but as they continued to descend deeper into the basement, the air began to grow chill. Her flesh pimpled and her finer hairs stood on end, only partly in response to the cold, damp air so deep below the surface.

After a few more turns of the stairs they reached another landing, which Husson once again bypassed to continue downward, until they finally reached a third level beneath the keep where the stairs ended at a door. Unlike the door above it was unlocked and clear of debris, and Husson held it open for her and ushered her through. She found herself in what at one time would have been a long storage basement for foodstuffs in the event of a siege, or for anything else that might need to be kept chilled.

"The vaults would likely be through here," Husson said in a low voice, which nonetheless echoed much more loudly than Elsabeth found comfortable, and limped forward again.

She hurried after him to a door at the far end of the cellar, which opened out onto a narrow tunnel. There was another door at the end, in which a narrow window with a sliding iron shutter had been set. This appeared to be pulled to, but as they drew nearer Elsabeth spied a small stone wedged into a corner holding it from closing entirely. Husson slipped his fingers through the jamb and hauled it open, with the stone carefully placed between the bottom and the floor to keep it from swinging shut.

"This way," Husson said, and plunged into the darkness beyond.

Elsabeth followed and found herself in another long hallway. The dim light of the lantern rolled back shadows in alcoves on either side, revealing cells set into the stone walls, each sealed with iron bars and a heavy iron gate, though these were visible only as a blacker shadow in the darkness. Elsabeth drew a deep breath and frowned; the air was oddly fresh, and not at all the musty smell of dust and stone she would expect from such an abandoned place. Once more her hand drifted to the hilts of her sword. She narrowed her eyes as she stared at Husson, little more than a shadowed figure blocking out the light of her lantern.

She followed him to a juncture at the end of the hall. To the left was a heavy iron door set into the wall at the very end of the passage. On the right were three other doors. Between each of the doors was an iron bracket that once held torches or lamps. Husson led her down the left turning, and on their left after a short distance was another door leading to what she suspected might have been a guardroom, to judge by the iron-barred windows looking out onto the hallway from within. The passage itself ended at an iron door.

Everything within was deathly silent except for the rattle of their gear, and Elsabeth's own anxious breaths.

"Come on," Husson said, and made for the door at the end of the hall. "This is it."

Husson put his good shoulder to the door and pushed against it. Slowly the heavy iron door swung inwards and opened onto a black chamber beyond.

He then stepped aside and sketched a mocking bow. "After you," he said.

Elsabeth eyed him suspiciously. "Why me?"

"Because you have the light."

Elsabeth glowered at him and raised the lantern. His eyes glittered in darkness, but she could make little of what was in them. He said nothing more, and merely waited silently.

She sighed, and the soft rasp of steel on wood filled the corridor as she slowly drew her sword. The lantern light flashed along the midrib of its naked blade, and with sword gripped tightly and light raised ahead of her, she stepped inside.

Beyond the doorway sprawled a large, open stone chamber. Brackets holding torches framed it on either side, but would do little to fully illuminate the space beyond. Shelves lined the walls, and at one time might have housed a vast store of supplies. Or treasure beyond count. But now it was all mostly empty. However, piled in the center was a collection of goods of the sort she might expect to see carted along the road by merchant traffic along with a few chests. Sacks, barrels, boxes, crates, and other stores were all assembled in haphazard fashion.

Husson brushed past her and headed straight for the pile, while Elsabeth scanned the rest of the chamber. There was no sign of anything else of tremendous value, leastwise no sign of the treasure Maerten had come for.

Elsabeth strode forward slowly, while Husson busied himself with one of the chests. He already had it open and was stuffing a sack full of whatever was inside. The jingle of coin broke the silence, and warning bells echoed through her mind as she stormed forward.

"All right," she said, and let her suspicions leech into her voice. "What in God's name is—"

She did not have a chance to finish. As Elsabeth came within the length of her sword, he wheeled around to face her. Before she could react, Husson sprung forward inside her point, thrust a hand around her waist and dragged her close to him, and all the air rushed from her lungs at once as Elsabeth felt something slam hard into her gut. Sword and lantern clattered to the floor from the force of the blow, and she felt herself lifted from her feet. Husson withdrew his hand and struck again, and she collapsed against him as she struggled and failed to draw a breath. He pulled his hand back a third time, and she watched the flickering light of the fallen lantern glint off the blade of a knife.

Before Husson could strike at her again, Elsabeth brought her knee up hard between his legs, and Husson doubled over with a howl of pain. They both stumbled away from each other; he nursed his wounded manhood, and she fought to steady herself, coughing and hacking in a desperate effort to start breathing again. She clutched her belly, and the metal scales hidden in the lining of her doublet that narrowly saved her from Husson's treacherous stroke.

He recovered first and rushed her with a snarl of fury. Elsabeth tried to duck out of his way and stumbled awkwardly to the side, but Husson managed to seize hold of her hair from behind, wrenched her head back, and pulled her tight against him.

"Bitch!" he hissed in her ear. "I warned you that I would make you pay for every one of your insults, and I have been looking forward to this!" She felt something prick the skin of her throat, and just made out the point of the knife pressed against the bare flesh of her neck in the lantern light. "I just regret that I shan't get to have a bit of fun with you first before I cut your pretty neck!"

With his hold on her hair Elsabeth was not able to escape his grasp, nor did she have the leverage to strike back against him before he cut her throat. With few other options, she threw all her weight backwards, and, unprepared for such a maneuver, Husson lost his balance and toppled over. She landed heavily on him, and all the air rushed from his lungs with a sickening grunt. His knife clattered away into the darkness as it flew from his fingers.

Elsabeth scrambled back to her feet and dove for her sword, but Husson recovered much more quickly than she expected and caught her by the ankle. She let out a yelp and fell face-first to the ground. Suddenly his weight was on top of her, and he pinned her to the floor and forcibly rolled her onto her back. His hands went to her throat, and she grabbed him by the wrists to keep them from finding purchase.

She wriggled against the ground in an effort to kick him off, but he was straddling her hips in such a manner that she could not use her legs against him. And with his full weight on her, Elsabeth was unable to move. One of Husson's hands found her chin, and he clamped it over her mouth and tried to wrench her head around. Elsabeth seized the opportunity, opened her mouth, and bit down hard on the side of his hand as it slipped between her teeth. Husson screamed in pain and rage, and Elsabeth tasted his blood as she tore a ragged chunk of flesh from him. He fell backwards, enough for her to free one of her trapped legs, and she leveled a kick at the side of his head. Her patten connected with the corner of his jaw and dropped him onto his back.

Elsabeth scrambled away from him and flailed about for whatever weapon she could find before he recovered. Just in time, she seized hold of the lantern and swung it wildly as he charged back at her again, catching him across the side of his face. He went down again, and she managed just enough of an opening to scrabble back to her feet. Unfortunately, once again, Husson was close behind, and charged her with hatred and murder in his eyes. He ducked past the light as she tried to thrust it into his face, and out of the darkness she saw something rather large swinging towards her. It was not until the sack of coin he had been filling connected with her temple that Elsabeth realized he, too, had managed to get hold of a weapon.

She did not particularly feel the impact. For a moment a white flash of light blinded her vision, and there was a persistent and aggravating ringing in her ears. She was also dimly aware of her body falling through the air as the force of the blow knocked her sprawling across the vault. This all passed momentarily, though a crippling dizziness remained as her head swam and the vault spun wildly about her. Elsabeth tried to find her feet, but neither they, nor the room, wished to cooperate to provide her with steady ground to stand on. Husson and his identical twin brother were back at the chest — or perhaps it was chests, there seemed to be two of them now — rushing to fill the sack with as much coin as he — or was it they? — could before she recovered from his blow.

Elsabeth put her hands beneath her and tried once more to get back up. This time the room managed to stabilize itself enough for her to focus on getting her feet to obey. Husson and his doppelganger slowly resolved back into a single individual, and he looked straight at her as she started towards him. He cursed sharply under his breath and took off in an awkward, hobbling run with his sack in hand for the vault door. He seized the handle as he fled through the open doorway, and hauled it closed behind him. She flung herself after him, but just as she reached the door, Husson pulled it closed, and she ineffectually struck it hard with her shoulder. The impact took whatever fight she had left out of her, and Elsabeth fell in a dazed heap to the floor.

A DULL THUD REVERBERATED THROUGH THE door from the damnable woman's futile attempt to pursue him, and Husson's lip curled into a smug grin. *That ought to slow her for a moment.*

He experimentally hefted the bag of coin, and his smile faded when he found it somewhat lighter than he had hoped. Unfortunately, he had not counted on her having armor on her person. And, he grudgingly admitted, if the fight had continued much longer, she likely would have gained the upper hand. Nonetheless, the haul would be more than enough to live on for a time.

Husson withdrew up the hallway, and hastily retraced his steps out the entrance to the dungeon and through the storage cellar. He mounted the winding stairs leading back to the ruined upper levels of the keep two at a time, with a steadying hand on the wall beside him to maintain his balance and keep him from falling. It was now utterly dark without Elsabeth's lantern, but he flew up the stairs guided by a familiarity that the passage of time could not completely dull. His bad leg throbbed in painful memory of old wounds at the speed of his flight, but he found the triumph of even this small vengeance enough to offset it.

Only a little moonlight managed to find its way through the narrow windows or the gaps in the crumbled ceiling. Nonetheless, with precision born of intimate familiarity with the keep's interior, he retraced his steps back through the hallways and chambers and made for the gap in the eastern wall.

Brother Hieronymus was sitting on a pile of stone with Maerten when he arrived, conversing in hushed tones. The boy jumped to his feet and spun around in alarm when he emerged from the darkness, but visibly relaxed once he recognized him. Without needing a word of instruction, Husson handed off the sack of coin, and Maerten grabbed it and slung it over his shoulder. Hieronymus observed the exchange with wary eyes and stood to lean on his staff.

"There you are," the friar said, "the boy was starting to worry despite my assurances that Tetty could keep you out of trouble." Hieronymus eyed him closely. "Where is she? Is she coming behind you?"

Husson brushed past him and leaned close to Maerten. "We are finished here," he muttered, barely above a whisper, and low enough that Hieronymus would be unable to hear him. Maerten nodded subtly.

"Did you hear me, my son?" Hieronymus said. "Where is Elsabeth? Was there trouble? Your hand has been wounded."

Husson turned back to the friar, and found him watching the pair closely, frowning at his hand. "No, there was no trouble with her at all," Husson said with a toothy smile, and inched his hand to the hilt of his sword.

Hieronymus tightened his grip on his staff and glared. "If nothing went wrong, then where is the boy's arms and armor?" He struck a nearby stone hard with the end of his staff. The crack echoed impressively across the ruined bailey, and even made Husson flinch. "And where is Tetty?" The last was added with a commanding shout.

"Half a moment, and you can join her," Husson said, and steel rasped on wood as he drew his sword. He charged and leveled a swing aiming to take the friar's head from his shoulders.

"Treacherous viper!" Hieronymus snarled. He leapt clear of the blow with agility belying his bulk, and raised his staff as if it were his own sword to deflect the blow. "The Dark One will take you for this!"

"I'll send you to meet him first! I am sure he has a special place in Hell for your sort of cleric!"

They were soon exchanging a flurry of blows, the friar wielding his staff in one hand with admirable skill despite his disadvantage, and Husson giving him no opportunity to draw his own sword. Small chips of wood flew each time Husson's blade struck the wooden shaft, and their fight circled for a moment before he slowly drove the friar towards the wreckage of the fallen tower.

Hieronymus ducked a blow aimed at his temple, guided Husson's sword safely past with his staff, and countered with a strike of his own which managed to catch him across the chin. Husson felt his head snapped around by the end of the friar's staff, and he stumbled to evade the follow-up.

Maerten watched the exchange, wide-eyed, from the gap in the inner enceinte.

"Damn you, boy!" Husson snarled, and ducked under a blow from the friar's staff. "Stop standing there gawking like a slack jawed half-wit and help me!"

"Cowardly rascal! You cannot fight me yourself so you would bring the lad into it as well!" Hieronymus shouted over the flurry of blows. "And I imagine you were in this from the beginning. Never mind denying it, for I shall deal with you as well once I have brought the Lord's justice against this two-faced villain!"

Hieronymus redoubled his efforts and sought an opening in his guard where he could bring the staff to bear for a crushing blow against his skull. Husson could only move his sword as best he could and seek an avenue of escape, slowed by the agonized burning in his shoulder stiffening his left arm. *Damn him to the depths of the Dark One's dominion! Why of all people did I pick a priest who wielded a sword before his staff?*

And then, by the Lord of All's intervention or pure chance, the advantage in the fight swung back in Husson's favor. Hieronymus struck towards the right side of his head, and when he shifted his sword to cover himself, it was followed with a second blow from the staff at the new opening on the left. Husson turned his hips to face the strike and brought his sword over. A sharp crack split the air. Husson was unsure whether his sword struck a natural weak point in the branch from which the staff had been carved, or if it had been weakened during the fight, but regardless the wooden shaft shattered halfway along its length in a shower of wood fragments. One end spun off into the ruins behind him. Hieronymus stared in horror and disbelief at the piece still clutched in his hand.

Husson pushed forward to seize the initiative, but was met by the remains of the staff flying at his face. He yelped in alarm as he ducked and shielded himself, then resumed his charge. That momentary delay was all the time the friar needed to evade Husson's cut at his own head. Husson pressed and cut at him again. The friar stumbled in his effort to evade the blow, caught his foot on a piece of ruined stone, and went to the ground with a cry. Husson raised his sword overhead for the fatal blow, but before he could bring it down again a shadow burst from the ruins of the keep.

Elsabeth delivered a furious blow to his side with her shoulder. Husson went down in a heap and lost hold of his sword when he struck the ground. He scrambled back to his feet and found himself looking up into the woman's angry green eyes with the awl-like point of her sword leveled between his.

"Hieronymus!" she snapped, and the hate in her voice was no less evident than what burned in her green eyes. "Watch the boy. Husson and I have an argument to finish."

The friar took one look into Elsabeth's burning eyes, then nodded and circled around him to do as she commanded, finally drawing his sword on the move. If Maerten gave any thought to taking advantage of the woman's preoccupation with his master and fleeing, such notions were quickly put out of his head when Hieronymus laid the edge of his sword across his shoulder. "Stay put, my lad," he said. "We will see to you in a moment."

Husson felt a ball of ice form in his gut while Elsabeth loomed over him. Maerten still had their sack of loot in hand, but he knew that he would not be able to make it through before she could cut him down.

"So you would strike me down in cold blood, then? I even imagine you want to see me beg for my life," Husson snarled at her. "I should have expected no less from a student of Soest."

Elsabeth smiled at him, but there was no mirth in the expression, and the lethal threat behind it sent a chill down his spine. "Oh, that would be no more than you deserve. After all, how appropriate would it be for someone who makes his arguments with a knife in the back to die whining at my feet like a beaten dog?"

She took a step back and kicked off her pattens. From his current vantage on the ground he could see that her boots were made of soft, thin leather well-suited to the duel.

"Though I am a woman," she continued, "'twill take precious little for me to prove I have a fuller pair than you. The least I can do is give you the opportunity to preserve what little of your shriveled manhood you still hold on to."

With that, she motioned with her point towards his sword lying in the grass a short lunge away. Husson stared at it as if it were a viper coiled to strike, then back to Elsabeth again. She watched him impatiently.

"Go on!" she said. "Pick it up!"

He hesitated again, the ball of ice in his gut spreading through his limbs as fear at the deadly intent in her green eyes, and of the very real possibility — denied in his gusto when she was not actively out for his head — he might suffer the ignominy of falling by the hand of a woman washed over him.

"Pick it up!" Elsabeth snapped again. "Pick it up or God help me I will cut you down where you lie like the coward you are!"

With nowhere to run, and never taking his eyes off the woman in front of him, he retrieved his weapon and returned to his feet as she warily slipped into a low guard not unlike the *Dente di Cenghiaro*; the hilt held at her hip with the blade angled towards the ground in front of her. He raised his sword behind his head in the *Posta di Donna* to counter her.

They circled one another for a few moments, each shifting from one guard to another while seeking for an opening to strike. Elsabeth found hers first, and exploded forward into him with all of Soest's aggression in a powerful falling blow from her right, aiming to cut him in two from his left shoulder to opposite hip. Husson replaced his footing and bound hard against her sword, and the ring of steel clashing against steel split the air. The moment their blades were about to meet, he stepped into his parry, lifted his sword, and passed under her blade, while Elsabeth stepped out and around to her left to deliver a rising cut to the back of his leg. Husson turned to face her, keeping his leg clear of her blow, and brought his sword around into *Dente di Cenghiaro* to cover himself. Again, their blades clashed, and Elsabeth lunged to her right and twitched her sword into a high lateral short edge cut aimed at his left temple.

Husson hastily cut one-handed through his left *Posta di Fenestra* for cover, and with an opening to interrupt her assault, followed with a quick spring to his right as he wheeled his sword into a falling right-hand cut from her teeth to her right knee. Elsabeth responded with fluid precision, and rolled her sword over and bound hard against him. She then raised her hilts and thrust the point of her sword into his face. He sprung backwards to clear her point, and wheel his sword around to cover.

Elsabeth pressed in aggressively, and her sword whistled towards him in a falling blow aimed to cleave him from his right shoulder to his opposite hip. Husson lunged to his left and brought his sword over to intercept her attack and bind her, but the expected blade contact did not come. Instead, his hands were jerked upwards, and he felt a sudden pain as Elsabeth's blade sliced through the flesh of his wrists. In his effort to defend her cut, Husson missed her sword falling off from its original line of attack and rolling into a rising cut at his hands. No longer in control of his fingers, he felt his sword fall from his grip, and he let out a cry of pain.

Then he was suddenly silenced as Elsabeth brought her sword back through in a lateral cut, and for a moment he felt the keen edge slice deeply through his neck. Husson's cry was strangled as he watched the fountain of blood spray from his opened throat, and spill hotly down the front of his neck and chest. He had no time to process what had just happened, and he briefly felt himself falling before the world went black.

21

LSABETH'S FINAL STROKE LAID OPEN Husson's throat, and a fountain of blood sprayed from the wound. Some of it reached her and splattered across her face, but most of it dyed the front of his doublet a dull crimson. Almost immediately his eyes rolled back in his head, and his body collapsed in an unconscious heap at her feet. He thrashed about for a few moments more, and then he lay still in the bloody grass. She panted from the exertion and rush of the fight, and stared down dispassionately at the treacherous bastard's limp form. The gash in his throat grinned at her like a gruesome mouth, and she gazed back in satisfaction at her handiwork before she finally, and wordlessly, turned away.

The course of the duel had taken her almost halfway across the grounds from where Hieronymus waited with Maerten. Hieronymus had sheathed his sword. He now stood with his head lowered, murmuring in prayer, while the boy regarded the scene before him from his knees with wide eyes and a pale face, clutching at his belly as if he were ill.

Elsabeth wiped Husson's blood from her face and started across the bailey.

"What are you doing?" she asked Hieronymus when she reached his side.

He paused in the midst of his prayer and looked up at her. "Someone must pray for the soul of that poor, misguided villain," he said. "Even if I suspect 'twill do him little good."

"You are more charitable than I would be, were our positions reversed."

Hieronymus merely shrugged and went back to his absolution, leaving Elsabeth to face Maerten. He did not even look at her, and instead stared queasily at Husson's still body lying in the grass. She forced down the thoughts and feelings threatening to well up as she gazed down on him, took hold of her sword in both hands, and placed the blade on his shoulder.

Maerten tore his eyes away from Husson and looked up at her with that same beaten dog look and tears coming to his eyes.

"'Twas not my idea. I did not wish to do it!" he whimpered, and she tried her best to ignore how the pleading in his voice tugged at her heart.

Hieronymus finished his absolution for Husson and turned his attention back to her. "Tetty?" he asked. "What are you doing?"

"Finishing this," she said. The words came out as a harsh croak as she forced down her own tears.

Maerten fell back and tried to scramble away, but bumped into the wreckage of the tower. "Mademoiselle, please! 'Twas not my fault! He made me do it!" he said in a panic when she closed the distance and readied her sword to strike. "'Twas all Husson's doing! I wanted to share everything with you, fairly!" The boy looked imploringly at Hieronymus, as if begging the friar to intercede on his behalf. "With both of you! But Husson would not listen!"

Elsabeth felt her hands begin to shake, and she hesitated. The desire to strike now warred with her affections for the boy, while his betrayal twisted in her bowels like a knife.

"Please!" Maerten cried, and threw himself forward on the ground and wrapped his arms around one of her ankles. "Please listen to me! I did not want to do it, he made me!" Elsabeth tried to shake him off, but he clutched her leg tightly, sobbed into her boot, and would not be removed.

"Elsabeth!" Hieronymus barked, and laid a hand on her arm. "Whatever becomes of the boy, you should not be the one to do it."

She turned on him and threw his hand off her arm. "You stay out of this!" Elsabeth snarled. "You were the one who involved me in this whole misadventure to begin with. I may as well end it."

He shook his head. "My dear, I have seen you do many things without blinking that would make even a hardened campaigner like myself squirm, but I can see in your eyes that if you do what you now intend, you shan't be able to live with yourself. I don't know why the lad has touched you so, but nonetheless, touched you he has."

"Then you would just let him go?"

"I would—"

A sudden sound that made Elsabeth's finer hairs stand on end cut the friar off before he could continue that thought, and they both snapped their heads in its direction. She strained her ears, and when it came again it was unmistakable: the voices of men approaching and drawing nigh to the ruined wall encircling the outer bailey.

"Bugger!" Elsabeth spat.

"We have no more time to argue," Hieronymus said. "We have to g—"

Once again, her companion was cut off, this time by a solid *whump* as something struck him hard from behind. Elsabeth turned in time to see the sack of coin tear after catching Hieronymus across the back of his shoulders and send him crashing into her, and they both tumbled to the ground while Maerten sped off. A rain of gold and silver fell across the near part of the clearing.

Hieronymus's sudden weight on her as he fell atop her nearly drove the air from her lungs. "Oof! That bloody manipulative little bastard!" she snarled, and swatted Hieronymus atop his head. "Get off!"

"Lord of All, damn that rotten brat to the depths of the Underworld!" Hieronymus added, and struggled to comply. Dazed as he was, and in no small part impeded by his weight, it took him a moment to find his feet again. When he finally did, he took Elsabeth by the hand and hauled her up behind him.

The voices grew louder and more distinct; too many for them to contend with alone. Elsabeth wiped Husson's blood from her sword on the tail of her coat and stared at the coin glittering on the ground. The sack that had been holding it had given out entirely, and there was nothing else at hand to gather it up in. As if sensing her thoughts, Hieronymus grabbed her by the hand and took off back towards their camp.

"Remember what the Lord would say of greed, my dear, and let us shun this temptation!" he huffed as he ran. "'Tis better to be satisfied with that which we have honestly earned than in such ill-gotten gains!"

"Which way did that lying rat make off in?" she asked as they left the inner bailey and rushed for their camp.

"Let us look to our own necks for now, Tetty! I say we get as far from here as possible. Besides, I am of the mind that these two were not alone in this conspiracy, and that there is another party we ought to see to. And I think I may have a guess as to whom!"

Elsabeth was about to open her mouth in protest, then thought better of it as the implication of the friar's words sunk in. Instead, she let out a strangled snarl of frustration and ran as quickly as she could back to the horses.

⁂

ARQUET STOOD IN THE FADING LIGHT AND surveyed the ruins of Castle Auch. He leaned on the sword at his hip, and the battered old coat of plates rattled beneath his cloak with every subtle movement. If one looked closely at the faded velvet outer covering of his armor the arms of the Baron du Auch — *Vert, on a chevron Argent five roses Gules* — could still be seen beneath years of wear and dirt. Its faded, frayed, and unraveling embroidery had long ago lost its bright and proud colors of days of noble service, and now remained only as a solemn ruin of the past, well-suited to the broken, burned, and tumbled remnants of his Lord's castle.

The rest of the band fanned out across the grounds and disappeared into the deepening twilight in search of the intruders. However, other than a solitary Hackney tied up within the shelter of the wall and signs of a hastily vacated camp in the outer bailey, they had vanished into the rolling hills of the Massís Miterre marching away to the east and west. They had enough of a start now that even over such rough terrain, Marquet was satisfied they would not be found unless they struck the road. But he dared not send scouts into the open now. He clenched his fists in frustration and scowled down at the black shape lying crumpled at his feet.

There was at least one other sign of their presence left behind.

"And you are sure he was with them at the ambush?" Marquet said to the man beside him.

"Yes, Marquet," the other replied. Though his features were lost in the shadow of his cloak and hood, Marquet could nonetheless make out the nodding of his head. "He was spit with a quarrel before the rest of us were cut down, but I guess the others patched him up."

Marquet nudged the corpse with his toe and flipped the man onto his back. He stared down into Husson's sightless eyes. His features remained twisted into a final expression of shock and incomprehension, and a dark line slashed across his throat like a gruesome second mouth. His death had come so sudden and unexpectedly, Marquet suspected he never had time to process the fatal injury.

"I don't know whether to be satisfied the treacherous snake is dead, or disappointed it happened so quickly, and I did not have the pleasure of killing him myself."

The man beside him shifted nervously, and Marquet let him squirm a bit longer. *I am not some cliché villain of minstrels' fancies to kill a man just for failing me. And if he had not escaped the scrap, I would never have known about this.*

"Well, I suppose I'll have to satisfy myself with this. 'Tis a fitting end for a twice-deserter rogue like you! I don't know why I ever accepted you into the band after you forsook his Lordship, bad leg or not."

A shadow broke away from the wall of the ruined keep and picked a careful path through the wreckage. Marquet tore his attention away from Husson's corpse.

"What have you?" he said.

"We had a look down in the vaults," the newcomer said. He wore his hood cast back, though there was little of his features to discern in the dying light, only a rough growth of beard around his chin and a shaggy mane of hair reaching to his shoulders. "There are signs of a fight down there, and one of the chests was raided. 'Twould be my guest two of them came to blows, though there is no sign of them now."

Marquet grunted. "Well, clearly that makes three treasons for dear, departed Husson. But there shan't be a fourth. All of his backbiting has finally caught up with him. How much was taken?"

"Not much, perhaps a sack. But it looks like most of it was spilled during the struggle here." He glanced off to either side at the men combing through the grass. Every now and then one would stoop and toss something into a sack held by another of their number, where it landed with the clink of coin. "The lads not out searching for the intruders are gathering it back up now."

Marquet shifted his weight and drummed his fingers on the pommel of his sword. A satisfied smirk tugged at his lips. "'Tis a welcome change of fortune then; our thieves were so caught up in squabbling over the spoils they ended up with almost nothing in the end."

The others chuckled in turn.

"Go and call back the others. 'Tis too dark now to chase them any further, and we shan't be catching them in this wilderness, anyway. Then gather everything up. The Legend of Auch did a respectable job luring a few fools out here for easy pickings, but after today I don't want to press our luck any further. Eze is bound to have wind of us 'ere long, and I'll not wait around to put my head in a noose."

"And what about him?"

The other motioned at Husson's corpse.

"Strip him of anything of value and leave him for the wolves and crows. I can't think of a more fitting place to leave his bones than in this ruin."

ALBOT LEANED ON HIS CANE AT THE archway leading into the Wizard's garden and watched the proceedings. It had been a quiet few weeks since the last visitors from beyond Checy had come to seek Sinopus. The miller's wife was back on her feet once more, and the newcomers to the area around the other side of the lake had been welcomed into the community, but of the young boy Maerten and his odd collection of companions, there had been no further word. Otherwise, life had returned to normal again after the brief excitement of the boy's visit.

His being invited to stay with the Wizard was met with quite a deal of gossip, of course. Never had Talbot heard of anyone being invited to stay the night, and most travelers from beyond Checy were obliged to return to the village when their business there was concluded. He, of course, paid little mind to the wagging tongues. Perhaps Maerten was part of some royal house traveling in disguise. Such things were certainly quite popular in minstrels' tales, though he himself had never seen such a thing. But the lad's business was for Sinopus alone, so he gave little heed to the rumors, which passed almost as quickly as the boy's party came and went.

Today's visitor was of the usual sort, a wandering chevalier and his lance — with him traveled his squire, a coutilier, and two crossbowmen — come to test the rumor for himself and see what manner of counsel the Wizard could offer. He was a tall and rugged-looking individual, with a clean-shaven face, neatly cropped black hair, and piercing blue eyes. A sword hung at his side, and he wore a coat-of-plates over his surcoat, with the rest of his heavier armor neatly stowed with his baggage in the village. His squire and coutilier were armed and armored in like manner, while the crossbowmen wore thick padded gambesons, with knives at their belts and crossbows in hand, though all his retinue were now lounging at their ease while being served by the Wizard's exotic companions, who were received with almost as much wonder as the Wizard himself.

The day wore into late afternoon. The sun had already passed its zenith and was beginning its slow descent towards the horizon. Talbot rocked gently from one foot to the other and did his best to maintain a respectful posture while in the presence of Sinopus. The Wizard conversed with his visitor before the stone altar.

"My wife and I have been married for better than five years now," the chevalier was saying, "yet she still has not conceived. I am desirous of a son, and I am growing frustrated with her failure to provide me a child. I have come seeking a solution as no one has yet suggested a satisfactory answer."

Sinopus murmured something unintelligible, and suddenly the surface of his altar burst into flames. The chevalier and his entourage all jumped in amazement at the sight, and one of the men snapped out an astonished oath to the Lord of All in response.

"Your wife is in good health?" Sinopus asked after a moment of gazing into the flames.

"She is," the chevalier replied.

"And you as well, my Lord?"

The man straightened indignantly, but wisely kept his hand clear of the hilts of his sword rather than take the Wizard's question as an insult. "Of course! There is no trouble with my faculties, Wizard," he said defensively.

"Oh, I had not implied otherwise," Sinopus said with an amused twinkle in his eye at the sharpness of the chevalier's response. "However, it is not in the woman alone in which dysfunction may occur, for both are responsible for conception, and if either seed should fail to take root, then childless you shall remain.

"If you desire my aid, my Lord, then it requires that I must be thorough in my questioning. If you should wish to take offense at my counsel, then perhaps we must end this consultation now."

That sufficiently chastened the chevalier, and he inclined his head apologetically. "Forgive me the hastiness of my reply, and do continue," he said, in a much humbler tone.

"Very well," Sinopus said. "Has your wife accompanied you to Checy, my Lord?"

"She has not. She does not even know that this was the purpose for my departure."

"I see." He waved his hands over the fire again, and with a rushing sound the flames flared up again and changed from orange to green. Accustomed as he was to the Wizard's displays of his power, Talbot did not jump at all, but the chevalier and his retinue once again startled at the sight. His lance shifted uneasily, their desire to be on their way once more evident on their features. But their master grew more determined with every showing of Sinopus's magic to see his question answered.

"Ch'u Niang," Sinopus said, and motioned to one of his assistants. The two women had finished tending to the chevalier's men and were just returning to his side within the garden when he called. "I shall need a clay pot, go and fetch it, please."

"Yes, Master," one of the women (despite having visited the Wizard's hut many times himself, Talbot could still not quite tell them apart) bowed stiffly at the waist and disappeared into the hut.

"I fear without your wife's presence my art is limited to what I may divine from you. I shall need a sample of your urine in order to proceed."

The chevalier blinked, and Talbot thought he saw a hint of color appear on the man's cheeks. "Is this some jest, Wizard?"

"Not at all, my Lord! For there is much I may be able to tell of this matter from your water."

Talbot smirked at the discomfiture in the chevalier's face. He had seen such reactions from others who had come to Sinopus for medical advice. They were always so eager for his wisdom that they acquiesced once the initial shock passed them by. He watched the same internal debate play out now in the visitor's eyes while he awaited the return of Ch'u Niang.

"Well, I see we have not come too late," an unexpected and familiar man's voice murmured from behind him.

Talbot nearly jumped out of his shoes at the sound, and his heart pounded in his throat. Standing in front of him was the friar and his lady companion, who watched the proceedings with indifference mingled with a sense of purpose.

"No," the woman — Elsabeth, if he recalled her name correctly — added quietly. In their current position along one wall just outside the archway, the Wizard would be unable to see them from his vantage. "It seems we arrived just in time."

Talbot quickly regained his composure and nodded to each politely in greeting. "Welcome back!" he said. "'Tis good to see you both well, how is your young master?"

The chevalier's lance had also taken note of their arrival, and watched them with curiosity that quickly turned to alarm at the rasping of steel on wood as the pair drew their swords. All four immediately had weapons in hand, and by now the disturbance had spread to the Wizard's private garden. Elsabeth's green eyes stabbed into his own, and Talbot flinched back at what he saw there.

"I suggest you stand aside if you are not a part of this scheme," she said. "I would rather like to avoid spilling innocent blood."

"What are you talking about?" Talbot stammered in confusion, but Elsabeth moved to shoulder him aside rather than waste time in answering his question. Hieronymus followed to clear her back and make sure the squire, coutilier, and crossbowmen did not interfere when she stormed into the garden. His effort was unnecessary in the end. All four were so taken aback by her very appearance that none of them seemed able to even consider barring their way, and she pushed past into the presence of their Lord with bared steel.

"What is the meaning of this?" Sinopus barked in as angry and commanding a voice as Talbot had ever heard, and immediately all the blood drained from his face at the lethal confrontation brewing before him.

"We have a grievance to discuss with you about your counsel, Wizard," Elsabeth said.

The chevalier, not about to be interrupted, drew his sword, and immediately placed himself between Elsabeth and the Wizard. "I don't know what grievance you hold, but I have paid good money for this audience, and Lord of All knows I shan't endure this intrusion," he said in challenge.

"Oh put up your sword, you bloody fool," she said, and though the woman had her back to him, Talbot could practically hear her eyes rolling in annoyance from the tone of her voice. "Or at least stand aside. If you have already rendered payment to this charlatan you shall soon have the same grievance as I."

"Charlatan? What do you mean?"

"This man is no wizard. A talented juggler, maybe, but I warrant there is nothing more to his magic than tricks you might see at any fair."

"Insolent quim!" Sinopus snarled, and the lethal ice in his voice sent a shiver down Talbot's spine. He waved his hand over the burning altar, and a ball of flame appeared in his palm, which he threw at the woman standing in challenge in front of him. She reflexively dove under his attack, struck the ground on her shoulder, and smoothly rolled back to her feet, having closed the distance enough to put her sword at his throat. The fireball struck the ground harmlessly and fizzled out.

The wizard's remaining assistant tried to come to Sinopus's defense, but with speed belying his girth, the friar circled round and intercepted her. He seized her by the wrist and leveled his sword ready to strike after a knife unexpectedly appeared in her hand.

"Now, now, my dear," he said. "Don't be foolish, unless you wish to be sent to the Lord of All's judgment before your time."

The woman let the knife fall from her hand, but the friar kept his sword poised to strike if she should try anything more.

"What is the meaning of this?" Sinopus demanded. Ch'u Niang emerged from his hut, gasped, and dropped the clay pot she was carrying at the scene playing out in front of her. Talbot felt the chevalier's lance press in close to watch them.

"Oh, I think you know quite well. In fact, I say you are rather surprised to see Hieronymus and me again." Elsabeth glanced at her companion. "Do you agree?"

"I do indeed, Tetty, though he hides it quite well. I warrant he has been at this business for some time now."

She turned her attention back to the Wizard again. "Yes, I suppose he has. You and I have certainly played a few folks, but he was even able to put one over on us. Of course, you had help in that particular endeavor."

Talbot paled at the accusation in her voice. "What do you mean, he had help?" he asked. "Surely you do not mean me?"

Elsabeth cut him off with a shake of her head. "No, love, I rather doubt you or anyone in Checy was a part of his Magnificence's scheme. Rather, I think you are as much a victim of it as we were. After all, I suspect that Sinopus made quite a comfortable living off the goods your people paid him for his services."

He gawked as understanding washed over him. "Are you saying that he has defrauded us?"

"That, my son," the friar said, "is precisely what we are saying."

"This is outrageous!" Sinopus snarled. "I demand you—"

His protest died in his throat when Elsabeth pressed the tip of her sword against it. "That is quite enough out of you. The boy was a fraud, you know. The amulet, his story, everything. And he set us up to take the fall for the whole business."

Talbot blinked and felt a ball of ice form in his belly. "You did not hurt the lad, did you?"

Elsabeth looked at him sharply, and it was impossible to miss the feeling of betrayal deep beneath the surface of her green eyes. "No, the little bastard got away. His guardian and I finally had out our argument, and he most certainly shan't be coming this way again." She turned her attention back to the Wizard. "So, you need not wonder about when that one will meet up with you."

"As for the lad," Hieronymus added, "I suspect, seeing as we find you still here, we are well ahead of him. Or else he abandoned you to your fate once the deceit was laid bare."

"But the magic!" Talbot said, as his head began to spin. "We saw his power! All of his remedies, his counsel ..."

Hieronymus grunted. "Oh, his leechcraft and herbalism are real enough, and I'll confess that he has knowledge of which even my Order would be envious." He swatted the woman he was guarding on the backside with the flat of his sword. She jumped at the contact and muttered indignantly in her native tongue while glaring venomously at the squat friar. Hieronymus just smiled at her and took a moment to look her over to emphasize his point. "And judging by the lovely company he keeps, I suspect 'twas no more magic than wisdom he brought with him from wherever he found these exotic beauties."

"As for the rest," Elsabeth said, and looked over Sinopus's voluminous robes, "I suspect 'tis no more than simple stagecraft."

And with that, she took her sword point from the Wizard's throat, slipped it into one of his sleeves, and with a deft flick of her wrists slashed it open. Immediately, several concealed pouches and small balls of fabric spilled out onto the ground. Elsabeth slid her sword back into her scabbard, (Talbot was conscious of the crossbowmen readying their crossbows on either side of him to keep the Wizard from attempting to flee) and picked up one of the fallen pouches. She hefted it in her hand for a moment, before opening it and peering inside. "I wonder what would happen if ..." she murmured, almost to herself, before she took a pinch of whatever was within and sprinkled it over the Wizard's altar. Almost at once the flames flared up and started to burn a pale violet color.

Elsabeth let out an excited squeak of amusement when the flames responded. "Oh, I really ought to have studied wizardry rather than the sword! I did find it right curious that you kept Hieronymus and me from joining you in your sanctuary when you spoke with Maerten. What was his explanation, love?"

"As I recall, Tetty, he called the Lord of All unwelcome, and had a few words to say about your virtue," Hieronymus said, and grunted indignantly. "As if God did not already have an eye upon whatever unseemly acts he performed, whether a servant of the Wheel was there to witness them or not. I rather think he used the opportunity alone with them to arrange the whole charade and find a way to interest us."

Talbot grabbed the sides of his head as the truth of what they were saying began to sweep over him. After everything the Wizard had done for the village, the remedies and counsel, for it all to be a sham? "But the boy, he knew he was coming, and sent me to meet you when he arrived."

Elsabeth leaned casually on her scabbard. "Of course he knew he was coming," she said, and the patronizing tone of her voice made Talbot feel quite foolish. "Because they were conspiring together the whole bloody time. He probably sent them down to the Four Ways looking for someone to swindle and was expecting them back." She spit the Wizard with her green eyes, and Sinopus flinched away from what he saw there. "I do wonder who you really are, though, and whether 'twas you who led your little band of outlaws."

Sinopus did not answer, but for the first time Talbot saw fear creeping into the old man's features, and the last of his disbelief at the woman's accusations began to crumble away. When it became clear the Wizard, or whatever he truly was, would not be forthcoming on his own, the chevalier stepped forward menacingly with his sword and seized him by the arm.

"Answer her, charlatan!" he snarled. "Or else you shan't speak again."

With almost arrogant indignation, Sinopus removed the chevalier's hand from his arm. "If it truly matters," he said, and his tone of voice and posture changed from that of a wizened sage, to smoothly cultured and not nearly as aged as he first appeared, "my name is Girart. And if 'tis vengeance you seek, Mademoiselle, then there is no need for it if I understand your meaning as to the fate of Husson, as the charade with the boy was his. Something about settling an old score with some former servants of the Baron du Auch."

When Girart spoke, any remaining doubt over the accusations were finally dashed in Talbot's mind, and he balled his fists tightly as anger blossomed over the revelations. "You lied to us!" he snapped, and immediately the attention of everyone atop the bluff turned in his direction. "We provided you with everything you desired, and you lied to us!"

"Oh, does it really matter? Did I not earn my keep listening to your people prattle on about their every little problem? And the good friar has already validated my leechcraft and herblore."

"You made my village accomplice to your swindling of those who came to you for counsel!"

"And even if she is avenged," the chevalier put in with a nod at Elsabeth, and seized Girart again, "I still have an argument with you, for I have already paid you for your services. Others may have turned a blind eye before, but I wonder now what the local bishop might do were a wizard brought before him?"

Girart swallowed visibly, and his efforts to extract himself from the man's grip proved futile. "I assure you, my Lord, that such threats shan't be necessary! I'll gladly return your offering."

"We are long past that, Sirrah!" Talbot snarled and started forward into the garden. "You made my people complicit in your scheme. We may have no local lord, but that does not mean we can't hang you."

Talbot did not make it more than a step towards the erstwhile wizard before he saw the flicker of motion from Ch'u Niang, who had gone largely forgotten in the doorway of the hut while everyone's attention was focused on Girart. Something arced from her hand to the burning altar, and the moment it landed among the flames the top of the bluff was split by a deafening roar. A brilliant flash of light blinded him. He felt a sensation like someone punching him in the chest, and then he was airborne, flung backwards like a ragdoll across the garden. Time seemed to still, and then he struck the ground hard, everything went black, and for a time he knew nothing more.

HEN HIERONYMUS REGAINED CONSCIOUSNESS the first thing he was aware of was the ringing in his head, and the sharp stench of sulfur hanging in the air. He found himself lying sprawled on his stomach, face down in the grass of the so-called wizard's garden, and lifted his spinning head with a groan. Thick white smoke hung across the top of the bluff, and he hacked and coughed when it burned his lungs and stung his eyes.

"Tetty!" he called. His voice sounded muffled in his ears.

The breeze off the lake slowly scattered the smoke, and when it cleared, he saw Sinopus's — that is, Girart's — altar had been shattered and its flame extinguished by whatever it was his second consort had thrown on the fire. Of the three villains he saw no sign, but Elsabeth and the chevalier lay crumpled near the south wall of the garden, and for a moment his heart leapt into his throat at the sight of his comrade lying stricken. But then they, too, stirred.

"Bugger!" she grumbled once she regained her senses. Talbot and the rest of the chevalier's lance picked themselves up as well. Those who were outside the garden had been spared the worst of it. The squire burst through first, headed straight to his master's side, and helped him sit upright, while the crossbowmen saw to Talbot.

"My Lord! Are you all right?"

"Yes, yes, thank you," the fellow replied as his squire helped him to his feet. When he saw Elsabeth sitting dazed and propped against the wall for support, the chevalier immediately shook his squire off, and hurried to offer her a hand up. "Here, allow me."

"Why, thank you," she said, and Hieronymus could all but hear her eyelashes fluttering when she accepted his aid. He just groaned and rolled his eyes at the sight. The coutilier had followed the squire in by now and turned his attention to Hieronymus.

"Are you hurt, Brother?" he asked, his face a mask of genuine concern.

"I thank you for your consideration, my son," Hieronymus said, "but the Lord of All has sheltered me, and seen me through unharmed." He did, nonetheless, accept the coutilier's hand in returning to his feet. His head still spun a bit, and he leaned heavily on the fellow for support until the dizzy spell passed.

"Fortunately, the Lord of All has also blessed him with an excess of padding around anything particularly vital in his body, while I imagine his own high opinion of himself has sheltered his brains," Elsabeth quipped. She, too, was leaning heavily against the chevalier, though Hieronymus suspected it had little to do with a need for the support.

"Blasphemous harpy!" he growled.

"Oh shush, you were supposed to keep an eye on those two. What in the name of the Dark One was that, anyway?"

"Blasting powder, I imagine," the chevalier said. "Where did those three villains disappear to?"

Elsabeth quickly swept her eyes across the garden as if realizing Girart and his consorts had vanished for the first time. "Oh, bugger!" she snarled. "That is the second time now one of those brigands has vanished out from under us! I swear to God if I ever get my hands on those two ..."

Hieronymus sighed and rubbed his temples. The ringing in his ears had passed, as had the dizziness, but a steady throb was taking its place. "If you please, my dear, having been brained by the boy and now this, I think I am content with foiling their scheme and escaping with our heads firmly attached. I rather fear to learn what mischief they have planned if we were to follow."

She sighed. "So you say we ought to turn the other cheek?"

"Indeed. At any rate, my dear Tetty, I think I could do with a drink."

23

HE COMMON ROOM OF THE FOUR WAYS was filled almost to capacity. The air was thick with cheers and shouts of merriment, and a fast, jaunty dance tune shook the heavy timber beams supporting the walls and roof. Elsabeth staggered and stumbled more than strolled over the threshold of the door opening out into the yard, and onto the landing of the stairs leading up to the room above. Her copper hair spilled loosely down her back. She left her sword, hat, and jacket behind in her room this night. It took her a moment to find the stairs, which were spinning and whirling about her. It was quite a miracle she found the market stall she had rushed out to visit at all after the vast quantities of drink she had consumed thus far.

Elsabeth started forward with a small bundle cradled protectively under her arm, and nearly tripped and fell when she misjudged the first step of the staircase leading up from the entrance. But she caught herself with a hand to the opposite wall, and let out a giggle before stumbling the rest of the way up the stairs.

The common room was lit with golden lamps, and the rejoicing of the patrons was almost deafening as they danced and drank. Swept up by the music, Elsabeth spun merrily through the crowd and sought a path to the corner from which the song originated. She danced among the other patrons and passed from partner to partner, laughing as she lost herself in the frivolity. Here and there she slipped past a groping hand or stole a kiss from one of the men dancing with her (at times to the consternation of his wife or mistress).

The current of merriment sweeping her along the sea of bodies soon led her near the side of the common room, where the way to her intended destination was mostly clear. As Elsabeth danced along in time to the steady beat of the music, a shadow (or was it a pair of them? One dancing about the other in a manner that made her quite dizzy) loomed up in front of her. She tried to slip to one side, but her feet refused to cooperate and caught on one another, and Elsabeth begin to fall. A pair of hands shot out to catch her and right her again, and the shadow pulled her close.

"Be careful, Mademoiselle," a familiar voice said, "I would hate to see you trampled underfoot should you fall."

Elsabeth blinked at the shadow, and she peered beneath the hood of the cloak and recognized Maerten smiling at her.

"You!" she slurred, and made a move to strike at him. However, in her inebriated state Elsabeth could offer little fight, and Maerten suddenly pulled her tight against himself in such a manner that pinned one arm, and she had to put another to his belt among the collection of pouches hanging there to steady herself and keep from falling to the floor again.

"'Tis good to see you again!" he said, and through the haze of drink she realized this was no longer the innocent, unsure youth she and Hieronymus had set out with.

"If I knew what it was I had done with my sword — and if I could stand up straight — I would take your head from your shoulders," she growled.

Maerten made a pout and tsked at her. "Now, now, that is no way to talk. I came here to offer my apologies."

"Your apologies?" She managed to free her hand from his grip and stabbed a finger hard into his breastbone. "You used me! And then you left Hieronymus and me behind!"

He grinned at her, and there was a playful arrogance there that reminded her too much of Cuncz. In spite of herself, the comparison drew up memories that suddenly made her feel quite awkward given the way the boy was pressed against her.

"And as I said, I really came here to apologize. 'Twas Husson's idea all along, you know. I argued against it, but he insisted."

"And why do you think I should trust your word now?"

Maerten reached inside his cloak, pulled out a small leather pouch, and stuffed it down the front of her shirt and doublet. Elsabeth's eyes widened in surprise and more than a little indignation at the uninvited contact when his hand lingered a little longer than necessary to secure the pouch between her breasts.

"I was able to rescue a little of what we took. I think 'tis only fair that you and Brother Hieronymus should have a share of it."

"Oh, you do? And do you really think that will make amends?"

He pouted again. "Well, I had hoped it would. And besides, I wished to extend to you my thanks for freeing me of Husson. He really was a right cruel bastard, and I am glad that I am no longer bound to him."

"And what of dear old Girart?"

"I suppose I'll not see him again. I thought you might have pieced the rest together, and even if I could have reached him, I doubt we would have had time to pack up before you arrived, so I knew I need not bother."

"You clever, manipulative, little bastard. Tell me, love, was anything you told me the truth?"

Maerten flashed that playful grin at her again, and in spite of herself, the look of it on his boyish features stole much of the fire from her anger at him. "Well, I truly am sorry that you fell into Husson's scheme. You really were very kind to me, though you needed not be. But now, I think 'tis time for me to go, farewell! Maybe we will meet again under more pleasant circumstances!"

He slipped away from her and Elsabeth nearly lost her balance and fell. By the time she recovered and spun around, he was lost in the crowd filling the inn, and the bodies pressed in around her and cut off any effort she might have made to chase him down.

Elsabeth stared after him for a moment, watching the surging crowd and listening to the raucous laughter and driving music, before finally turning back to continue in the direction she was headed before the interruption.

Finally, she reached the edge of the crowd, and stood before the group of musicians while they played. The music swelled, building in volume and tempo. The patrons of the inn danced and cheered around her, and suddenly the entire establishment burst into applause when the final note hung in the air. Elsabeth clapped her hands together, then gleefully burst from the crowd to approach the men and their instruments, singling out the face she had been seeking; a shawm player with bright blue eyes, dark hair to his shoulders, and a handsome chiseled face seated on a chair.

When she reached him, she dropped into his lap and pulled him into a kiss to the raucous approval of the crowd around her, and heedless of the catcalls and whistles resulting from her display.

"Ah, there you are!" he said, when she let him up for air again. "I was wondering where you disappeared to!"

Elsabeth favored him with a throaty giggle. "I had to find a little something for later, love," she said, and flashed him a suggestive smile. "Now why don't you find something more enjoyable to play with? I think they shan't miss you too much for a while."

She pulled him into another deep kiss, not for a moment caring that she and her paramour were fully in view of much of the establishment. He kissed her back, and Elsabeth was immediately aware her attentions had the desired effect on him. "How could I refuse such an offer?" he said when their lips parted again.

Elsabeth slipped from his lap and took him by the hand, and immediately his attention fixed on her other fist. "Now, what is that you have got there?" he asked.

She looked at her clenched fist, and a mischievous grin spread across her features. Elsabeth tossed the pouch she secretly removed from Maerten's belt while he was distracted slipping the other down her shirt up into the air, and caught it again to the sound of the coin within jingling together.

"Oh, this? Never you mind, love, just a little payment for a job well done. Now, come along and let us see what sort of music I can make on your shawm!"

Presenting a special first look at

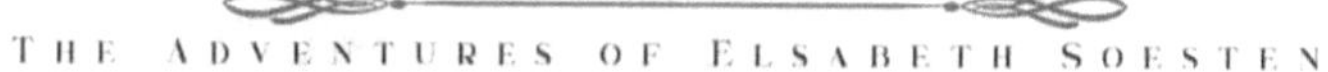

THE ADVENTURES OF ELSABETH SOESTEN

PRIZE PLAY

1

IS FIST CONNECTED WITH HER GUT, AND with a sickening grunt all the air was driven from her lungs at once. Elsabeth felt herself falling and watched the ground come up to meet her, but she did not quite reach it. Rough hands grabbed her under the armpits, and hauled her with no particular gentleness back to her feet again before she could collapse. She gasped in desperation for a breath, but another blow to the belly just beneath her ribs cheated her of the effort. She might have regretted misplacing her doublet and enjoyed the satisfaction of her tormentor's bare hand smashing against the concealed metal scales, but all her attention for the moment was focused on gasping for big gulps of sweet, lovely air, while stars danced around her eyes

Elsabeth slumped in the hands grasping her bloodied shirt. Her hands were bound behind her, and her legs threatened to collapse beneath her. Blood from an open cut above one eyebrow dripped into her eye, and when she finally managed a random, hacking breath her mind turned itself to more practical matters, like outrage over the thought she might be left with a scar. She was not given long to gather her thoughts before the back of his hand flew and landed across the corner of her jaw.

"Quim!" Caspar von Bech snarled, his Boehman spoken with a cultured and generally superior accent, wholly at odds with the vulgarity of the curse.

Elsabeth spat blood from her mouth, and smiled up at him. "Oh Caspar, whatever is the matter today?" she said.

Caspar seized her roughly by the chin and wrenched her head around to face him. Eyes blue as ice bored into hers, and his lips twisted into a scowl beneath his well-manicured mustache. His hair was the color of straw, and was silky and neatly groomed. She might ordinarily have found him a quite handsome man from across a tavern, but unfortunately for him she also knew him far too well already to be fooled by such appearances.

"You know 'whatever is the matter,'" he snapped. "I want it!"

"Well if that is the way you ask for it, then 'tis no wonder every woman from here to Köln has refused your bed."

The words were no sooner out of her mouth than his hand flew again. He delivered a powerful cuff to her temple that snapped her head around, and momentarily blinded her with a flash of light across her eyes. Only the firm grip of Caspar's men kept the impact from driving her into the dirt. Elsabeth shook her head to clear away the ringing in her ears, decided his reaction had been worth it, and grinned up at him again.

"Where is it?"

"I don't know, maybe you should ask that idiot Vorfechter of yours," she said.

That earned her another solid punch to the stomach, and again Elsabeth gasped for breath. Caspar seized her roughly by the hair and pulled her head back. "Take a good look around," he hissed between his teeth. His ordinarily fair-skinned face turned bright red as his temper got the better of him.

They were in a small clearing of widely-spaced trees, grass and wildflowers. It was a beautiful autumn evening, aside from the company, with a wide and clear sky set on fire as the sun slipped down into the west, while a cool breeze wound between the trees and set their branches in motion. The area was also conspicuously absent of any sign of human life. There was no road or trail, no sound of voices or other activity, no abandoned carts, garbage, or anything else associated with people having passed this way any time recently.

"If you wished for time alone with me you could always have asked," she said, when she managed to regain her breath. The last blow left her belly tying itself in knots, and her last meal threatened to claw back up her throat.

Caspar seized her by the throat and squeezed, just tight enough Elsabeth felt the blood flowing through the veins in her neck strain against his grip, and she had difficulty drawing a breath. "You are alone, whore! The Master is no longer here to take care of you. I could crush your throat here and now and leave you for the wolves, and no one will ever find your miserable carcass."

He released her with a violent shove. Elsabeth's neck throbbed in protest at the manhandling, but she refused him the benefit of reacting to the pain.

She tsked him. "Ever the jealous sort, Caspar. How many times need I tell you Master Paulus did not share your sort of affection?"

Another crack echoed across the wood as he rounded on her again. Elsabeth spit out more blood, and ran her tongue over the gash torn in her lower lip. Caspar grabbed her by the chin again and put his face in hers. The veins in his neck and temple were bulging. "Don't you dare insult me like this now!"

"Well, you always were envious of my closeness to the Master, and you certainly never made a move on me, though you had plenty of opportunity. Not that I ever would have accepted, of course. Even then you were a disgusting pig, and you certainly have not improved in our years apart. But it does make one wonder."

This time when his hand flew, it was not the back of his hand to the side of her face or a fist to the gut. Instead he balled his hand and delivered a vicious hook to her temple, and once again Elsabeth saw stars. Such was the force of the blow that the men holding her lost their grip, and she spun face-first into the dirt.

Her ears rang, her vision swirled about her, and Elsabeth was only vaguely aware of the hands seizing her and dragging her to her knees while Caspar stepped around in front of her. Had she the mind, she might have considered delivering a solid head-butt to his groin, for which she found herself at the convenient height. But, dazed as she was, Elsabeth could not even remain upright, much less formulate any particular strategy to avenge the battering. So instead, she just hung suspended from the men gripping her arms, spat the blood out of her mouth and fought back the rising urge to vomit while the world spun about her.

Caspar crouched in front of her, seized a fistful of her hair, and wrenched her hanging head around to force her to look at him once more. There were now two of them spinning in circles about each other, and the idle thought of *two* Caspars in the world made her suddenly desperate for him to go on and kill her, even if it did mean his countenances would likely be the last thing she would see.

"I tell you one last time: Return it, now!"

Elsabeth winced against the strain the awkward turn of her head put on her neck. "And I am telling you one last time I have no idea where it is!"

He released her once more with a rough shove, and nodded to the men behind her. They yanked her back to her feet, and dragged her towards a large oak tree with several branches of convenient height. She made an effort to break free, but her captors were too many, too strong, and with her hands bound she was left with only her feet as weapons. Elsabeth kicked at whatever shin, knee or groin presented itself as a target, and tried to smash the back of her head against anyone standing behind her. But her struggling quickly proved futile, and any fight she had left in her was ended by yet another solid blow to her belly that drove the air from her lungs, and left her gasping for breath and on the verge of vomiting.

A length of rope was thrown over one of the branches perhaps twice her height above the ground, and one end was knotted into a noose. Elsabeth fought down the surge of panic as the full realization of Caspar's intent settled over her. "Oh, really, Caspar?" she said when she managed to draw enough breath again to talk. She made her best effort to keep her voice level and her anxiety out of it. "Is this really supposed to convince me to tell you something I have already told you I know nothing about?"

"You had your chance, bitch," he snarled. "You are a thief and a liar, and 'tis long past time someone treated you as such."

Perhaps I am, but damned if I die like this.

"And I tell you I dispute your charge," she said. "Give me a sword and let us argue the point like civilized folk so I can cut your head off rather than listen to your slander any longer."

He glowered at her. "Do you take me for a fool? I know what will happen if I put a sword in your hands, and I shan't let you slip away again."

"Oh, so you are still a coward, then. You would not dare fight me as a student, and you daren't fight me now. It defies belief the Brotherhood ever made you Master in Soest."

He snapped his fingers, and the noose was unceremoniously lowered over her head and tightened. Three of Caspar's men took hold of the other end and tested it and the branch, and Elsabeth felt the rope tug against her throat. Desperation to delay what was to come so she might find a means of escape overrode her revulsion of what she now considered.

Elsabeth made a pout and gave him a quick bat of her eyelashes.

"Come now, Caspar, I am sure there must be something you and I could work out together ..."

She trailed off suggestively, but grimaced inwardly. *I think I may be ill...*

However, Caspar just gave her a vicious and humorless smile. "Oh no, you don't cry, kiss, or fuck your way out this time. Your charms are wasted on me. Hang her!"

The next thing Elsabeth felt was the rope pulling taut, and she was hauled roughly off her feet by the neck. Her body thrashed and kicked in a desperate attempt to find some sort of purchase to lift the pressure off her throat as the noose tightened around it, but the effort was in vain. She gasped in anguish, and her blood surged against the rope cutting off the flow to her head. Pressure built in her head and face, and her tongue swelled and tried its best to force its way out of her mouth. Her last conscious thought as darkness intruded on her vision was how grey and lifeless everything around her now seemed.

Then all she knew was black.

APPENDIX: READING BLAZONS

The coats of arms herein are presented in the form of the blazon. This is a particular heraldic language used to describe a coat of arms in a succinct manner that will automatically be understood.

The arms are always described in a specific order:

1. Any divisions of the shield which exist.

2. The field is described:

    a. In the case of a solid color, the tincture of the field (capitalized, even if the color is not the first word of the blazon) is given, followed by a comma.

    b. In a complex field, such as *chequy* (that is, checkered of two colors) the pattern is described, followed by a comma.

3. The principle ordinary or charge is given, followed by in order:

    a.   Its attitude (IE the pose of a bird or beast)

    b.   Its tincture

    c.   Parts that might be colored differently

    d.   A charge may have another charge placed on it.

4. Any additional charges placed around the primary charge described as above with their positions.

5. Any additional charges *on* the principle charge, again described as in the principle charge.

A blazon is always given from the *bearer's* perspective, not the viewer's. Thus dexter refers to the part of the shield on the bearer's right (viewer's left).

On a divided shield, the divisions are described beginning at the chief, (top) from dexter to sinister, then the base (bottom) in the same fashion, much like reading a book. Thus in a quartered shield, the top row would be quarters I and II, while the bottom row is III and IV.

For example, the blazon — *Quarterly 1ˢᵗ and 4ᵗʰ Azure, on a bend Or three bears statant erect Sable Quarterly 2ⁿᵈ and 3ʳᵈ Gules, two longswords in saltire proper in chief a gauntlet Or —* would describe the following shield:

The bearer's upper right and lower left quarters are blue, each with a gold diagonal band from (bearer's) upper right to lower left. On this band are three black bears standing on their hind legs. The bearer's upper left and lower right quarters are red with two crossed swords with points angled upwards. The swords are colored naturally (silver blades and gold hilts). Above the swords is a gold gauntlet.

There are other elements of a coat of arms, including achievements, mantling, and supporters, but these do not appear on the shield itself.

GLOSSARY

ARCHITECTURE

Crenel — The gap between merlons on a battlement.

Enceinte — The main enclosure of a fortification, including the main defensive wall and towers.

Merlon — The raised portions of a battlement.

ARMS AND ARMOR

Arming Sword — A one-handed, double-edged sword, with a blade averaging about thirty inches. The classic "knightly sword" of the Middle Ages.

Buckler — A small round shield seldom more than a foot in diameter, typically made of metal, and held using a center grip. It was often paired with an arming sword.

Longsword — A two-handed, double-edged sword with a blade generally ranging from three to three and a half feet in length. Longswords are generally well-balanced between cutting and thrusting, and are quite fast and agile swords.

Rondel

A dagger with a long, slender blade of lenticular, diamond, or triangular cross-section ending in a fine, needle-like point designed for punching through mail or penetrating the gaps in plate armor. The grip is cylindrical, with a disk or similarly-shaped guard and round pommel. One or both edges could be sharpened. It was particularly favored by knights, and often served as a sidearm or personal defense weapon.

ARTS OF DEFENSE

Dente di Cenghiaro

"Boar's Tooth." A principle guard of the longsword in Italian fencing traditions. The hilts are held on the left side near the hips with the point downward, with the right foot leading.

Half-Sword

A technique by which the wielder of a sword places one hand on the blade and the other on the grip, allowing him to wield the sword in a fashion like a spear. This shortens the reach of the sword, but improves control of the point when thrusting.

Pflug   "Plough." A principal guard of the longsword in German fencing traditions. The hilts are held at either the left or right hip, with the point angled up at the opponent's face. The lead foot is the opposite side from the sword (thus if the sword is on the right, the left foot is leading).

Posta di Donna   "Maiden Guard." A principal guard of the longsword in Italian fencing traditions. The fencer holds the hilts high and winds the sword up behind the head with the blade resting across the shoulders. The sword is on the side opposite the lead foot, so if the sword is on the right the left foot is leading, and vice-versa. The fencer may shift his weight towards the back foot.

Posta di Fenestra   "Window Guard." A guard of the longsword in Italian fencing traditions. The hilts are held above the left or right shoulder, with the blade pointed forward towards the opponent and angled slightly inward. The lead foot is the opposite side from the sword (thus if the sword is on the right, the left foot is leading).

Vom Tag   "From the Day." A principal guard of the longsword in German fencing traditions, held either with the sword above the head, or with the hilts just below the left or right shoulder. The blade is held point-upward and angled back slightly. It is typically assumed with the sword on the fighter's strongest side, with the opposite foot leading (thus a right-handed fencer leads with his left foot, and the sword is held at his right shoulder).

HERALDRY

Argent
: One of the two recognized metals, either silver or white.

Azure
: One of the five recognized tinctures, referring to blue.

Bend
: An ordinary in the form of a diagonal line, from upper dexter (bearer's upper right) to lower sinister (bearer's lower left). A bend sinister is a diagonal line in the opposite direction (from bearer's upper left to lower right). In addition to an ordinary, multiple objects can be placed diagonally, described as "in bend." A charge described as "bendwise" is rotated to follow that angle. A bend can also describe a diagonal division of the shield, "per bend."

Chevron
: An ordinary in the form of an inverted V across the shield. In addition to an ordinary, multiple objects can be placed "in chevron," in which case they are positioned in an inverted V. A chevron can also describe a division of the shield, "per chevron."

Chief
Referring generally to the top portion of the shield. A chief is also an ordinary across the top of the shield. A charge can also itself be placed "in chief," meaning that it is placed towards the top of the shield, rather than in the center.

Erect
An animal depicted standing upright.

Escutcheon
Either the shield on which a coat of arms is painted, or a separate charge within the coat of arms. When used as a charge, the Escutcheon may have its own blazon.

Fess
An ordinary in the form of a horizontal band running across the shield. In addition to an ordinary, multiple objects can be positioned "in fess," meaning lined up across the shield. A fess can also be a line of division; "per fess" would mean the shield is divided in two along a horizontal line.

Gules
One of the five recognized tinctures, referring to red.

Or
One of the two recognized metals, referring to gold.

Ordinary
A simple charge or device, generally in the form of a line, bar, cross, or other simple geometric pattern. An ordinary is considered a primary charge, and can have another charge placed on it, for example "on a fess."

Proper
Indicating that the referenced object is in its "correct" or "natural" colors, as opposed to using conventional heraldic colors. Proper colors for many objects are officially defined in heraldic tradition. IE *a sword proper* always has an *argent* blade and *or* hilt.

Quarterly
A shield divided into quarters. Each quarter is numbered 1st through 4th from dexter to sinister, and then chief to base. Each quarter of the shield can have its own blazon.

Sable
One of the five recognized tinctures, referring to black.

Saltire
An ordinary in the form of a St. Andrew's cross. Two objects can also be described as "in saltire," meaning diagonally crossed (IE, *two rods in saltire*).

HORSES

Hackney
A powerful, but attractive, general purpose riding horse. Their trot made them better suited as war-horses than amblers.

Jennet
A small, compact, and well-muscled riding horse of good disposition, noted for its ambling gait. It is smaller and frequently less expensive than the palfrey. The modern Spanish Jennet is very similar in appearance and gait, though the historical jennet was not a specific breed.

MEDICAL

Aqua vitae	A Latin term meaning "Water of Life," and used in reference to distilled ethanol alcohol, most commonly made during the Middle Ages and Renaissance by distilling wine. It was originally used medicinally before coming to be consumed as liquor in its own right.
Arrow Spoon	A medieval surgical tool for extracting arrows, consisting of a metal shaft connected to a diamond-shaped spoon with a closed tip, so it can catch the point of an arrow or bolt.
Cauter	An iron probe or bladed implement used for cauterizing a wound.
Fleam	A sharp, thin lancet specifically used for bloodletting.
Trephine	A surgical tool with a cylindrical blade designed for making circular cuts.

TITLES AND RANKS

Chevalier	The French term for a member of an order of chivalry; a knight.
Comte	The French term for a count.
Coutilier	A light armored horseman in Medieval French armies also known as a serjeant-at-arms, who was part of the entourage of a knight or squire.

Huángdi	The Chinese term for emperor.
Duc	The French term for a duke, and whence the English word derives.
Ritter	The second-lowest rank in German nobility, below *Freiherr* (Baron) but above *Edler*. A hereditary knighthood roughly analogous to the English baronet.

WEIGHTS AND MEASURES

Denier	A silver French coin roughly equivalent in value to a penny (about 1/240 of a pound).
Pfennig	A silver German coin roughly equivalent in value to a penny (about 1/240 of a pound).
Sou	A silver French coin roughly equivalent in value to a shilling (1/20 of a pound).
Span	A unit of measure defined as the distance between the tips of the outstretched thumb and little finger. It equates roughly to nine inches.

OTHER

Lance	Short for *lances fournies*. A military unit originating in Medieval France, based around a knight and roughly analogous to a modern squad. A lance generally consisted of a knight, his page or squire, two or three archers, and a coutilier.

Nunnery	Ironic slang for a brothel.
Pattens	Raised wooden soles attached to shoes, often by lacing or straps, to lift the wearer out of the mud and protect the softer, thinner soles of the shoe itself while traveling.
Small beer	Beer with little or no alcohol, often drank with meals in place of water. *Why* it was drunk in place of water is the subject of myth and debate, ranging from providing extra calories for field workers, to being safer to drink than water in pre-industrial societies because of the brewing process.

ABOUT THE AUTHOR

D. E. Wyatt was born and lives in St. Louis, Missouri. When not writing he is an occasional gamer, a student of German swordsmanship, a saxophonist, and works in IT.

www.ingramcontent.com/pod-product-compliance
Lightning Source LLC
Chambersburg PA
CBHW021236310726

48971CB00006B/1851